TITLES BY DAWN ADDONIZIO

Novels Of The Faerie Realm:

A RISKY PROPOSITION, Book 1 of
The Third Wish   Duology

SOUL SEDUCTION, Book 2 of
The Third Wish Duology

PASSIONATE MAGIC

GREY'S MAGIC

Published by Nouveau Ventures Unlimited
3606 Woods Walk Blvd
Lake Worth, FL 33467

Edited by DM Eburn

SOUL SEDUCTION
Book 2 of The Third Wish Duology

First paperback printing February 2014

For information contact:
Dawn Addonizio
Dawn@DawnsBoutique.Org

The Third Wish Duology is dedicated to:

Dr. Amy Kaufman—Who read it first as both a friend and an English professor, and kept me going with a priceless combination of encouragement and good feedback. I couldn't have done it without you!

My Mom—Who has always encouraged me to think bigger and better and to believe that anything is possible.

My Husband—Who inspires my fantasies…and makes them come true.

Ann C. Crispin & the attendees of her 2008 Writers Workshop at Dragon*Con (which was Amy's idea)—Thanks for the feedback & encouragement!

Much Love & Faerie Blessings Upon You All!   -Dawn

Table of Contents

Chapter 1—Last Resorts

Panting and cursing the stupidity that had possessed me to call the Hell Ride, I pushed myself into an upright position. I put my weight on my left forearm instead of using my shredded hands, the searing pain along my right side making me wonder if I'd broken a rib. I'd never had a broken bone in my life so I didn't know what it felt like. But as I moved the pain receded into more of a sharp ache, and I was able to draw air into my chest, so I figured I was only badly bruised.

I seemed to have landed on the deck of a massive, badly weathered wooden ship. A broad, heavy mast rose from an elevated base several yards away, towering high into the black, starless sky above. Its spindly arms stretched out to either side with what was left of their tattered sails hanging off of them like withered flesh. The shapes of ragged clouds sped by overhead, adding to the eerily shifting shadows teeming across the surface of the deck.

An abandoned captain's wheel stood forlorn and motionless between the spot where I crouched and the stairs leading up to the mast platform. Dark, bulky shapes lined the sides of the ship and another platform rose behind me as the bow of the ship narrowed, making me feel trapped within the shallow pit between.

I winced as I pulled out some of the larger splinters that were biting into my palms, identifying them as bits of the deck's dark timber planks. My hands were bleeding and, although it was dim, I could see that I would have some work to do with tweezers later to get the rest of the splinters out.

A scratchy whispering rose up around me, making my skin crawl. Already tense, I jumped when an eerie, high-pitched cackle rang out. A low rumbling growl sounded in response, like taunting laughter rolling up from the bowels of the ship.

I heard a scuttling sound, like tiny claws scampering along the surface of the deck. I cringed, overcome by the creeping feeling that I was surrounded by unseen creatures scurrying through the shadows around me. The scuttling grew closer, a rapid pitter-pat that set my teeth on edge, and I felt a sharp pinch on the tender spot above my right elbow.

"Ow!" The sound left my throat on an indignant scream of fear. I struck out in panic, whipping around to fend off my attacker, but nothing was there—only the quickly receding sound of claws clicking against wood. The whispering grew louder and a chorus of laughter broke out, a mad tittering interspersed with dim chuckles and cruel giggles.

I rubbed at the stinging ache above my elbow and my fingers came away wet in the darkness. Apparently I had been right about the claws...or possibly teeth. I stood shakily, struggling to get my feet beneath me as fast as I could.

It might have been my fevered imagination, but for a moment it seemed that a figure loomed up out of the dimness behind me, mocking my attempt to gain protection from my height. I spun in a circle, my eyes darting wildly between the thick puddles of shadow spilling across the planks. I thought I caught other glimpses of movement as well, but every time I whirled for a closer look, there was nothing there.

Something flew by my head, rushing past my ear in a gust of wind. I gasped and jerked away as my eyes made a futile attempt to follow it. Whatever it was disappeared into shadow and hit the deck with a soggy splat. A rancid odor wafted through the air as tittering laughter erupted around me once more, followed by a chittering growl of displeasure.

Something else flew at me, low and fast, this time hitting its mark as it smacked into my jean-clad leg with a squelchy thump. The scent of decay rose, stronger now, as I reached down in horror to slap away the wetly clinging mass. It soaked through the denim to my skin as it dripped in moist, clotted clumps down my leg. Confusion coursed through me as I identified the mess as a rotten orange.

I was pelted again and a second smelly, disintegrating object exploded against my left shoulder—this time a tomato.

My mom and I had lived near a tomato field when I was in high school, and I still remembered the overpowering stench it gave off every year after harvest time.

I was speechless. I had landed myself in the clutches of what was supposedly the most powerful force for evil in the faerie realm and they were throwing rotten fruit at me. Was this really the best they could do?

I could only hope.

Raucous, snickering laughter spewed forth from my unseen audience as I was belted with a putrefied apple. For the first time since I had been so unceremoniously dumped on the ship's deck, a spark of anger burned brighter than my fear. I marched forward, in the direction from which I thought the fruit bombs had been flung.

"Show yourself!" My tone rang forcefully through the night, giving me an extra shot of bravery.

With a determined step, I approached one of the large, shapeless lumps resting against the side of the ship. My heckler had to be hiding behind it. The dry, crackling whisper of voices grew louder and a shrill squeal broke out as the lump dissolved into a mass of smaller, mismatched forms that scattered before me like cockroaches beneath a kitchen light.

I leapt back in surprise, then recovered and sprinted after a single trailing figure. The creature appeared to have fallen on its misshapen head. It righted itself and waddled after its companions, ducking behind another crouching lump further along the deck with a terrified squeak.

I skidded to a halt beside it. Not knowing whether this lump would also dissolve into a jumble of shadow creatures, I reached out to prod it with the tip of my sneaker. It gave slightly against the pressure, but remained stationary and whole. I squinted into the gloom, leaning down in an attempt to see where the little devil had disappeared to.

I realized that it had grown eerily quiet, as if the whisperers held their collective breath in anticipation. I stared harder into the darkness, willing my eyes to discern the shapes hidden within it. A minute shift of movement jerked my gaze to the lump beside me.

A malevolent eye looked back at me, mere inches from my own, wide and unblinking like a mouth frozen in a silent scream. It studied me from between long, bony fingers ending in cruelly sharp nails. I ceased all movement, including breath.

A second skeletal hand was folded over the first, the clutching fingers clamped together to obscure its other eye, like the legs of some monstrously long-limbed spider wrapped around its prey. Now why did I have to go and think that? Goddess, I hated spiders.

But even worse was the thought of it spreading those claw-tipped appendages and *both* of those soulless eyes staring back at me. The idea made my heart race so fast that my chest hurt. I was literally paralyzed by fear, afraid to blink or breathe beneath the gaze of the nightmare beside me.

I remained motionless for long moments, praying it would do the same. Rigid muscles quivered and cramped from being held tight and immobile. My lungs burned and my eyes watered, but the terror was so unspeakable that I couldn't move. Dark spots swam across my vision and a warning echoed through my oxygen-starved brain, demanding I either breathe or lose consciousness.

Malicious knowledge glared back at me, and I was filled with a horrible comprehension. The nightmare knew its own power. It knew that as long as it fixed me with its stare, I couldn't move, couldn't breathe—not even to save my own life.

Some fading part of me cried out in denial, shrieking a demand that I fight back. But its struggles receded into the distance, eclipsed by an overwhelming relief that within mere moments, I would feel neither fear nor pain.

As blackness claimed me, hissing whispers fractured the silence once more. They sounded excited, almost frenzied, but I couldn't bring myself to care.

"That's enough." A soft voice pierced the din, like sharpened steel sheathed in black velvet.

The whispers ceased and I collapsed to the floor, squeezing my eyes shut and gasping for air as the leaden weight on my lungs dissipated.

"It would not do to exhaust our guest's potential for amusement so quickly. You must curb your eagerness, my pet." It was a woman's voice, cold as winter snow, yet filled with an unmistakable fondness.

As soon as I was able to move, I scrambled away from the nightmare creature, crawling to a stop mid-deck when I glanced back and saw that it wasn't following me. It had returned to a lifeless, non-descript lump resting against the side of the ship.

I noticed that the night had grown lighter and looked down to find myself bathed in a frosty glow, as if from an errant sliver of moon. Twisting around, I discovered that I had halted at the bare feet of a woman draped in a clinging, sleeveless gown of translucent lavender.

Her lithe naked body was visible beneath, her skin like blue-veined marble, grey and bloodless, yet beautiful to behold. Raven hair spilled long and thick down her graceful form, twining around to caress her limbs on its journey toward her ankles.

A sickle moon gleamed upon her brow, the blades of its arms turned upward in sharp peaks. She was both lovely and terrible, with eyes like death, of lightest lavender tinged with poisonous red.

Hard lips curved in a merciless smile. "And who might you be, my dear? It has been longer than your paltry lifetime since a human has willingly joined us on the Hell Ride. I see that you have already acquainted yourself with Gochi, our resident *bug*. I would advise that you not threaten the imps again, or the next time I may not be able to contain his enthusiasm. And his games are so much deadlier than theirs."

She laughed, an icy chime that sliced through the air to be accompanied by a host of answering hoots, chortles and snickers.

"Yeah, I much preferred being pelted with rotten fruit," I muttered, peering warily around the now illumined deck.

The whispering horde had revealed itself—and they were a bizarre and motley collection. As if in answer to my comment, a decomposing grapefruit splattered onto the wood beside me, liquefied pulp splashing onto my arm.

My gaze darted toward the perpetrator as harsh catcalls and giggles rang out again. A small ugly creature, not much bigger than the fruit it had just pitched at me, sat perched on the edge of a large basket of fresh produce. Its beak hooked sharply and mean little eyes burned like chips of coal beneath its scowling brow.

As I watched, it leapt nimbly into the basket to land beside a ripe orange. Grasping the fruit in both tiny hands, it leaned forward to take a bite. As soon as its beak pierced the rind, the orange began to rot before my eyes. A brown spot appeared at the point of entry and spread outward until its firm ripeness was lost to soft decay.

The creature spun the fruit between its paws, studying it, then gave a sour grunt and lobbed it over the side of the ship before turning its attention to a new piece.

My eyes roamed the deck to take in the creature's companions. They surrounded me, piled along the rails of the ship, staggered upon the stairs leading up to the mast and bow, and even swinging from the mast itself.

Hundreds of mismatched eyes stared at me from myriad grotesque faces. They ranged in size from the tiny fruit flinging fiend to the largest, whose head doubled for its body, making it resemble a jack-o-lantern with a crooked mouth.

They tumbled over each other, jostling for position, no two alike. Their fleshy, leering faces varied from broad to narrow; some had long pointy ears while others had no ears at all; some had button noses and others long protruding beaks.

Squabbles broke out between them constantly, and they pushed and poked each other with spiteful glee. I watched as one vicious little devil punted its smaller opponent across the deck. It landed with a thump, rolling several times, its three goggling eyes making it impossible to tell which side was up.

My wonder almost outweighed my fear. So these were imps—the things Angelica had wanted to set loose on Jeremy before we'd ended up in our bizarre little love triangle. I was glad I hadn't consented to her releasing them in our house.

I decided, however, that I wouldn't mind sic-ing the whole lot of them on that succubus tramp, Edie.

"The imps truly are entertaining creatures," the dark woman said affectionately. "But I am being discourteous. I am Lady Nightwing, mistress of the Hell Barge. Please rise and introduce yourself, little human. You have the scent of magic upon you. Are you a witch?"

I pushed to my feet, doing my best to ignore the complaints of my aching body as I debated the best way to answer her. It might not be a bad idea for her to believe I had some magical power. I executed a stilted bow, hoping the courtesy was appropriate.

"Pleased to meet you, Lady Nightwing. My name is Sydney. And I have been known to cast the occasional spell."

'Tell the truth' had always been my motto. And if you happened to mislead someone—well, that didn't make it a lie.

Her crimson-tinged eyes flashed with interest. "Few are the secret ways to join the Hell Ride uninvited." She smiled, a slight baring of teeth. "Fewer still are those brave enough...or foolish enough...to make use of them."

I held onto my calm facade with a death-grip, hoping she couldn't hear the accelerated beat of my heart—or smell my fear the way she had smelled the magic. "I apologize for my presumption, Lady, but I am searching for a goblin. And I have been told that he is a frequent guest on your ship."

A hissing murmur went up and a gravelly voice spoke from behind Lady Nightwing. "I told you Nugratz must have sent her."

"Silence!" she demanded imperiously, irritation darkening her tone.

Nugratz...why did that name sound familiar?

I peered into an unnatural patch of shadow behind Lady Nightwing. A pair of glowing blue eyes looked out at me, feral in their intensity. I had to force myself not to step back when the shadows dropped away like a discarded cloak and revealed the creature behind them.

The thing was a perversion of a forest spirit, like the demonic incarnation of a rotten-hearted tree. Jagged, branch-like antlers sprouted from a mane of hoary moss atop its head. Its arms extended the length of its body, studded with foot-long thorns that angled upward in wicked spikes. Fingers grew out of its wrists like crooked sticks sharpened into spears, and its thick trunk sat atop bowed legs ending in gnarled, root-like toes.

It fixed me with its hateful blue gaze, but paid obeisance to Lady Nightwing's demand for silence.

"Now then, Sydney, was it?" Lady Nightwing continued in a cloying tone. "What is the name of this goblin you seek?"

"I'm afraid I don't know his name," I answered, keeping a nervous eye on the wicked-looking creature by her side. "But he has a mark on his hand, like a tattoo, of an infinity symbol."

She fixed me with an odd look. The imps began chattering again and the tree creature stepped forward menacingly. I couldn't stop myself from taking a step back this time.

"You dare to try the Lady Nightwing's patience," it growled. "Goblins do not allow themselves distinguishing marks. What is your real purpose here, human? Do not take me for a fool. I know that you have been in contact with Nugratz. What does that pitiful excuse for a goblin think to gain from us?"

I stared at the creature, the name Nugratz like an ember burning a hole through my mind. Then my eyes widened in recognition.

"Nugratz was the goblin that killed the Unseelie leader and started a rebellion against the Seelie Court," I murmured, my confusion warring with excitement over remembering the name from Sparrow's story about his parents.

The creature narrowed its feral blue eyes at me, crossing its thorn-spiked arms in a threatening stance.

Lady Nightwing gave the thing a dismissive wave, genuine amusement curving her chiseled lips. "Can it be that you don't know?" She clasped her fingers together and regarded me with a delighted expression that I found unsettling.

"I truly don't believe that you do. It will be my pleasure to educate you further on this matter, Sydney. But first, answer me one question—and I shall know if you lie," she warned. Her voice was light, but the underlying threat made my stomach drop.

"Did the human, Leslie Horowitz, have anything to do with your visit here this night?"

Surprise shot through me. "He owns the store I work for. But no," I answered with a frown. "He knows nothing of this. What does he have to do with..."

"I thought not," Lady Nightwing interrupted. "Next time, Hob, you will hold your tongue, or you shall find yourself without one."

"Yes, my lady," the tree creature grated with a bow of its mossy, antlered head. I shifted my feet uneasily at the look of unbridled fury it directed at me.

"Now, let me see," Lady Nightwing mused, tapping the end of one lavender-lacquered fingernail against the curve of her lower lip. "It is true that Nugratz murdered our weakening leader and made an unsuccessful bid for power by stirring up a rebellion against the Seelies.

"In actuality, many of us shared his sense of outrage that our Court had allowed itself to become so cowed by them. If he had bothered to recruit the older members of the Court, it is likely that many of us would have followed him. Just as it is possible that, had he taken the time to plan his attack better, he might have been victorious.

"But, alas, goblins have never been known for their foresight. They tend to get wrapped up in the moment and play their hand far too quickly, which is perhaps why most of them are such enthusiastic, yet poor gamblers."

Lady Nightwing offered a tongue-in-cheek smile and the imps erupted in raucous laughter. Even Hob barked out a gruff snort of amusement.

"Sadly, Nugratz was no exception," she continued with an exaggerated sigh of regret. "I'm afraid that after the dismal failure of his plot, not to mention the loss of many of our strongest young warriors at his command, he became rather unpopular. No longer welcome in Unseelie society, he disappeared into the goblin territories and set about drowning his regrets in drink and gambling. However, it was not long before his luck ran out completely.

"You see, one drunken night, Nugratz made the mistake of engaging in a high-stakes game with a death djinn. He bet a large sum, which he was unable to cover, and lost. Not only did he lose, but being ever prideful and incapable of keeping his foolish mouth shut, he gravely insulted the death djinn.

"Were it not for that, the djinn would have likely let it go. But in the fire of his anger, he demanded satisfaction from the only thing that Nugratz had left to offer—his immortality. Nugratz had so offended the djinn, in fact, that he took it a step further and cursed him into human form, forcing him to leave the faerie realm and live amongst the humans he so despised."

I stared at her, still at a loss as to what any of this had to do with me.

Lady Nightwing's smile deepened. "Nugratz has been living amongst the humans for nearly the past twenty years. I believe that in your realm he goes by the unfortunate name of Leslie Horowitz—a name with which we have already established your acquaintance."

I was so shocked the fruit flinger could have knocked me over with a rotten strawberry. I'd always considered D.J.D.'s owner to be inhumanly nasty, but I'd never suspected just how accurate an assessment that was.

"Close your mouth, dear, before the imps attempt to use it for target practice."

My teeth came together with a click.

"Judging by your reaction, I presume that you were unaware of your employer's dual identity. Well, he has fooled those less naive than you. I have seen the wretch, and although he still carries faint goblin characteristics, the djinn's curse did a remarkable job of making him appear human." Her laughter was like the tinkle of shattering icicles.

"In truth, it was ingeniously cruel. Nugratz was driven from the goblin territories, for to his people, his human appearance was an abomination. And due to his unfortunate history, he had long been unwelcome by both Unseelie and Seelie societies. His weakness for gambling prevented him from living his days out in isolation, and I suppose he was unwilling to end his miserable life—so the only choice left to him was to join the reviled humans." Lady Nightwing's eyes sparkled with spiteful amusement.

"But...he's still a goblin underneath, right?" I asked, unable to hide my grimace.

"Oh, yes. Although the djinn's curse altered his appearance, it could not change him into something he is not."

"But he married a human—and had a child with her." The disgust in my voice was unmistakable.

Lady Nightwing shrugged. "Nugratz is nothing if not a survivor. He was wily enough to realize that the appearance of having a normal human family would aid him in your world. I believe he befriended the man who sired his human wife, a drunken gambler like himself, then wormed his way into their lives and made their riches his own. As for the child, it must have been begotten some other way. A goblin and a human cannot breed."

Thank Goddess for small favors. At least I didn't have to walk around carrying the knowledge that Mickey was unaware of his goblin parentage. But poor Cindy. How did you tell someone that their husband of almost twenty years wasn't just an abusive asshole, but quite literally an evil goblin? And would it really do any good to try?

"But I grow tired of discussing Nugratz," she said in a bored tone. "Let us return to the far more interesting subject of why a human would invite herself to one of our nightly soirees. I must admit, it is something of a curiosity. I find that humans generally do not enjoy their time spent with us."

The imps cackled and Hob's blue eyes glowed with an eagerness that sent prickles down my spine.

"I can barely remember the last time a human willingly sought us out. In my experience, such an act is always rooted in desperation. You claim to be searching for a goblin bearing the tattoo of an infinity symbol on his palm. What desperation, Sydney, drives you into my domain to look for such a creature?" Lady Nightwing's eyes glittered with anticipation.

She was right, of course. I *was* desperate. But I trembled with the knowledge that giving her the truth would be like handing her a weapon crafted specifically for my destruction. My mind whirled with half-truths, as I searched for an explanation that wouldn't reveal too much.

"He cheated someone close to me while the two of them were gambling," I said finally.

"Fie!" she exclaimed with an impatient snort. "You will have to do better than that, Sydney. Such things are an everyday occurrence in this realm. What did this goblin take that holds a high enough value for a human to risk searching the Hell Ride for it?" Her lips twisted in an eager smile as she awaited my reply. Even the imps had gone eerily quiet.

I was suddenly glad that I wasn't looking for something the goblin had stolen. For in that moment, I had no doubt that it would be Lady Nightwing's greatest pleasure to make sure I never recovered it.

"It was not what the goblin *took*," I answered with feigned composure, "but the quality of what he gave as payment that is the problem."

Lady Nightwing glided closer and I had to force myself not to retreat. Her expression conveyed annoyance, but the emotion seemed at war with avid interest. I prayed her interest would win out.

"You deliberately lead me on with your vagaries, Sydney. And while I can appreciate the rare human that does not dissolve into a gibbering heap at my mere presence, my tolerance only extends so far. What did the goblin *give*, then, that was of such importance that you would come here looking for him?"

The imps chittered softly and Hob's stance made it clear that nothing but sheer will held him back from striking at me.

I bowed my head, trying not to give into the sudden weakness in my knees. "Your pardon, Lady Nightwing. I have no desire to offend."

I could do this. If there was anything I'd learned from my daily conversations with Cindy, it was how to direct attention away from the things I didn't want to discuss. I took a deep breath, hoping against hope that my next words wouldn't be a mistake.

"The goblin lost a bet to a death djinn and gave a soul in payment. The soul turned out to have far less worth than it had first appeared, and this has caused a great deal of trouble for the death djinn. The djinn wants revenge."

I forced all expression from my face as I awaited Lady Nightwing's response.

The upturned sickle moon upon her forehead grew bright with a corrosive light. I gasped as a fiery pain shot into my chest, like acid burning a hole straight through me. The sensation abruptly ceased, and I was once more pinned solely by her piercing gaze.

"Revenge I can well understand. But the question remains—why would a human with an intact soul be seeking revenge for a death djinn?"

"We have an...arrangement," I said haltingly, still trying to catch my breath after her painful probing. "He was unable to come himself, and I have sworn not to reveal certain details that he entrusted to me."

Nightwing's poisonous lavender eyes narrowed upon me as if she was trying to detect a lie. My heartbeat crashed through my ears in the waiting silence.

Finally she spoke.

"You fear this death djinn more than you fear the Hell Ride." It was said with a grudging respect—not for me, but for the one who wielded such power over me.

She tilted her head and gave me a considering look. Then she seemed to come to a decision.

"Many goblins pass through the Hell Ride. I do not recall having seen one with the mark you describe, but I rarely concern myself with such creatures. I do, however, know of another being who has such a mark, and perhaps this one will be able to lead you to your goblin. I will give you a choice, Sydney.

"I will grant you passage home now, safe, but having failed in your quest. Or you may choose to stay, and we will have a little wager, you and I. If you win, I will send you to the one who bears the mark of infinity without further delay. However, if I win," she paused to moisten the curve of her upper lip with her tongue, as if savoring the thought. "Well, I am not an ungenerous host. I will still send you to the one who bears the mark. But you must first remain my guest for the night."

The voices of the imps rose in an excited crescendo, evil howls of laughter ringing out around me. But the smile that spread across Hob's bark-roughened countenance was what really made me shiver.

"Enough." Lady Nightwing's voice was moderate, but it commanded instant obedience.

"Think well on your choice, Sydney. You have drawn the attention of not only Hob, Gochi and the imps this night. I can feel the curiosity of the other hob-goblins, as well as the gleaners, as they go about their work below. I daresay—everyone wants a turn with you.

"Playing with a human that will remember their games, instead of passing them off as a fading nightmare, will be a singular amusement for them. Needless to say, I do not think you will find the experience so enjoyable."

Her lips drew up in sadistic pleasure and her eyes gleamed at me mockingly. "Make your choice, little human. Disappoint your death djinn, or take a chance with us."

Chapter 2—Negotiations In The Dark

Disappointing Balthus was my most fervent wish. But although I had managed to mislead Lady Nightwing on that point, I wasn't sure how much good it had done me.

The only thing I knew for certain was that I wasn't going home without whatever she could tell me about that infinity tattoo.

"What kind of wager?" I croaked.

Lady Nightwing's vicious grin grew broader with the knowledge that I had chosen to stay.

"Well, let's see. We could have a riddle game," she offered with a nonchalance that I trusted about as much as I'd trust Leslie Horowitz with my life savings.

"I'm not very good with riddles," I answered in a careful tone. "And I'm not sure how much sense a human riddle would make to you, and vice versa."

Lady Nightwing gave me a nonplussed look and Hob grumbled his displeasure.

"No, Hob, perhaps Sydney is right. A race, then?" she suggested. The calculating light in her eyes made me suspect that, of the two, this was the option she would have preferred anyway.

I rubbed my palms against my jeans in a nervous, unthinking gesture, feeling as if a vise was closing ever tighter around me. The rough denim reopened the drying cuts and the friction pushed the splinters deeper. Cringing, I stilled my shaking hands and lifted them away from the fabric.

The renewed sting was forgotten when I looked up to find that the imps had begun to creep closer on all sides, a writhing wall of misshapen flesh moving to box me in. Hob was sniffing the air, his gaze fixed hungrily on my torn and bleeding skin.

I stuffed my hands into my pockets, unmindful of the pain. What was a little stinging compared to the possibility of being eaten alive?

"Your pardon, Lady Nightwing," I sputtered in a high voice. "But I don't think I'm in any shape to run a race at the moment. Maybe a game of chance, rather than skill, would be the best choice to even the playing field?"

"I did not mean for you to join in the race, Sydney." Lady Nightwing's dry words were accompanied by a derisive snort from Hob. At least he had stopped scenting for my blood. "We would choose our contestants from the slave stock below and pit them against each other."

"Oh," I said, still not enamored of the idea. I definitely wouldn't put it past Lady Nightwing to rig a race in her own favor. Nor was I especially hot on the idea of participating in the forced racing of her slaves.

"Um, I'm afraid I wouldn't even know where to begin as far as picking out a suitable contestant," I ventured apologetically. "I've never been much of a gambler." As a matter of fact, I had taken more chances in the past twenty-four hours than I probably had in my entire life. "How about something simple, like..."

My finger brushed the edge of thin metal deep within my pocket and an idea hit me. "The flip of a coin," spilled from my lips, just as Lady Nightwing decisively said the word, "Dice."

She blinked at me as I pulled Sparrow's silver coin from my pocket, knowing it was likely my best chance at receiving fair odds. After hearing stories about weighted dice, I had a feeling I wouldn't fare any better with that suggestion than I would with races or riddles.

"What do you say? It's straightforward and quick, with a fifty-fifty chance for each of us." A storm-cloud of suspicion drifted across Lady Nightwing's brow. "And you can call your side first, since it's my coin," I added hurriedly. "You can't get a fairer wager than that."

"Let me see that," she demanded, presenting me with the outstretched fingers of one marble-veined hand.

I balked at the idea of placing something that I knew was so precious to Sparrow in her possession. What if something happened to it? How would I tell Sparrow I'd lost his good luck charm and the last thing his mother had ever given him?

Lady Nightwing's face darkened with my hesitation and I realized it was too late to change my mind. If she knew the thing was important to me, I would be in even more danger of losing it. I schooled my expression and reached out to drop the coin in her palm.

She snatched it away from me and held it up, flipping it over to study both sides. Bright silver glinted in the pale light spilling from the crescent moon upon her forehead. She grimaced as if the coin offended her, and I scrambled to catch it as she flung it back at me.

"How came you by such an old sidhe coin?" she asked, her distaste evident.

I shrugged, trying to make it seem insignificant. "I saw it and thought it was interesting, so I held onto it. But you can see that it's just a plain old coin. No tricks. You choose the sun or the tree, and we'll toss it in the air and see where it lands."

"You have strange friends for a human," Lady Nightwing said with a thoughtful gleam in her eyes. "I am not best pleased that you brought this Seelie token into my domain, but fine—if it will make you more comfortable with our wager, then this is what we shall use."

She gave me an ingratiating smile that made my skin prickle with unease. "You are, after all, my guest, Sydney. Now, let us venture below to the arena. Our contest will take place there, for the amusement of the

Hoarde."

She turned and glided across the deck toward the raised mast platform, the hem of her transparent gown fluttering around her pale ankles in the breeze. Hob smirked at me nastily and gestured for me to follow her with one thorn-spiked arm. I had no choice but to comply.

The imps drew apart in order to allow Lady Nightwing through. A rotten peach sailed past, narrowly missing my head as the night grew darker with the retreating light from the Lady's crescent moon. Laughter and grumbling faded to silence as the imps blended into the shadows once more.

I followed in Nightwing's wake, past the mast and down the opposite side, where a door had been cut into the platform wall. It opened onto a steep, narrow stairway that descended into blackness. There was no railing, only rough walls crowding in on either side, close enough for me to brace my forearms against as I ventured deeper into the belly of the Hell Barge.

The climb was endless, the dank air disturbed only by the rasping breath of Hob at my back. Absolute darkness enfolded me, clinging and sticky like tar. It felt sentient, a heavy waiting presence that gradually suffocated life and hope. On and on I pushed through it, straining to keep moving despite the voice in my head screaming for me to turn around and run back, toward the feel of wind on my face and the familiar darkness of the night above.

A steady rising panic engulfed me, leaving me breathless and dizzy. I stumbled, scraping my arms against the invisible walls of my prison as I steadied myself. A grunt sounded close behind me and something sharp pricked the back of my leg through my jeans. I gasped as I forced my feet to continue forward.

"Hob!" Lady Nightwing grated from somewhere below me, a warning peal in her tone.

The sound was a relief to my ears as I struggled blindly toward her voice. It was a dark comfort—the seeming lesser of two evils.

"Your pardon, Mistress," Hob mumbled. "On my life, it was an accident."

Lady Nightwing huffed irritably in response. "It is not much further, Sydney," she assured me.

I managed to propel myself onward for several more minutes with those words repeating in my head.

Just as I was sure I couldn't take another step, an abrupt brightness ripped across my eyes and a cacophony of voices assaulted my ears. I squeezed my eyelids shut against the resulting ache and lurched forward. Finally the ground leveled off and my fingertips moved past the edges of a doorway. I floundered into the shock of an open space, reverberating with sound.

Fumbling to a halt, I cracked one eyelid, willing my pupil to adjust faster to the light. Although it was painfully bright after the blackness of the stairwell, in reality the space was dim—lit only by the hungry licking flames of swaying iron chandeliers and scattered torches.

We had arrived in a marketplace of sorts, crushed with a bizarre assortment of creatures. The whole space must have been magically enlarged, because it sprawled out far beyond the size of the deck above. Merchants hawked their wares behind ramshackle stalls and tables. Most I recognized as goblins, bow-legged and standing about four feet tall with pale, beady eyes, flat noses and too-wide mouths.

A few wore their wiry reddish-blonde hair in long, straggly strands past their shoulders. Something about their features seemed softer than the others, and I guessed they were the females.

Imps scrambled or waddled past, their bodies low to the dusty wooden floor. They wove between the legs of the crowd, grunting and squealing when they were kicked or stepped on. Creatures like Hob were scattered throughout the throng, all appearing as the perverted embodiments of various trees or shrubs, as different from each other as the species they mimicked.

There were tall, thin creatures with long emaciated limbs, who bore an eerie resemblance to the popular images of aliens. Their large black eyes gleamed hard and shiny like onyx, but were disturbingly cold and lifeless. They were given a wide berth by the rest of the masses.

"Come, Sydney," Lady Nightwing instructed as she continued forward through the crowd. Most acknowledged her, inclining their heads respectfully as she passed. But even among those who didn't, not one dared touch her or bar her way.

As I moved along behind her I received reactions ranging from disinterest, to avid stares, to sneers of contempt. Hob followed in my wake like a sinister bodyguard, growling with menace if anyone ventured too close to me. I was grateful for his protection, though I doubted its sincerity. He was probably just hoping to reserve the pleasure of tormenting me for himself.

Sickly sweet aromas assailed me from vendor stalls offering unidentified meats with bone and gristle poking through charred flesh. Several hobgoblins gathered to the side of one such stall, tossing glistening, pinkish-white objects the size of gumballs into their mouths like candy. The orb-like morsels popped between their teeth with a squelchy sound.

I thought it best not to dwell on exactly what manner of meat was being sold.

We passed shrill-voiced goblin merchants, striving to outsell each other as they boasted the quality of their weighted dice. Others stridently touted the potency of various spells. There were tables lined with jars of herbs and powders, along-side others displaying colorful assortments of pipes with which to smoke them.

Daggers and deadly-looking blades of every description rested on stands or were laid out in haphazard rows. Some had hilts encrusted with jewels that winked fitfully in the unsteady torchlight; others sported grips wrapped in tanned hide; while still others looked to be carved from bone and inlaid with strange, twisting symbols.

I watched as a faerie-like creature, with skin glistening a venomous green and wings resembling bug-eaten leaves, alighted on one of the tables and began haggling for a tiny, saw-toothed knife. It came to an agreement with the merchant, and was exchanging a small drawstring pouch for the blade, when shouts rang out somewhere ahead of us.

The crowd exploded like a hive of angry bees.

Idle browsers suddenly surged forward toward a growing knot of spectators that were gathering around the unseen commotion. A few smaller, more timid-looking creatures ran in the opposite direction. But most charged toward the disturbance, jostling anyone in their way and yelling violent encouragements.

The merchants stayed behind to guard their goods, but craned their necks and climbed on stools and tables to see above the mob. Through a break in the throng, I could see one of the tall alien creatures with the dead black eyes. A thick, pulsating aura bled from its skin, turning the air around it into a nauseating corona of shadows.

Lady Nightwing sighed. "It appears that Lathos is once again at the center of some disagreement. Come, Hob. Let us see what all the excitement is about. I require his overseeing services for my wager with Sydney."

She continued forward, then slowed and looked back at me. "It would be best for you to remain here, Sydney. Nasty accidents have been known to befall humans in the midst of such mobs."

Hob glowered at me as he moved to join Lady Nightwing. "If you are not here when I return you will regret it, human," he growled under his breath.

I hung back and watched as the crowd parted to allow them through. I glimpsed a haggard and pitiful creature cringing at the feet of the menacing Lathos. It resembled a goblin in body and hair color, but its features were more elegant, its bone structure finer, and two velvet-tipped horns protruded from its hairline. Clad in only a loin-cloth, it writhed against the wooden floor as if in the throes of a nightmare, unmindful of the jagged splinters tearing at its skin.

The mob stilled as Lady Nightwing pushed her way through. Lathos, however, was unaffected. He continued to stare down at the creature with his intense, pitiless gaze. The shadowy nimbus surrounding him grew stronger, spreading from his body to caress the trembling wretch at his feet. It cried out and I cringed involuntarily. The sound was the embodiment of utter terror and pain.

Lady Nightwing allowed it to go on for a few moments more before interrupting in a bored tone. "Lathos, I require your services at the arena. Be done with this half-breed and join me."

Lathos raised his head to fix his soulless eyes on Lady Nightwing. The shadowy aura surrounding him grew fainter and began to gather back toward his body. The creature at his feet wrapped its arms around itself and sobbed.

"This half-breed attempted to purchase a spell that I am interested in obtaining." Lathos' voice was soft and expressionless, and all the more unsettling for the fact that his small slit of a mouth didn't appear to move when he spoke.

"Your pardon, Master Gleaner," the half-goblin begged, its voice catching in misery. "I would most certainly have stood aside, but I did not see you at the table."

Lathos tilted his head and considered the creature impassively. "That is because I had not yet reached the table."

Malicious snickers sounded throughout the crowd.

"I shall have that spell," Lathos stated.

Lady Nightwing shrugged. "So take the spell and throw the half-breed into a slave ring. We have more important business to attend to."

The half-goblin whimpered and the mob jeered in excitement.

"The spell remains at the merchant's table," Lathos said without inflection as he turned to approach a nearby stall.

Lady Nightwing shook her head in exasperation and turned to Hob. "Take the half-breed to Ogre Malfecus' slave ring, and then rejoin us," she instructed, pointing to an area with a high chain-link fence around it.

Hob stomped forward and jerked the poor creature to its feet. It grimaced in pain, and I could see bloody gashes where the rough wood had ripped its skin. I winced in commiseration, gingerly running my fingertips over my own stinging palms.

The crowd began to disperse and Lady Nightwing trailed after Lathos. I remained where I was, standing alone and trying not to appear as nervous as I felt. A few of the retreating hobgoblins narrowed their glowing eyes at me as they approached, whispering amongst themselves.

"Hey Gorbuz!" a heavily barbed one called out in a loud, gravelly voice. I followed its eyes toward one of the meat-selling goblins.

"Jab Thornbriar," the goblin answered with a courteous bow. "What can I sell you this night?"

"Gah—I've had my fill of flesh for the moment. Just thought I'd let you know—one of your livestock has escaped."

The hobgoblin inclined its thorny head toward me and the group broke into evil laughter. The goblin vendor snickered and wiped his hands on a blood-stained cloth before continuing about his work. I waited for the hobgoblins to pass, and then inched backward toward the merchant tables, easing my way out of the more exposed thoroughfare.

"Human," a cracked voice grated out behind me.

I spun to find myself at one of the spell tables. It was scattered with frayed scrolls tied with multi-hued pieces of string, and dusty, mismatched jars of different colored powders...as well as more unpleasant-looking ingredients. The merchant standing behind the table was an ancient goblin woman. Only a vague hint of red remained in her straggly grey hair. Her skin was leathery and worn, and one eye was a blind, milky white.

She spread her wide lips in a grin, revealing a mouth that was missing most of its teeth. "I am Ezrega," she croaked. "Come closer, human. I have a proposition for you."

My heart was still racing from the hobgoblins and the look I gave her was dubious at best. "What sort of proposition?"

"You seek a goblin with the mark of infinity on his hand."

I blinked at her, unable to disguise my shock. "How...You know him?"

She broke into a wheezing laugh. "Ezrega knows and sees much, child." She sobered abruptly and fixed me with her piercing, one-eyed gaze. "Firzag is no longer in this world. I have seen his passing, although the manner of it eludes me."

She cracked her gnarled fist down onto the table in frustration, rattling the clusters of jars, and I started.

"Something clouds my vision," she grumbled in irritation.

"He's dead?" I asked, my heart sinking.

She cocked her head and pinned me again with her one bright eye. "Aye, I've said so, haven't I?" she demanded. "But he's left something behind, he has," she continued in a low tone. "Something you may find useful." The look she gave me was calculating.

"What is it?" I asked, afraid to hope.

"A book. Of no use to me, but he left it in my care. He won't be returning for it now." She cackled madly. "But the voices in the fire say that if I give it to you—if you survive this night—Firzag may be avenged."

"What kind of book?" I whispered, refusing to speculate about whether I'd survive the night.

Ezrega grunted. "Don't read. And don't trust no-one to read it for me. So either it stays with me, closed forever, or I give it to you." She tapped one twisted knuckle against her wrinkled chin. "But not for nothing. You must give Ezrega something in return."

My face fell. "I don't really have anything with me."

Her gaze narrowed on me, the milky whiteness of her blind eye swirling like the surface of a disturbed pond as it focused in on my pocket. "Coin," she croaked.

My hand flew protectively to my pocket. "I can't give you that. It belongs to someone else. And Lady Nightwing and I have a wager on the flip of this coin."

Her face grew blank, as if she was listening to something no one else could hear. Then her lips cracked into a crooked smile. "Wise human. You may survive this night after all. But if you want the book, and will not give me the coin, you must allow me to tap your vein."

"What?" I blanched when I realized what she was asking. She wanted my blood.

"Come now, child. I will only take a little," she encouraged in a grandmotherly tone. "You can't have something for nothing."

"But what will you do with it?" I sputtered.

"Why, sell it to the highest bidder, of course," she answered with relish. "Human blood is a key ingredient in many powerful spells. But the Seelie Court makes it difficult to get away with spilling it. Freely given, however, it is legal."

She grinned, showing off her few remaining teeth, and I blinked at her.

"Make your decision quickly, child. Nightwing returns soon."

The old goblin woman pulled a thin, well-honed dagger from her belt and waited. My stomach gurgled with acid, and I closed my eyes as I held out a trembling hand. She grabbed it and pulled it toward her, her bony grip surprisingly strong. I felt the cold bite of metal across my wrist, swift and deep, and I flinched.

"Make a fist," she ordered, turning my arm sideways and holding it immobile.

I did as she instructed, feeling the sting of air on the wound and the flow of blood across my wrist. I didn't really want to see, but morbid curiosity forced me to look. I stared in fascination at the rapid, unstaunched stream of bright red spilling into the glass jar she had placed beneath my arm. It was filling up fast.

I began to feel lightheaded and nauseous, not surprising since I always had the same reaction when they took blood at the doctor's office. It didn't take much to make me feel that way. I had never even bothered trying to donate to the Red Cross.

An ache began to plague my arm—a helpless, shrinking feeling that spread through my veins as my body struggled against the loss of its life fluid. I inhaled through the discomfort, telling myself it was almost done.

Then the old crone moved the full jar out of the way and pushed a fresh one beneath my wrist.

"Ezrega, no!" I gasped, my voice growing unsteady. "I can't give any more—I'll pass out!"

She clucked her tongue, and with her free hand she reached into one of her display jars. She pulled out a palm full of ruby powder and blew it into my face with one strong breath.

I choked and sputtered as it went up my nose and down my throat, searing delicate inner passages along the way. Ezrega continued to hold my arm still with a ruthless grip. My eyes watered and my nose and throat felt burned and raw. But I felt stronger.

"Fire orchid powder—toughens and purifies the blood," she told me with a wink. "This will be the last jar."

Soon enough the second jar was full and she sprinkled a different, darker powder over my wrist. It stung like acid, but the blood stopped flowing immediately. She dipped one bony finger into the first jar of blood before sealing it and storing it out of sight. I grimaced as she stuck her finger in her mouth and tasted it.

She hissed and made a face. "What's this child?"

Hob's growling voice sounded behind me and I stiffened. "I thought I told you to stay put, human."

Before I could form a reply, Ezrega grabbed both my wrists and yanked me forward. She nimbly stuffed something square and flat into the waistband of my jeans, and then sprinkled more of her dark powder over my splinter-shredded palms. It burned like fire and I let out a yelp of complaint, just as she blew more of the fire orchid powder into my face, making me tear up and gag.

She gave me a warning look as she scooped some of the darker powder into a drawstring bag and pushed it into my hand before releasing me.

"Have a care, Hob Nightshade," she croaked. "Risky to leave your human unattended in this place with the stench of blood on it. Nightwing would not be best pleased to lose her evening's entertainment."

She fixed him with the milky, swirling gaze of her blind eye. "But then, your carelessness may have already robbed Nightwing of her nightly pleasures." She let out a hearty cackle.

Hob was visibly startled, but recovered quickly. "Mind your own affairs, you meddling old hag!" he barked.

He looked as if he would say more, but he was interrupted by Lady Nightwing.

"There you are. Come Hob. Come Sydney. We have an appointment to keep at the arena. Lathos will join us there." She turned back the way she had come, expecting us to follow without question.

Hob gave Ezrega one last glare before turning on his heel and hastening me away.

I shivered, both at Lady Nightwing's icy tone and at the thought of meeting Lathos face to face. Ezrega's insane laughter rang out behind us as we left her table, and I wondered uncomfortably what she had meant about

Hob robbing Nightwing of her entertainment.

I felt in my pocket, relieved to find I still had Sparrow's coin. My fingers traced the outline of the small book Ezrega had tucked into my waistband, pushing it down more securely. I was dying to pull it out and look at it, but that would have to wait until later...assuming there would be a later.

As we approached the tall chain-link fence that Nightwing had referred to as 'Ogre Malfecus' slave ring', I could see the half-goblin with the velvety horns huddled alone in a far corner. His side was pressed into the grating of the fence and he trembled as he attempted to lick at his wounds.

"Hob!" called a high, child-like voice.

I turned to see a massive figure shuffling toward the inside perimeter of the fence near the miserable half-goblin. Its body was wide and round atop thick, stubby legs. Towering at least eight feet tall, its broad forehead jutted out over pin-prick eyes and a gaping mouth with large, uneven teeth. It held a long, cruel whip in one enormous fist.

"Hob!" it called out again, its tinny voice belying its girth. "They told me you just dropped this one off!" It aimed a well-placed kick at the half-goblin's ribs, and the creature moaned.

"Fresh slaves are always appreciated—we seem to go through them so quickly." It giggled, a grating sound that set my teeth on edge. "Lady Nightwing," it added with a bow of its corpulent head. "As a small show of appreciation, I have a tip that you may like to take to the betting pools."

"Thank you, Master Ogre," Lady Nightwing answered graciously. "I have always found your tips to be quite useful."

She and Hob approached the fence and began speaking with the ogre in low voices. I sidled over to the half-goblin and gazed down on him in pity. He clutched his side, no longer attempting to staunch the blood flowing from his wounds. I pulled the little pouch Ezrega had given me from my pocket.

"Here," I whispered. "This should stop the bleeding."

He flinched and gazed up at me with startled eyes. They were a lovely shade of blue-green, soft and wide beneath his down-fuzzed horns. I pushed the bag through a hole in the fence, blocking the view with my body. Slowly, he reached out and took it, the expression on his face a painful mix of fear and gratitude.

"But why?" he asked in confusion.

I shrugged. "Because you need it more than I do."

"Thank you." His beautiful eyes were bright with unshed tears. "I am Barnaby. And I will never forget your kindness."

I blinked my own tears back. I needed to stay strong, now more than ever. "I'm Sydney."

"Thank you, Sydney." He sprinkled the contents of the bag over the numerous cuts and gashes on his arms and legs, wincing as the powder hit his skin, but not making a sound.

"Sorry. I know it stings," I whispered with a sympathetic grimace. "Some old goblin lady used it on me after she took my blood."

"It is nothing," he dismissed, as he emptied the bag and stuffed it into a crevice in the dirty wooden floor. Then he flashed me a sad smile and tilted his head behind me in warning before turning away as if we'd never spoken.

I didn't know if it was the discovery of a kind soul in all the madness, or the loss of blood, or simply the hour—but I was suddenly overcome with weariness.

∞∞∞∞∞∞∞∞

By the time we reached the arena, a roughly circular space bordered by a low plank fence, I was literally dragging my feet. My bruised right side was a mass of soreness, and the chaotic atmosphere was doing nothing to alleviate my pounding headache. I plodded after Lady Nightwing, each step more difficult than the last, until we reached a roped-off area near a gate in the fence.

Spectators ringed the enclosure on all sides, yelling and jeering at the contestants within, who appeared to be engaged in some sort of free-for-all fighting match. A pair of unconscious goblins was being dragged off to the side by an ogre, his meaty fists large enough to carry each one by a leg.

As I watched the remaining contestants, a satyr-like creature was knocked to the ground as well. It had horns like Barnaby's, but its lower half was covered in shaggy brown fur and it had cloven hooves instead of feet. It lay there motionless and, after a moment, it too was dragged away.

Three fighters were left—a female centaur with a bare-breasted torso and the body of a horse with small, stunted wings; a creature that resembled an ogre, but with about three feet missing from its height; and a strange, feral-looking man that moved on all fours and had dark wings sprouting from his back.

The winged man and the ogre creature were ganging up on the female centaur. The ogre swung a club at her head while the man flitted back and forth at her rear haunches, striking out with what appeared to be metal-tipped claws. She reared back to dodge the club, roaring in anger and pain as the claws ripped deep furrows into her left flank.

The crowd screamed its approval, but just as swiftly the centaur shifted her balance and struck out behind her with a vicious kick, catching the man in the chest and sending him flying into the wooden fence. He smacked against it with a loud crunch, then sank to the ground and didn't move again. Her eyes held fire as she advanced on the ogre, who stepped back uncertainly. In that moment of hesitation she plowed forward, knocking him to the ground and trampling him.

The uproar from the audience was thunderous as gamblers rushed forward to settle their bets. The prevailing sounds consisted of booing, cursing and ear-splitting insults. The centaur stepped back from the lifeless ogre and held her head high, as if unaffected. Despite my growing weariness, a small smile stretched my lips. They shouldn't have bet against the only female in the ring.

The body-dragging ogre came to lead the winner from the arena as others quickly cleared away the losers. The crowd began to settle and a disembodied voice rang out over the murmuring din.

"And now, fellow members of the Hoarde, we have something very special for the next event of the evening. A fairly unexciting contest, perhaps—but for interesting stakes. Please welcome our own Lady Nightwing to the arena as the sponsor of, and a participant in, this challenge..."

The voice was drowned out by raucous cheering and the vigorous stomping of feet. Lady Nightwing smiled and waved one pale-veined hand in acknowledgment. When the noise died to a dull roar, the speaker continued.

"The contest will consist of a simple coin toss. The challenger—a human female."

There was a collective grumbling, but the crowd held their objections to a minimum, as if afraid to offend Lady Nightwing.

"Hoarde bets will not be taken on the outcome." The grumbling went up several decibels and the announcer was forced to raise his voice. "The wager on this contest has already been agreed upon between Lady Nightwing and the human. It is as follows: if the human wins the toss, Lady Nightwing will transport her from the Hell Barge to the destination of her choice."

The audience exploded in avid displeasure. Malicious eyes sought me out, burning in a multitude of ugly, leering faces. Fists were raised and angrily shaken. I was suddenly glad the fruit flinger wasn't there to pass out rotten fruit.

"BUT..." the announcer broke in loudly, "If Lady Nightwing wins," the cacophony lessened and the leering faces turned eager, "the human must remain with us for the night. And this is no ordinary human, my friends. She has dared to embark upon the Hell Ride willingly.

"The gleaners will not be required to remove her memories at the end of the night. She will leave us with full remembrance of the Hoarde's games."

The response was deafening, and I closed my eyes against it as I forced down a wave of nausea. I was beginning to feel really sick, and I didn't think it was solely from the fear. My head hurt, my stomach gurgled unpleasantly and my skin was clammy with sweat. It almost felt like food poisoning.

I was making a concerted effort just to breathe, slow and deep, when the announcer's voice broke through my misery once more.

"And since Lady Nightwing knows how eager you will all be to participate, she has chosen to allow the Hoarde to bid for equal time slots with the human. Her only stipulation is that winners curb their amusements so that the human remains conscious when they are finished. After all, we don't want any of our time slot winners to feel cheated.

"The gleaner, Lathos, will preside over the coin toss. Time slot bidding will begin at the conclusion of the contest." The speaker paused for emphasis. "Pending, of course, Lady Nightwing's victory."

If the mocking tone of those words hadn't made my stomach pitch with misgivings, the evil cackles and howls of laughter from all sides would have done the job.

"Come, Sydney, it's time." Lady Nightwing's cool voice was a balm compared to the harshness of the voices from the crowd.

I followed her through the gate and toward the middle of the dusty arena. The roar of the spectators barely reached my ears; I was so intent upon not stumbling, and avoiding the congealing puddles of blood and other bits of gore. I swayed to a stop beside Lady Nightwing and looked up to find that we were at the center of the circle.

The crowd, held back only by the short wooden fence and Lady Nightwing's will, seemed even louder and more intimidating from here.

"The coin please, Sydney," Lady Nightwing said softly.

I attempted to shake off the fog that was taking over my brain and reached numbly into my pocket for Sparrow's coin. As soon as I touched it, I felt a little better. It wasn't much, but it helped.

When I raised my head, I realized that Lathos was standing beside me. His lifeless black eyes seemed to leech away my brief sense of comfort.

Lady Nightwing turned to the crowd and smiled, gesturing to me as she spoke. "As you are my guest, Sydney, you may choose your side and perform the coin toss."

"Thank you," I said faintly, trying to conjure a weak smile of gratitude that probably came out more of a grimace.

I blinked at the bright silver coin, turning it over in my palm. The sun, beautifully depicted, seemed to swirl with heat. It symbolized the antithesis of this place of endless night, and Goddess knew I wanted nothing more than to escape and feel the light upon my face again.

But I was drawn to the tree.

The multitude of shimmering leaves, captured in minute detail, seemed to blow in the wake of a mystical breeze. It was gentle and comforting. My eyelids fluttered shut, and for an instant it was as if I could feel Sparrow's presence, the hint of his warm breath mingling with mine.

"The tree," I whispered. I cleared my throat and said it louder. "I choose the tree."

"Very well," she agreed. Again she addressed the crowd. "The sides have been chosen. Sydney will toss the coin and Lathos will confirm the result." She turned back to me expectantly.

I rubbed the coin between my thumb and forefinger, feeling it grow surprisingly hot with my touch. Then I flipped it high into the air, following it with my eyes and catching it on the back of my hand as my other palm came down atop it. Lathos leaned in closer, the dark shadows of his aura pulsing outward toward my hands. As I uncovered the coin, a silent prayer spilling from my lips, an indistinct halo of light radiated from it, pushing away the seeking darkness.

I let out a painful breath, almost sobbing with gratitude. The side with the tree was showing. I looked up at Lady Nightwing with undisguised relief. The expression on her face was one of triumph.

Confused, I glanced down at the coin again. The shadows surrounding Lathos thickened and the image on the coin wavered, the sun flickering there for a single nauseating moment. Then it strengthened indisputably into that of the tree.

"It's the tree. I won." Suspicion rode my tone and I held the coin out for both of them to see.

The crowd thundered its discontent. But what captured my attention was the look that passed between Lady Nightwing and Lathos. Anger flashed in her lavender eyes, and his emotionless visage came close to reflecting discomfort.

"Two out of three," she snapped.

"What? No! I won!" I insisted. It came out defensive and louder than I intended.

Lady Nightwing reined in her anger, but just barely. "Yes, Sydney," she agreed with a hard smile. "You won the first toss. Now we will have two more to decide the contest."

"But that's not what we agreed," I stammered in denial, clutching the coin tightly in my hand.

She narrowed her red-rimmed eyes at me and I was suddenly more frightened of her than I was of Lathos and the entire mob combined. "It is customary for such a contest to be decided in two out of three tosses. If you wanted the final decision to be based on a single toss, you should have specified that before we began."

I stared at her, unable to speak.

She smiled again, her icy composure restored. "But I am not an ungracious host. To make up for this misunderstanding, if you win, I shall grant you an additional boon.

"What shall it be, Sydney?"

I tried to swallow past the lump in my throat. I felt faint, my skin now flashing between fever and chills. The crowd still roared, but it sounded hollow in my ears. I looked around, trying to think, trying to hold onto fading hope. New creatures occupied the roped-off waiting area by the gate. There were several vicious-looking hobgoblins, a gleaner and.... Barnaby.

His striking blue-green eyes met mine, and the sympathy I saw there was nearly my undoing. I brutally forced back a sob and looked away, steeling my face as I turned back to Lady Nightwing.

"Alright. If I win, in addition to our original agreement, I would also have you release that half-goblin, the one Hob brought to the slave ring earlier, and transport him—unharmed—wherever he wants to go." I pointed toward Barnaby so that there would be no mistaking who I meant. But I didn't dare look at his face again.

Lady Nightwing's smooth forehead creased as if she couldn't quite fathom my request. "You desire that I free a half-breed slave as your second boon?" she repeated, as if to make sure that she had heard correctly.

I nodded my assent.

"What is this slave to you?" she asked, her voice a mixture of curiosity and suspicion.

I shrugged, hoping my request wouldn't make things worse for Barnaby if I lost. "He's nothing more to me than any other slave I'd want freed."

The crowed snickered and jeered at my response. A mocking grin spread across Lady Nightwing's features. It was tinged with what might have passed for pity, had it been someone else.

"Agreed," she stated aloud for the benefit of our audience. "Let us continue."

Then, for my ears alone, she whispered, "Sometimes I forget how pathetically amusing you humans can be."

I ignored her derision and unclenched my palm, rubbing the coin between my fingers again before flipping it up into the air. Lady Nightwing and Lathos edged forward. "The tree remains my choice for this and the next toss," I clarified, not wanting to leave them room to change any more rules.

Lady Nightwing glared at me impatiently. "Understood."

The shadowy nimbus around Lathos writhed and reached toward me once more. I held my breath and removed my hand from where I'd caught the coin. My stomach roiled and my heart sank. I didn't know if it was Lathos' doing or the coin's natural fall, but there was no doubt as to what my eyes were seeing.

"Sun," I said in a choked voice.

"Once more, Sydney," Lady Nightwing said with a calm smile.

I fingered the coin one last time, a desperate prayer on my lips as I tossed it. I uncovered it quickly, like ripping a band-aid from a wound. Lathos' black aura seethed forward and I blinked. Shadows swirled violently around my hand, but the silver of the coin only shone brighter against them. It grew hot against my skin, insistently revealing the tree.

"It's the tree," I said with a strength I didn't feel. "I win."

The crowd erupted in uncontrollable wrath, and the fury on Lady Nightwing's face was terrifying. My knees gave out and I collapsed to the filthy ground. The voices washed over me like a raging sea, hatred crashing against me in unrelenting waves. Sparrow's coin was my life preserver, and I clutched it in desperation.

"I won," I said, my voice sounding faint to my own ears. "You have to send us where we want to go." I tried unsuccessfully to swallow. "What's wrong with me?"

Lady Nightwing looked down on me with utter contempt. "You think you have outsmarted me, human, but I shall have the final victory. You may have cheated the Hoarde out of one night's diversion, but by the looks of you, you wouldn't have been good for much anyway.

"What is wrong with you?" she mimicked nastily. "The deadly poison from Hob Nightshade's thorns burns through your veins. So I will send you to the one who bears the mark of infinity as promised. And your pitiful soul shall trouble me no more."

My vision tunneled as I tried to grasp what she was saying. "The half-goblin. You will also send him wherever he asks," I insisted weakly.

She ground her teeth. "As agreed. Now be gone."

Dark fire seared through me. I tried to scream but my voice wouldn't work. The tunnel around my eyes narrowed to blackness. All my senses collapsed into a single awareness—pain—and it tore through me as if I was being ripped apart.

And then there was blessed nothingness.

<u>Chapter 3—Adrift</u>

"I am The Shepherd. There is nothing to fear. Come, bright one, it is time to rest after your journey. Rest and let go."

The voice was comfort and warmth. I settled into it—became the words, sank into the depths of their meaning. And I was content.

After a while I felt a gentle shifting, inexorably forcing me out of my newfound contentment as if someone was waking me from a pleasant sleep. I transitioned into a dissatisfied grumble, and the voice I had thought to join with chuckled softly.

"Your pardon, bright one. I cannot take you into me, but you will be united with the others soon."

I accepted, existing along-side the voice instead of within it. A vague curiosity stirred me and my awareness expanded to reveal the space around me. It was darkness, soft and thick, fogged with dim color. Entities floated past, each with a unique form, but all of them shimmering with the same inner light. It was as if their essence was the light and their forms were fluid and inconsequential.

They were beautiful and strange, familiar yet not. I was drawn to them on an elemental level. It seemed natural to want to flow into them and nestle within their glow.

A smoldering orb soared past on gossamer wings, sparking trails of energy that flew out behind it like the tail of a comet. Another being trundled by, almost amphibious in appearance, as if the head of some sea creature had been joined with the body of a man. Its dark, soulful eyes stared through me, wisdom brimming in their depths.

The figure of a woman danced through the gloom, her inexhaustible essence spilling out from her in bright waves of joy. A distinctly feline form slunk past, its face glowing like a cautious moon.

Another young woman's form peered out at me from a shadowy corner, and she seemed strangely familiar. She glowed golden, but her light was dimmer than the others'. Her long blonde hair billowed around her ethereally as she turned away. A heart-rending sadness radiated from her entire being.

A chubby-faced little girl smiled at me, haloed by points of tiny stars that formed a constellation around her. Her expression shone with innocence, yet worlds of knowledge smoldered in her child's eyes. A thought flitted past, a fleeting memory of a tiny, wrinkle-faced woman I had once called Grandma.

"These souls are waiting to be reborn and must learn to stand alone once more. You will be together again, perhaps, but now is not the time."

Then a face with strong male features appeared and looked out at me from a flaming ball of radiance. His eyes, intensely blue, burned with desperation. They struck a chord deep inside me, imploring me to remember who I was and rejoin him.

His fear confused me as I drifted away from him through the multi-hued fog. And then he was gone, replaced by the ocean of light that called to me.

It grew brighter and brighter and I felt myself quicken as I flowed toward it, eager to pour myself into it. But again, something held me back.

"Easy now, bright one. We'll be there soon."

Impatient at the delay, my focus shifted to the being that belonged to the voice. A figure drifted close behind me, benevolent and ancient as time itself. A drooping, walrus-like face, dripping with whiskers and studded with large round eyes of deepest midnight, hovered above me. His body was covered in sparse grayish feathers, the skin mottled a dark pink where it shone through them.

The bulbous fingertips of one three-fingered hand were curved above me protectively, and I realized that he cradled me within his palm. Swaying gently with his movement, I watched the being in awe, the ocean of light forgotten. Finally he stopped.

"Here we are, bright one. I now release you into the Sea of Souls."

He held me away from his body like an offering, and I turned to look out onto a vast sea of purest light. I realized in wonder that it was made up of countless beings like the ones we had just passed. Their endless manifestations were in constant flux as they flowed through each other in waves. They seemed to briefly adopt physical likenesses from one another when they touched, as if they could become each other for a moment before moving on.

I had never felt such utter love and acceptance in my life, and I suddenly wanted to join them more than I had ever wanted anything. I felt myself flowing forward, as if on a sigh—the last sigh of a long and weary day, uttered while sinking into my own soft pillows.

And then all thoughts of earthly existence broke apart and began to fade. I was shining and free. The Shepherd held up a hand in farewell, and I hovered for a moment, mesmerized. A brilliant symbol glowed there on his palm like a beacon. A faraway memory seemed to tug at me. I reached for it, struggling to recall what the symbol meant and why it was important.

With a regretful glance at the beckoning sea, I turned and began drifting back toward The Shepherd's hand, searching myself for the significance of that strangely compelling symbol. Its meaning was as vast as the sea behind me. It went on forever, like...infinity.

Memory crashed over me and I felt myself buzzing with agitation as I rushed toward The Shepherd. I didn't belong here. I tried to tell him—but I had no voice. His walrus' face hung down in puzzlement as he attempted to urge me forward with his hand. Brightness beamed from the infinity symbol there, and I felt it nudging me back toward the Sea.

Panic overtook me as I resisted the push. The air began to glow brighter around me, and I realized that it was my own light, pulsing in time with my fear.

The Shepherd blinked his midnight eyes at me and the infinity symbol dimmed as he slowly lowered his hand.

"Seals of the magi," he mumbled, shaking his head and sending his long whiskers quivering. *"I won't force you, bright one, but the wait will be long and lonely if you do not join the Sea."* He watched me for a moment before he sighed and turned away. *"I suppose you'll move on when you're ready."*

I hovered there, lost and alone, as he shuffled back up the tunnel. Not knowing what else to do, I drifted after him. He continued to mutter to himself and I floated closer so that I could hear him.

"Only has one other soul ever refused to join the Sea like that. Strange happenings here lately. More souls being reborn than usual. Maybe it's time to pay a visit to the Seelie Court. Probably been at least a century since I poked my head out."

He grumbled, seeming caught up in an argument with himself. Then he shrugged and puffed out his whiskers.

"No. Surely they would call on me if there was a problem. Must be getting paranoid in my solitude and old age." He chuckled softly. *"I'm sure everything is in good order. Still, I suppose I am past due for a visit. Maybe sometime soon..."*

He fell silent. I continued to drift along behind him, back up the passage, past the myriad souls that waited to be reborn. He turned to the left and disappeared through an opening in the wall that led into a small, sparsely furnished space. I watched him settle, cross-legged, onto a cushion in the middle of the floor. He closed his eyes and remained there, perfectly still, like a wizened old monk lost in meditation.

I was forgotten. Despair and loneliness settled over me. What was I supposed to do now? How was I going to get home?

And then it hit me.

Oh Goddess.

I was dead.

I flew further up the twilit passageway, this time paying no heed to the glowing entities wandering in my wake. I was desperate to find an exit— and not into the newborn body of a screaming baby. I had to get back and tell Sparrow, Sunny and Lorien about the goblin and the infinity tattoo—I couldn't be dead!

As I neared the end of the tunnel, fog swirling with dark rainbows gradually thickened and condensed into an amorphous barrier. It looked like a heavy mist, but it was as unyielding as a rock wall. I floated up its length, my anxiety growing as I explored its edges but found no escape.

Two waiting souls approached—one thin and fey, graceful as a butterfly; the other short and round, with the look of a plodding forest creature, an orb of light at the tip of its tail. They were different as sun from moon, but they held hands as they traveled alongside each other, their mingled bliss shining from their faces. They seemed to belong together, like two mismatched peas in a pod.

I thought, in wonder, that they must be twins.

They floated right at the barrier and I swept down to rush after them. But the mist gently pushed me back, even as it allowed their forms to pass through. I could have cried with the frustration of it, but just as I had no voice, I had no tears. I sank down to the floor, utterly disheartened.

I remained there for a long while, limp and hopeless, my consciousness beginning to drift. A sound, so faint I thought I might have imagined it, caught my fading attention. It came again, nearly inaudible, like a cry heard from too far away. I rose, gliding back down the tunnel with listless curiosity, and coming to a halt before the orb of flame with the man's face that had drawn me earlier. Its brightness had dimmed to almost nothing.

As I focused on it, the pale impression of masculine features reappeared. Eyes looked out at me in desperation and something inside me recognized their heat. They pulled me forward into the intensity of their gaze. The cry sounded again, resonating deep within me, calling my name.

I melded into the orb and was instantly engulfed by its warmth. Then I was flying through the nothingness of space at an impossible speed, too fast to think, too fast to see. It ended in an abrupt jolt of physical awareness that left me gasping for breath.

Heaviness settled into me, paralyzing and unbearable at first. But gentle hands moved over me and soft crooning words whispered through my ears. Gradually the heaviness began to ease, and I opened my eyes to find Sparrow hovering over me. He tried to smile, but his face was stiff, his eyes haunted.

I wanted to reach up and smooth his worried frown, but my body felt awkward and unresponsive, and my hand flopped uselessly at my side. He must have seen my panic, because he moved closer, whispering words of comfort in Gaelic as his palms swept down my arms, his fingers finding mine and twining with them.

I felt wetness on my face and realized that the tears I had been unable to shed now streamed from my eyes.

"Sydney," Sparrow whispered brokenly, holding me with his gaze as he leaned in to brush his lips against mine. It was the lightest touch, meant only to soothe, but electricity arced between us with the contact. My lips responded the way my limbs wouldn't, desperately moving against his. I drank him in as if I was dying of a thirst only he could quench, my flesh craving proof that it still lived.

He groaned softly into my mouth, his tongue seeking mine as he returned the kiss with a slow-burning intensity that sent me spiraling out of my body once more.

A muffled sound, half laughter, half sobbing, broke through the burgeoning haze of desire that threatened to sweep me away.

Sparrow gentled the kiss, cupping my face in his palms as he broke it, the stroke of his thumb across my lower lip easing the vacancy left by his mouth. "We thought we'd lost you."

I felt the mattress dip beneath me as Sunny scrambled onto the bed and threw her arms around me in a tight hug. When I whimpered at the pressure against my aching right side, she instantly pulled back, her tear-streaked face contrite.

"Sorry, Syd. Did I hurt you?" She sniffed, her green eyes rimmed with red and cloudy with worry.

"Just bruised where I fell," I mumbled, trying to manage a reassuring smile.

She gingerly lifted my dirt-crusted shirt and sucked in a breath. I craned my neck, grimacing at what I saw. No wonder I was sore. My entire side was an ugly mass of discoloration, blooming with shades of black, green and blue.

"Are you sure nothing's broken?" Sunny asked, looking horrified.

"Let me see," Sparrow insisted as he leaned over me. He passed his hand just above the bruising, closing his eyes as he did so, his words becoming an inaudible hum. A curious heat traveled down my side beneath his palm and a soft, silvery light bled from the Celtic tattoos on his bare, muscular arm. Except for the one just beneath his elbow, which pulsed with a bright yellow.

My own arm was still a little shaky, but I reached up to trace my finger over the pulsing design. It was almost hot to the touch and a tingling energy vibrated through my hand with the contact.

"Why does this one always glow yellow, when the others glow different colors?" I mumbled.

"Hmm?" he murmured as he completed his examination of my side. He blinked at me, and then ran an absent hand over the inked flesh I had touched. "Oh, that just means I'm a bit tired."

His blue eyes captured mine and he reached to smooth his fingers over my forehead, the touch both soothing and stirring. "No broken bones, I think, and no internal bleeding. I can probably heal some of that bruising later, but I'm afraid I'm a bit tapped out at the moment."

I studied Sparrow's handsome face, noting the deepened lines of strain and exhaustion.

"I'll get you something for the pain," Sunny offered, rolling to her feet and heading toward the medicine cabinet in my bathroom.

I felt a flutter of air against my side and looked down to see Lorien hovering there, a look of sheer determination on her face. Her wings quivered and dark purple faerie dust sifted from them in a heavy stream.

"Lorien!" I exclaimed, overjoyed at the sight of her. Just as quickly, regret twanged through me over the way I'd spoken to her earlier.

"At the very least, I can manage this." She swiped angrily at a tiny, crystalline tear.

She reached into her little silver pouch and pulled out a pinch of glittering silver dust. A look of fierce concentration took over her pale face as she moved above my side and sprinkled the silvery powder onto the bruising.

I felt a faint shimmer of relief. "Thanks, that helped," I assured her.

She ignored me, staring at my injuries with an irate gleam in her tear-filled eyes. She withdrew a second pinch of dust from her pouch and repeated her actions with forceful intensity. A golden glow transmuted the silver of the powder, growing brighter than flame as it landed against my side.

It remained there for a moment, drawing out the pain, a skein of light lying over my skin like a healing balm. Then it flashed outward, knocking Lorien back onto the bed, before it winked out of existence. I stared down in amazement at the unblemished flesh it left behind. My eyes drifted to Lorien, her small limbs sprawled out as she lay in a stunned heap beside me.

Sunny stood motionless halfway to the bathroom, having abandoned her quest for the medicine cabinet. Sparrow whistled into the silence. "That was quite an impressive bit of healing magic, little sister."

Lorien swallowed, then her face crumpled and she burst into tears. Feeling helpless, I sat up and gently scooped her into my palms—which were also now smooth and splinter free. I held her close, wondering how I was supposed to properly hug a three inch tall faerie, and felt my own tears start again.

"It's okay Lorien. And I'm so sorry—I didn't mean what I said before. I know all you've ever done is try to help me."

"Useless is what I am." She sniffled. "I knew you were in danger and I couldn't do a blinking thing to help. And then you just disappeared," her pitch rose, "and I couldn't feel you at all." She shook her head and hid her face in her small hands.

Sunny came back and perched on the side of the bed, pulling her thin robe more tightly around her. She placed her hand against my shoulder as if she needed the contact to steady herself. "What the hell happened to you? Lorien woke me up. I ran in here and you were just lying there, with your clothes and face all dirty, as still as death. I thought you *were* dead," she said, her speech strained. "But then I realized you still had a pulse, even though we couldn't wake you."

Sunny paused and then whispered, "Lorien said your soul was gone. We thought a death djinn had..." she tapered off as if she couldn't bear to say the words.

"I thought I was dead too," I replied in a small voice. "I felt so far away... and light. And there was this old walrus guy carrying me. He wanted me to join the Sea of Souls. It was so beautiful and bright," I breathed, memory coursing through me.

Lorien let out a gasp, her violet eyes startled, and Sparrow reached for my other shoulder, his hand tightening around it like he was afraid I might float away.

"I almost went into it," I continued, hearing the awe in my voice as I remembered my intense desire to join with all of those combined souls.

"If you had, I wouldn't have been able to call you back," Sparrow said, emotion deepening his brogue.

"Something stopped me." I frowned, trying to gather the fading fragments of the experience in my mind.

"Did you hear me calling you?" he asked gently.

"Yes, but..." I frowned, trying to squeeze the memory from my muddled brain, and then my eyes widened with excitement. "The infinity symbol! The Shepherd had the infinity symbol on his hand!"

"Was he a goblin?" Sunny asked in confusion.

"No," Sparrow answered and my eyes shot to his. I could almost see the thoughts spinning behind them. "The Shepherd is an ancient mage who was assigned to watch over the Sea of Souls by the Seelie Court long ago. Very little is known about him, and I had forgotten this small piece of lore, but it is said that he carries the symbol of eternity upon his palm to aid him in tendering mortal souls to and from the Sea."

"It makes sense," Lorien said with an animated nod, rising from where she had been resting in my hands. "The symbol of eternity—*infinity*. Whoever's been magically tampering with the souls must be using the symbol as a way to gain power over them."

"The Shepherd's symbol is a mark of the magi," Sparrow said slowly. "Only a highly accomplished mage would be able to harness its power. No goblin should be able to fully wield such a mark—there isn't enough magic in their blood."

"There *was* a goblin with the symbol on his hand," I interjected. "His name was Firzag. But he's dead."

Three pairs of eyes turned on me in the sudden deafening silence. "You still haven't told us what happened to you," Lorien said, suspicion warring with the concern in her gaze.

I squirmed, knowing that no one was going to be happy with where the conversation was about to go—least of all me.

"I met an old goblin woman who knew him. She didn't know why he had the symbol, or how he died. But she gave me a book that belonged to him." My breath caught in panic as I reached down to my waistband.

I exhaled in relief as I felt the thin, square shape beneath it. "I didn't get a chance to look at it," I said as I pulled out a small, green writing journal. The cover was heavily stained, the edges of the pages yellowed with time.

Sparrow looked at me questioningly and took the notebook when I nodded my assent. He opened it with caution and then scanned a few of the pages. "It's part of a journal," he confirmed.

"It doesn't look like it was written by a goblin—it looks like it was written by a mortal woman. She talks about a bargain made, granting three wishes and immortality in exchange for pledging service to a 'highly charismatic man, with eyes of fiery green.'" Sparrow's gaze rose to mine.

"Death djinn," Sunny intoned.

"Is there a name?" I asked anxiously.

Sparrow flipped through the thin notebook, shaking his head as he went. "I'd really like for our mages to take a look, if you don't mind me borrowing it for a few days. But at first glance I'm not seeing any names or other specifics. Only about a quarter of the journal was used." He held up the book to show us mostly blank pages.

"Take it for however long you need. There better be something of use in there, considering what I went through to get it," I added in a grumble.

"No dates either?" Sunny insisted in frustration.

Sparrow shook his head again as he leafed through the notebook, his expression grim. "I'm afraid not. It looks fairly old, though. Where did you meet the goblin woman who gave it to you?" He looked up to pin me with his gaze.

Well, I hadn't thought I was going to get off that easily. And I might as well spill it now, while there was a chance they'd take pity on my weakened condition.

"She was a merchant on the Hell Ride." I was surprised by how steady my voice was, though I couldn't force myself to meet anyone's eyes as I said it.

Lorien let out a strangled gasp.

"You didn't tell me you were going to do that!" Sunny accused.

"So that's why I couldn't get to you! Sydney—how could you do that?" Lorien exclaimed.

I accepted their censure in silence, bracing myself for Sparrow to join in. When he didn't, I raised my eyes to his, expecting to see fury there. His blue gaze locked with mine, so many things swirling within it that I could barely put a name to them.

"You nearly died tonight, Sydney. It was a foolish move—and an immeasurably brave one. And I haven't the right to judge you."

It was almost an apology and I knew I didn't deserve it. "Sparrow, I'm so sorry I didn't tell you about Jeremy. I didn't keep it from you on purpose, I just wasn't thinking. I..."

"Shhh." He stroked the backs of his knuckles down my cheek and I leaned into his touch, squeezing my eyes shut against the tears that threatened to fall again. "I know," he said simply. Then he folded his arms around my shoulders and pulled me into the solid warmth of his chest.

Peace settled over me, followed by a stirring awareness that curled through me at his touch. Goddess, he smelled *so* good. And he felt even better.

After a minute, Sunny cleared her throat and the mattress shifted as her weight left the bed. "Come on, Lorien. We can tell her what a dumb idea it was in the morning. She's had enough for tonight."

Lorien pointed to the alarm clock on my nightstand, where glowing red numbers proclaimed it was 3:47 am. "It *is* morning," she said obstinately.

Sunny coughed a laugh. "Yeah, but I think we should leave these two alone."

Lorien's pale cheeks pinkened at Sunny's significant look.

"Don't worry, though—I'll be right there with you when she wakes up later. I can't *believe* you didn't tell us you were planning to go on the Hell Ride." Sunny glowered at me as she shooed Lorien toward the door, her tone promising retribution.

I gave her an apologetic half smile, my chin still resting on Sparrow's shoulder. "You would have talked me out of it."

"Damn right," she grumbled, closing the door with more force than necessary.

"I love you guys—you're the best friend and faerie guardian a girl could have!" I called out after them.

"Yeah, yeah. Save it for the inquisition tomorrow," Sunny groused back.

Sparrow chuckled softly in my ear. "Looks like you're in trouble."

"Looks like," I agreed.

"Then I guess we'll just have to make sure this night was worth it." His low voice vibrated through me, an arrow of desire piercing deep into my core.

He scooped me off the bed and carried me toward the bathroom.

"What are you doing?" I demanded on a peal of laughter.

"First, I'm going to wash the Hell Ride off of you. And then I'm going to do something I should have done days ago."

"What's that?" I asked, breathless with anticipation.

His eyes were searing as they looked down into mine. "I'm going to make love to you properly, Sydney. And this time, nothing is going to stop me."

Chapter 4—A Worthwhile Diversion

My passion was diluted by my reflection as we passed the mirror above the vanity sink. I looked up at Sparrow in horror. "My Goddess, Sparrow, why didn't you tell me I was hideous?"

He choked back a laugh and dropped a kiss on the tip of my dirt smudged nose as he reached into the shower to turn on the spray. "Only temporarily hideous—nothing a little hot water and soap can't handle."

I gaped at him. "Aren't you supposed to lie and tell me that I could never be hideous? You *are* hoping to have your wicked way with me tonight. Shouldn't you be whispering sweet nothings in my ear, regardless of their veracity, and..."

His mouth swooped down to silence me, his tongue coaxing my lips apart and then sweeping inside to stroke against mine. He lowered me down his body until my feet touched the floor, supporting my weight as I clung to him.

He pushed my dirt-caked shirt up my body in an unhurried slide, his long fingers branding a path of need as they glided over my sides and back. His hands slowed as his thumbs swept up the curves of my breasts, pausing to brush my nipples into hard peaks through the thin fabric of my bra. I moaned and his kiss deepened.

He pulled away to rid me of my shirt, capturing my eyes with his as he dropped it to the cool tiles of the bathroom floor. "You are always beautiful to me, Sydney," he whispered as his arms came around me and his hands moved to deftly unhook my bra. His eyes held mine as he discarded the scrap of fabric and pulled me closer.

He brushed my lips in a feather light caress. "And I do fully intend to have my wicked way with you tonight," he added in a heavy brogue. The top button of my jeans came free with a flick of his fingers and my body clenched with heat.

His mouth drifted across my cheek to my ear, where his teeth grazed and nibbled at the sensitive flesh behind it. Sparrow released my zipper and slid my jeans down over my hips. "I'm going to make you come until you beg me to stop, Sydney." A little cry escaped my lips as his hand moved between my legs and his fingers began stroking me.

"And then I'm going to make you come again."

My knees turned to water and Sparrow held me up with one arm banded low around my back. His fingers slid through the slickness at the entrance to my body, circling but not penetrating. He growled deep in his throat, whispering to me in Gaelic as he nuzzled the spot behind my ear.

Then he groaned, "You're so wet, Sydney." His finger plunged inside me as his thumb brushed over my clit, once, twice, a third time before dipping

two fingers into me. My body was a tangle of exquisite sensation as my
hips rode his hand faster, taking him deeper, until I was soaring and crying
out in pleasure.

He held me until my trembling calmed, and then reached behind me
to slide open the shower door. Steam billowed out around us, its damp
warmth caressing my bare skin. I sighed as he placed me beneath the
flow of water, the shock of heat making my muscles tighten for a moment
before it soaked in to melt away the tension. I leaned bonelessly against the
shower wall, letting the hot water stream over me, as I watched Sparrow
strip.

Well-defined muscles shifted in a symphony of motion beneath tanned
and inked skin as he lifted his black t-shirt up and over his head, leaving
his dark hair careless and mussed. He pushed his jeans and boxer briefs
down his thighs, and my eyes riveted to his thick, hard shaft as it sprang
free of the material.

And then he was walking toward me through the heated mist, like a
naked Celtic god stepping from a dream. He slid the shower door shut
behind him, his blue eyes bright as they held mine, and I suddenly found
it difficult to breathe. His hand came up, his fingers lightly grazing over
my neck, until the pad of his thumb was gliding across my lower lip and
pulling it down to open my mouth for his.

"You're not having second thoughts, are you Sydney?" he whispered as
his tongue traced where his thumb had touched and then dipped into my
mouth. He pulled me under the spray and slicked his fingers through my
hair as he lifted his head and smiled questioningly down into my eyes.

"Not at all," I denied with a quick shake of my head. "This just feels so...
intense," I breathed, hearing the words leave my mouth and hoping they
didn't sound as corny as I feared.

Sparrow's eyes darkened and grew serious. "It's the same for me,
Sydney."

Relief moved through me and I whispered, "Good." Then I forced a grin.
"Of course, it might also have something to do with the fact that I have the
most gorgeous naked man I've ever seen in my shower with me."

Sparrow raised his eyebrows playfully. He reached behind me to take the
soap from its dish, wetting it and beginning to scrub slow circles over my
back. "Flattery will get you everywhere, Sydney."

He gave me a wicked smile. "So where would you like to go?"

I nibbled my lip as the corners of my mouth twitched upward.
"Everywhere."

I ran my hands along the corded contours of his arms, his Aegishjalmur
tattoo glowing red and tingling beneath my palm as it traveled up toward
the firm width of his shoulders. My fingers tangled in his damp hair as I
pulled his lips down to mine, rising up onto my toes to meet them. Our

mouths joined at the edge of the shower's spray, the water heightening the eroticism of the kiss.

Sparrow's hands went still at my back and I reached behind me to steal the bar of soap so that I could lather the solid wall of his chest. He shuddered beneath my touch as I washed him, running my fingers over his body with the flowing water as it rinsed him clean. I worked up a froth between my palms and put the bar aside. Then I trailed my hands lower, rubbing one soap-slicked palm over the length of his shaft and cupping his sac in a gentle massage with the other.

My gaze drank in his stubble-darkened face as his eyelids fell shut and his head tipped back in pleasure. I leaned forward to kiss the intricate patterns on his skin, licking at droplets of water as I tasted him, the clean fragrance of my soap mingling with his own spicy scent beneath. His intake of breath was sharp as I circled his nipple with my tongue, pulling it between my lips to suckle it before kissing a path across his chest to lave its twin.

I sank slowly to my knees, allowing the water to rain down between us until the soap was washed away. Resting on my folded thighs, I lifted his heavy shaft and delicately ran my tongue from the base up its full length. When I took the tip of him into my mouth, he let out a hoarse shout that sent a jolt of desire rebounding through me.

I swirled my tongue around him, bathing him with its lush heat, tasting his salty essence. He muttered low and fast in Gaelic, his tone as reverent as a prayer, his hands coming down to caress my face. I took him deeper, my thumb gliding a slick path along the bottom of his shaft as I moved my lips over him. I felt the need for release building within him and spilling into me as I quickened my pace.

My hips thrust in time with my mouth, and I felt myself grow wetter as I imagined him driving into me with the same urgency. A haze of passion fogged my brain until I could no longer tell whether it was Sparrow's pleasure I felt, or my own. And then he was gently tugging at me until I rested my cheek against his hip, cradling him in my hands as he came in a warm, pulsing rush.

He pulled me to my feet and crushed me to his chest, our bodies melding as he dipped his head to take my lips in a long, lingering kiss beneath the cleansing spray.

We took our time finishing our shower. Sparrow found my shampoo and massaged it through the heavy length of my hair, his long fingers working magic upon my scalp as they soaped it and then rinsed it clean. He worked the conditioner through the ends with such care that I couldn't help but smile.

Then I asked him to give me a few minutes alone so that I could finish the rituals of shaving my legs, smoothing on lotion and brushing out wet,

tangled hair. I chose my most flattering piece of lingerie from a drawer and
pulled the partition closed between the vanity and the bedroom.

My stomach fluttered as I took a last glance in the mirror before opening
the partition. My red silk negligee floated above my knees, hugging my
curves perfectly as it dipped into the hollow of my back and swept down
in a flat line above the swell of my stomach. My hair, toweled dry, fell
long and straight behind me, swaying against the gauzy material with my
movements.

Sparrow made me feel beautiful, but I wanted to *be* beautiful for him.

I took a deep breath and stepped into my bedroom to find myself in the
midst of a romantic fantasy. Sparrow was touching a match to the last unlit
candle in the room, soft classical music spilled from the television speakers,
and rose-petals were strewn across the linens of the huge canopied bed.

Shaking out the flame, he dropped the match beside the ivory pillar he'd
lit. Intricate inked patterns rippled over his taut muscles as he turned to
face me. Scattered points of candlelight glinted off his damp hair and lent a
golden sheen to his bare flesh as he stood before me.

I drifted toward him, speechless with wonder as I paused by the bed to
rub a ruby velvet rose-petal between my fingertips.

"Sparrow, this is amazing," I murmured on an awed breath. "Where did
you find roses?"

My heart fluttered at his charmingly boyish grin. "I'm magic, remember.
Do you like it?"

"I love it," I answered, humbled by his consideration, a rush of emotion
swirling through me.

He closed the distance between us and his hand came up to cup my
cheek, his touch reverent, as if he was handling something precious.
The fingers of his free hand brushed across the red silk of my negligee,
skimming over the stiffening peaks of my breasts before meandering in a
path across my stomach.

He leaned in, his breath a caress against my ear as he whispered, "I like
this very much."

His lips moved softly against my neck as his hand roamed lower, his
fingers splaying over my hip before gliding down my silk-covered thigh.

"Have I told you lately how incredibly sexy you are, Sydney?" His voice
shivered through me, making my womb clench. Tight and needy for him, I
moaned in response, melting into the hard length of his body.

His palms brushed over the curves of my ass, and then he lowered me
onto the edge of the bed. He knelt before me, his hands stilling at the edges
of the gossamer fabric that rested above my knees. He rubbed the supple
cloth between his fingers, and then grasped it in both hands, the muscles of
his arms flexing with controlled force as he slid it up my thighs. His pace
was excruciatingly slow, the sigh of cool silk against my sensitized skin

pushing me into a painful state of awareness.

I trembled, my body tense and hot, as he forced the negligee up over my hips. Then he stilled and simply stared at me, my most intimate place lying open to his gaze. I instinctively moved to close my knees, and his searing look transferred questioningly to my face.

Sparrow's hands slid down my inner thighs and, with a gentle pressure, he urged them wider apart. He moistened his forefinger with an erotic stroke of his tongue, and my lips parted on a shallow breath as his focus traveled lower again. He reached forward to rub his damp finger against my already slick opening, and I sank back onto my elbows with a groan.

Then his head was between my thighs, his tongue moving over me, tasting and probing at the entrance to my body, flickering over my clit, and returning to torment me with a long, slow exploration of the folds beneath. A fierce ache built within my core and a whimper of need escaped my throat. Sparrow parted my tender flesh with his fingers, opening me to the thrusts of his tongue, penetrating me deeper.

I let out a little cry of pleasure as the ache eased, transforming into a sensation of ecstasy that thickened and expanded throughout every nerve-ending in my body. My hips bucked against Sparrow as his fingers massaged the swollen nub above his mouth, his tongue continuing its merciless plundering.

My consciousness dissolved and I fell back onto the bed with a sob of assent as my orgasm ripped through me in a rush of liquid. I bit my lip with a groan and raised my head to wince down at Sparrow, afraid that my body's fluid release would shock him. He merely gazed up at me, a smile of satisfaction glowing in his eyes as his tongue trailed toward my belly button.

HIs hands caressed my sides as he lifted me to a sitting position and pulled the wispy negligee up over my head, dropping it to the carpet in a silken heap to leave me fully bared before him.

His eyes caught and held mine. "You taste earthy and sweet, like wild honey."

A fresh jolt of desire shot through me at his seductive tone and the quiet reassurance of his words.

"Wrap your legs around me, Sydney," he ordered softly.

I slid my ankles up his sides to lock them behind his back. The friction of his body rubbing between my legs was exquisite, and I gasped as he rose in one smooth motion, bringing me with him. His arms raised me higher, until the thick head of his shaft was positioned at my entrance.

I would have given my soul to have him inside me then, but years of ingrained caution kicked in. "Wait," I said on a reluctant breath.

He froze. His biceps bulged beneath his swirling tattoos, but didn't betray a tremble as he held me poised above him. The look on his face, however, was pleading.

"Condom," I gasped, "Top drawer in my nightstand."

His expression turned comical, and when he spoke, his voice was thick and raspy. "Uh, Sydney. I know this might sound like a line, but you don't have to worry about that with me. My sidhe blood keeps me free of those types of diseases, and I won't get you pregnant unless I choose to."

I blinked at him in shock, his words taking a minute to sink into my brain. "You won't get me pregnant?" I echoed faintly.

His eyes darkened to cobalt and the corners of his mouth turned upward playfully. "Not unless you want me to."

I shook my head and he leaned forward to take my lips in a lingering kiss. "Do you still want me to get the condom?" he murmured.

"I want to feel you inside me." My voice was so hoarse I barely recognized it.

Sparrow backed me up against one of the wide, rounded bedposts. There was so much heat in his eyes that I thought we'd both go up in flames.

"Put your hands above your head and hold onto the post, Sydney."

Nearly panting with desire, I raised my arms and wrapped them around the bedpost, clasping my hands behind it. My back arched, thrusting my breasts upward, and Sparrow dipped his head to take one of my nipples between his lips, swirling his tongue around it as he eased the thick head of his shaft into me.

"Sparrow, yes!" The words left me on a helpless shout, the feel of him stretching and filling me as he lowered my body down onto his almost too intense to bear. When our hips met, his shaft so deep inside me I could feel him brushing my cervix, I had to squeeze my eyes shut against tears of relief.

"Look at me, Sydney," he demanded worriedly. "Did I hurt you?"

"No," I gasped, my body a tangle of sensations as my hips squirmed fitfully against his and I struggled to pull myself back up the bedpost. "You feel so good. I need...I need more."

He grinned as his lips descended toward mine. "Impatient little witch," he breathed into my mouth. And then his tongue was stroking against mine as he lifted me up his length and began a smooth, thrusting rhythm that left me mindless with pleasure. He gradually increased the pace, sliding deeper into my wet passage as my hips rode him, my body straining for release.

The concentration of pleasure became painful and my eyelids squeezed together as I urged him faster, reaching in frustration for a closure I feared wouldn't come. I was wound so tight, I nearly sobbed when he slowed his thrusts and gentled his kiss.

"Shhh, Sydney," he intoned in a quiet brogue. "Look at me, *a chuisle*."

I opened my eyes to find him watching me intently. I was so close to orgasm that my nerves felt shredded and raw. But I didn't know how to find it.

If I had been with Jeremy, he would have finished by now. He had left me on the brink so many times that my body had learned to shut itself down after a while to avoid disappointment. I couldn't bear the thought of that happening with Sparrow.

I looked at him, hating the silent plea I knew was in my eyes.

"It's okay," he whispered, slowly rocking his hips up into me. My breathing steadied and deepened as I held his gaze. His leaned in to move his lips over mine, but he pulled back when my eyelids fluttered shut again.

"Open your eyes, *anamchara*," he coaxed. "Stay with me."

I did as he asked, the unguarded connection of his stare making me feel self-conscious. I stiffened, my hands clutching involuntarily behind the bedpost. His eyes burned bright in the flickering candlelight. They pulled me in, unashamed, freely offering what I needed. Sparrow continued the gentle rocking of his hips, stroking deep inside me, our bodies so close that the crisp dark hairs above his shaft brushed my clitoris with each movement.

"Stay with me," he murmured again, shifting so that he slid deeper, increasing the pressure against my clit.

He smiled at my sudden pleasured inhalation and rocked into me faster. The sensations built and I took full, even breaths to steady myself. The air around us seemed to vibrate with color and energy. And Sparrow's eyes stared fixedly into mine, breath-taking in their openness, looking past my vulnerability and calling to something deep within me.

An expansion began at my center, unfolding and flowing outward, rushing through me as bands of light moved across my vision. "Sparrow," I gasped his name like a prayer, our eyes remaining joined even as my body shuddered and trembled, clenching and milking his as he rocked harder into me, increasing and prolonging my climax.

He caught me as my arms fell from the bedpost, cradling me against him and raining soft kisses over my face as he whispered beautiful words that I didn't understand.

He lowered me to the bed, slipping out of the sheath of my body as his hands urged me to turn onto my stomach. His fingers brushed over my hair and along my back, my skin so sensitive now that his every touch sizzled through me with shattering intensity.

The scattered velvet of rose-petals caressed my flesh where I lay against them. Their lingering fragrance was an aphrodisiac that whispered seductively to my overloaded senses. Sparrow drew my hips back so that I rested low on my arms, my knees at the edge of the bed with him standing behind me.

"Once more, Sydney," he rasped as he bent over me, his voice sending a shiver across my skin. "I want to be so deep inside you that you'll hold a part of me there forever."

He plunged into me and we both cried out, our pleas mingling in the thickened air. He pulled back until his tip barely brushed my entrance, and then plunged into me again. Every pleasure center in my body was heightened to the breaking point. Once more Sparrow pulled out and thrust himself deep inside my sensitive passage. I groaned, unsure how much more I could take.

"Sparrow, you're killing me," I gasped unsteadily.

He leaned closer, running his fingers down my spine and over my sides, making me want to purr with ecstasy. "Just a little death," he whispered, his tone wicked. His palms lifted and kneaded my breasts as he stroked into me again.

I drove back against him, begging him to move faster. His hands swept across my stomach, spreading shivering fire wherever they touched. Then he wrapped an arm around my hips and pulled me into a steady rhythm. I moaned my assent, my body opening wider as I took him deeper.

He quickened and his need rushed through me, intensifying my own. My muscled clenched around him just as he let out a husky shout, his shaft pulsing inside me as my inner walls tightened and released against him.

Lost in a sea of sensation, helpless little gasps escaped my throat as I sank to rest on the bed, still holding Sparrow within my body. Clasping me to him, he rolled onto his side. His warm hands skimmed over my belly, lazily drifting upward to cup the weight of my breasts.

My back arched into his chest, a languid, cat-like stretch of satisfaction. Then I nestled against him, my limbs filled with delicious exhaustion. The room was growing brighter outside the shutters of my eyelids. I smiled as the familiar lilting of a flute drifted from the speakers, playing the opening cadence of Grieg's 'Morning'.

I'd just had the most amazing sex ever. And I was so tired I didn't think I could move. I debated about sliding up the sheets so that our heads were on the pillows and we could pull the covers over us...

And with that thought, I was fast asleep.

<u>Chapter 5—The Handwriting On The Wall</u>

When I woke it was after noon and I was alone in my bed. I groggily focused on my nightstand, where a large Starbucks cup loomed over my head. I pulled it toward my lips and took a sip, hoping I hadn't somehow spent my third wish on it in sleep induced delirium—but grateful for it none the less.

Ahhh...peppermint mocha, still warm and just how I liked it. Already a little more excited about the prospect of being awake, I propped myself up on my pillows. A single deep burgundy rose lay atop a folded slip of paper further back on the nightstand.

I smiled, a tingle of excitement teasing my insides as I reached for the perfect bloom and its accompanying note. The flower's aroma was rich and sweet, and I closed my eyes to savor it before unfolding the message. In crisp, bold script it said:

Sydney,
Sorry I couldn't be here when you woke—I had to go into the office for a while and didn't want to disturb your rest. Not that I'll be able to stop imagining making love to you for long enough to actually concentrate on work.

Last night was amazing.

Sunny said this was your favourite coffee. I hope it's how you like it.

I borrowed the journal so that our mages can examine it. I'll return it to you when they are finished.

I will try to come by this evening, or as soon as I can slip away. But Lorien knows how to reach me if you need me sooner.

Sparrow

P.S. Good luck with the Inquisition. I'm rather eager to question you myself. But I promise you'll enjoy my brand of torture...

Mmm...I had no doubt I would.

Feeling giddy, I rose to get dressed and face whatever Sunny and Lorien had to dish out. Not even the prospect of their combined anger and disappointment over my impromptu journey on the Hell Ride could dent my good mood after last night.

Coffee in hand, I headed up the hallway and into the kitchen. I brought Sparrow's note too—mostly because I couldn't seem to stop re-reading it.

I bounced past my dining room/office, ignoring the fact that my appearance immediately halted my friends' discussion. I plunked onto the couch next to Sunny, my grin still firmly in place. Angelica sat with her knees crossed in an elegant pose on the loveseat, no doubt having been enticed into a gossip break by Sunny and Lorien.

I lay Sparrow's letter on the glass table top next to Lorien, undaunted by the scowl on her face. Angelica, I noticed, seemed to be trying to hide her own guilty expression of pleasure.

Then, before they could say a word, I launched into a cheerful apology.

"I know you guys are mad at me, and I deserve it. I'm not sure what got into me—I just couldn't stand feeling so helpless. And the Hell Ride seemed like my last hope of finding out about the goblin and the infinity mark. I should have told you both what I was planning, but I was afraid you'd talk me out of it. And you know how stubborn I can be. Anyway, I'm really sorry. It was wrong for me not to include you."

Sunny narrowed her eyes at me and shook her head. Lorien floundered for a response, then her scowl deepened and she turned to glower at Sparrow's note.

"What's that?" Sunny asked testily as she leaned forward to join Lorien in reading the letter.

Lorien fluttered her wings and floated back from the table, so she could make out the words. The piece of paper was large enough to cover her like a blanket. Sunny finished first and dropped her head into her hands with a sigh.

"It's so unfair," she mumbled.

"What?" I asked with a widening grin.

She peered at me from between her fingers, giving me what could only be described as the stink eye. "Here I was, all ready to lay into you—as you so richly deserve—and you have to go and bring this example of unadulterated sap into it. I can't be mad at you *now*." She exhaled irritably. "And I had such an impressive tirade planned, too."

Lorien finished reading the note, and seemed torn between anger and concern. Even the sparkling dust that sifted from her wings kept alternating colors, shifting between an aggravated orange and an anxious purple.

"Going on the Hell Ride was, by far, the most ignorant, troll-brained bit of insane dragon dung you've ever pulled, Sydney!" she sputtered.

"I know. You're right," I agreed in a contrite tone.

"And if you *ever* do anything like that again, I'll...I'll make Sparrow put you over his knee and spank the dust out of you!" she exclaimed.

Sunny snickered and I tried very hard not to laugh.

Angelica looked perplexed. "I thought you wanted to *discourage* her from doing such a thing again," she murmured in confusion.

Lorien turned on her with an outraged glare and I collapsed against Sunny with the laughter I could no longer contain. Lorien threw her small arms into the air and abruptly sank back to a seat on the edge of the table. "I give up," she grumbled.

"So, how was it?" Sunny asked with a suggestive wiggle of her raven brows.

"Incredible," I exhaled in appreciation.

"I am so happy for you, Sydney." Angelica beamed with sincerity. "The passion between you and your lover when you finally came together this morning was an inspiring thing. It woke me from sleep and I couldn't help but share in your joy."

"Uh...thanks, Angelica," I said, trying to adopt the pleased manner of someone who had just received a compliment. I wasn't entirely sure I wanted to know how she had 'shared in our joy', though. I cleared my throat.

Lorien made an annoyed sound. "Well, since you've managed to cheat your way out of being properly reprimanded for it, you could at least tell us what happened while you were out all night on your idiotic quest," she grumped.

I grinned at her. "Yes, ma'am."

"And don't leave out any details!" Sunny demanded.

"I wouldn't dare," I agreed in a meek tone.

Having diffused their anger, it was kind of fun telling them about my adventures on the Hell Ride and in the Sea of Souls—although I wasn't eager to repeat either experience in reality.

All three of them were on the edges of their seats as I recounted what had happened on the Hell Barge. And they shuddered gratifyingly at my descriptions of Gochi, Lady Nightwing, Hob and Lathos.

"It sounds like Gochi was a bugaboo," Angelica mused. "They're rare and horrible creatures with the ability to paralyze their victims through fear."

"I wondered why Lady Nightwing called him a 'bug'!"

Lorien hung her head when I got to the part about giving my blood to Ezrega in exchange for the notebook. "That was ill advised, Sydney," she said quietly. "Let's hope that whoever purchases it from her uses it for a generic spell, and not to gain power over you specifically."

I felt a chill of discomfort at her words, but I shrugged it off. There was nothing I could do about it now. I certainly wasn't going back to the Hell Ride to reclaim my blood. It was a miracle I'd survived the first time.

"So Hob accidentally poisoned you when he ran into you on the stairs!" Sunny exclaimed in dawning horror, when I recounted Lady Nightwing's parting words before she sent me to the Sea of Souls.

"Troll-brained hatchling," Lorien muttered angrily. "Titania's wand! *Everyone* knows you should never get that close to a hobgoblin!"

Angelica nodded vigorously, her blue eyes huge and round above her rose-tinted cheeks. "You are lucky that the goblin woman gave you her blood strengthening cure, or you may not have lasted as long as you did."

"That sneaky Nightwing hag was going to send you to your death whether you won the coin toss or not!" Sunny snapped indignantly.

I nodded. "She was the most horrible, frightening woman I've ever met. But I guess you don't become the queen of the Hell Ride by being all sweetness and light."

Sunny and I were the only ones who seemed to find that observation amusing.

I frowned. "If the poison was so deadly, though, shouldn't it have taken more than Ezrega's powder to cure me?"

"It did." Lorien's voice was so soft I almost didn't hear it. "Agent Sparrow nearly burned out his power trying to heal you and call you back from the Sea of Souls. I wasn't strong enough to do it. In the end, he had to combine his soul with yours to save you."

I stared at her in shock. The whole Sea of Souls thing was strangely hazy in my mind, as if it was a fading dream. "He's okay though, right? He still has his power?"

"He tested it to its limits, but it held." Lorien looked troubled, despite her reassurance.

"What aren't you telling me?" I asked, anxiety nipping at my throat.

"Nothing," she insisted. "It's just that, combining your soul with another's like that...it's an incredibly intimate act. It creates an unnatural bond. And then you two," she paused for emphasis, "bonded even more closely right afterward."

I grinned at her in relief. "Is that all you're worried about? I think Sparrow and I were well on our way to doing *that* regardless."

Sunny smiled, but I couldn't help noticing Angelica's thoughtful look and the concern still shining in Lorien's violet eyes.

My forehead crumpled in a frown. "What are you saying, Lorien? That Sparrow only slept with me as a side effect of the soul combining thing?"

"No. Not necessarily." She shook her head, looking uncomfortable. "All I'm saying is that he carried your soul in his. Sometimes a little distance is called for after that sort of thing—to ease the separation for both parties and allow them to regain their individuality." Her eyes were pained. "I just don't want to see you hurt again, Sydney."

I shrugged, trying not to give rise to my growing trepidation. "Okay, I'll keep it in mind. Thanks."

I told myself that her concerns didn't matter. I wasn't going to let her fears ruin my happiness over making love with Sparrow. Nonetheless, my elation was dampened.

Lorien's words whirled insistently through my mind, no matter how hard I tried to push them away. Last night was the first time I'd seen Sparrow since he found out I was married. And he'd forgiven me awfully quickly for keeping it from him. Could his sudden renewal of interest really be because his feelings for me had been artificially manipulated by calling my soul back?

And what were we supposed to do—not see each other until it wore off? How long would that take, and how would we know when our feelings were our own again?

The idea was so upsetting that I ended up excusing myself and retreating back to my room.

I claimed exhaustion from the previous night's ordeals, but I didn't think my friends were fooled. I could feel Sunny's sympathetic gaze following me until I disappeared into the kitchen. Angelica even offered to leave the cleaning of my bedroom for next time.

Lorien just watched me go with a silent, unreadable look.

∞ ∞ ∞ ∞ ∞ ∞ ∞ ∞ ∞

In truth, I was still pretty tired. I knew I should call Cindy and let her know I'd be back to work tomorrow, but I just didn't have the energy. I crawled between the sheets and it wasn't long before I drifted off again. I expected nightmares, but I managed to slip into a dreamless sleep.

"Wake up, my *anamchara*."

I awoke to Sparrow's whisper and his breath tickling my ear with warmth. Lorien's warning flew right out of my head.

I smiled and turned toward him, my arms snaking around his back to pull him the rest of the way onto the bed. He laughed as his weight joined mine and I scooted over to give him room. We lay on our sides, our faces inches apart.

"Haven't you had enough sleep yet?" he teased.

"Hey—I happen to take my sleep very seriously. The more, the better." My tone was indignant, but I couldn't hide my grin.

A playful light came into his eyes and he shrugged, as if to bait me. "Sleeping's for old folks and bairns."

"Oh really?" I huffed, giving him an offended look. "Well, you must not be on close terms with many succubi then. Just the other day, Angelica offered to send her two incubi friends into my dreams and…"

Sparrow growled and rolled on top of me. "Is that so?" he inquired in a silky voice. "I suppose I'll just have to work twice as hard to take your mind off of them, then."

His mouth descended to cover mine, kissing me long and slow. Then his lips moved down my jaw to explore a tingling path across my neck before they recaptured my lips.

"Have you forgotten about your dream lovers yet?" he murmured, his tongue dipping into my mouth to caress mine.

"I told Angelica I wasn't interested," I breathed with a laugh.

Sparrow kissed the tip of my nose. "Good," he whispered.

He lifted his hand and I caught a flash of white between his fingers. "By the way—I found this on the floor earlier," he said in a dry tone. "I wondered how you'd managed to call the Hell Ride."

I gave him a guilty grin as I realized he held the crumpled slip of paper with the Hell Ride incantation on it.

"Where did you get this, Sydney?"

"Lauringer gave it to me." He scowled and I added hurriedly, "She told me it was a bad idea, but I insisted."

"This a very dangerous bit of knowledge," he said, his expression growing dark. "I don't think it's a good idea to leave it lying around, or truth be told, to have it at all. I don't want to tell you what to do, but…"

I snatched it from his hand and ripped it into several pieces, which I wadded together and tossed to the side. Then I grabbed him by his starched collar and pulled him down to plant a kiss on his lips. "I'll burn it later," I promised, with a heated smile, "but right now I have other things on my mind."

"Such as?" he enquired in a voice like roughened velvet.

"Well, I never did properly thank you for that coffee you left me this morning—it was perfect." I gave his lower lip a delicate nibble.

"And the rose was beautiful." I traced the seam of his lips with my tongue.

"And your note was lovely," I added huskily, my mouth hovering just beneath his.

"*You're* lovely, my *anamchara*," he whispered. His hands moved up to frame my face, his thumbs caressing my cheeks, his eyes bright with tenderness.

"What does that word mean?" I murmured, brushing my lips against his, feather light and teasing.

"Soul mate," he replied softly.

Lorien's warning came rushing back to me and I pushed it away with a painful breath. "Make love to me again, Sparrow. Now."

Sparrow gazed down at me for a moment, a question flickering in his eyes. And then, wordlessly, he did as I asked.

I watched in silence as he undressed, rising to pull his buttoned white shirt over his head, and then sliding his dark slacks and briefs down the muscled lengths of his legs. He was already thick and hard beneath, and I reached out to run my fingers over his firm, satiny flesh as he moved to strip me of my shorts and t-shirt.

And then he was beside me, his skin hot and alive against mine as our bodies settled together like two incomplete fragments becoming whole. Our joining was a dance of languid comfort, our mouths never parting as he shifted above me. I wrapped my legs around him, rising to meet him, opening myself in warm welcome as he rocked smoothly into me.

His Aegishjalmur tattoo tingled with electric sparks beneath my roving fingers. I rested my palm against it, drawing its energy as I drew Sparrow's breath into my mouth. I returned it in deep, even exhalations as the sensations built, and then in short gasps of pleasure as my desire crested, rolling through me in waves as I shuddered against him.

And still he continued to move within me, pushing through my climax in deep steady strokes, prolonging and strengthening it, until I was lost in a mindless whirl of ecstasy that allowed for neither fear nor sorrow. He joined me in one powerful surge, penetrating me so profoundly that I nearly screamed with the intensity of it.

Then he rolled me on top of him, holding me close and remaining buried inside me.

"Thank you, Sparrow," I said softly, after a long while.

"My pleasure, Sydney." His voice held a hint of quiet amusement.

He ran his fingers through my hair, making me shiver and my muscles clench around him as I held him within my body. I tilted my head to smile up at him as I lazily traced the planes of his face with the fingers of one hand. He felt so good against me that I never wanted to move again.

Unfortunately, necessity called.

"Would you excuse me for a moment?" I asked with a regretful grin.

He sighed. "I suppose. If I must."

I released him gently, kissing him before I left him alone in the bed.

I felt better, even though I'd been too much of a coward to voice my concerns about the soul combining thing.

Sparrow watched in silence as I exited the bathroom and moved across the thick carpeting to the sliding glass door, my body still languid and relaxed from our love making. Dusk painted the sky with broad strokes of pink, orange and a deepening blue. A gentle breeze cooled the air and I stood in the doorway, reveling in its soft touch against my bare skin. He joined me, wrapping his arms around me as I leaned back into the warmth of his body.

"I returned the vial of immortality," he said softly. "It's on your nightstand. Regrettably, it had no bearing on the investigation. And since you found it, it belongs to you." He paused. "I did, however, discover something quite interesting about its original owner."

I looked up at him questioningly.

"It came from Nugratz the goblin."

I gasped. "You're kidding!"

He lifted a brow at me in bitter amusement. "You remember who Nugratz is, then."

I turned in his arms. "I remember he was the one indirectly responsible for your father's death," I said, reaching up to caress his stubble-roughened cheek. "And that reminds me of something I meant to tell you that I found out on the Hell Ride last night. Do you know how Nugratz lost his immortality?"

Sparrow shook his head.

I took a deep breath and gave him the consolidated version. "Lady Nightwing told me a story about how he couldn't pay on a bet he lost to a death djinn. Apparently he got mouthy, and the djinn got pissed and took his immortality as payment, then cursed him into human form. He left the faerie realm and he's been living here as a human named Leslie Horowitz for about twenty years now. She told me this because Leslie Horowitz owns one of the stores I work for, and she thought he might have sent me to her."

I gazed worriedly into eyes that had hardened into icy chips of cobalt. "Are you okay?"

He hissed out a long stream of air. "That's interesting news, Sydney. Nugratz disappeared from our radar years ago when my superiors downgraded him to non-threat status. I always wondered what happened to the little bastard."

I bit my lip. "Can you believe his immortality just dropped into our hands like that? Whoever's in charge of karma must have a sick sense of humor. I wonder if Balthus was the one who cursed him."

Sparrow made a noncommittal sound in response, his jaw still tight.

"Do you want it?" I asked uncertainly. "You're welcome to it."

"No," he said in a clipped tone. "I want nothing to do with that miserable creature. And you should watch yourself as well. He may no longer be immortal, but that doesn't mean he's lost his penchant for stirring up trouble."

"Believe me—I have as little to do with him as I can. He's an asshole no matter what form he takes."

Sparrow gave a rigid nod. "I also brought the notebook back. It's over there." He indicated my nightstand with a nod, seeming to want to change to subject.

"That was quick," I commented, stepping away from him to retrieve it. I stuck the vial out of sight in a drawer before coming back to sit on the end of the bed.

Sparrow gave me an apologetic grimace. "I'm afraid the journal didn't reveal anything with regard to the identity of its owner. It appears to be just another sad story of a woman giving up her soul to a death djinn."

Disappointment twisted my insides. I had risked my life for the stupid thing. I flipped listlessly through the pages. I had little hope that I'd find something where the Seelie mages had failed to do so.

"They couldn't tell you *anything* about the woman who wrote it?" I asked in frustration.

Sparrow reached out to squeeze my shoulder, his touch warm and soothing against my skin. "Sorry, Sydney. There was no traceable magic on it. We also had our staff empath try to tap into the emotional quality of the writing, but despite its personal nature, the journal is so old that she wasn't able to access anything conclusive either."

"What about the goblin, Firzag," I asked with cautious optimism.

"He seems to have vanished completely. We're in the process of several inquiries as to who and what he was involved with before he disappeared—but so far, no luck."

I sighed in defeat, looking down to read a random excerpt from the journal. Sparrow disappeared into the bathroom, leaving me to my bleak curiosity.

He is highly charismatic, with eyes of fiery green. He has promised to grant me immortality and my three greatest desires, in exchange for my services thereafter. I am drawn to him as I have never been to another man.

Yep. That sounded like Balthus and his friends, alright. I reread it, feeling as if there was something familiar that I couldn't quite put my finger on. But what could I possibly have seen that related to this? I skipped forward a couple of pages.

I proved them all wrong! I had my moments of doubt, but my benefactor was as good as his word. And success is better than I ever dreamed it would be...

She sounded pleased with her bargain so far. But I wasn't holding out for a happy ending for the mystery author—especially after a couple hundred years, when the insanity kicked in. I turned a few pages and read more, still trying to identify what was tweaking my memory.

I am beginning to wonder if I have not made a terrible mistake. My fiery-eyed lover has not come to me for many weeks, and during his last brief visit he merely demanded some spells and then left. I fear he grows tired of me, yet I continue to crave his touch to the point of pain. I have agreed to keep our arrangement a secret for both our sakes. But I grow lonely without him. If it weren't for M.J., I think I might go mad.

Sparrow padded barefoot past the end of the bed and I glanced up, my eyes following his progression. Goddess, he was magnificent. All toned muscle and tanned, tattooed skin gleaming in the lamplight. He was completely at ease in his nakedness—and deservedly so.

I was a little surprised at how comfortable I was with my own lack of clothing. It probably had something to do with the fact that my stomach was unusually flat at the moment, since I hadn't eaten anything all day. It suddenly grumbled loudly in recognition of that fact.

Sparrow's lips quirked up at the sound. "Hungry?" he asked.

"Uh, yeah—I guess I am," I mumbled in embarrassment. "But wait, this is more important. There *is* a name in here. Someone called M.J." I held out the notebook and pointed to the page I'd been reading.

Sparrow's smile faded and his expression turned rueful. "I know, Sydney. Believe me; we went over that thing with a fine-pointed wand. But figuring out who this 'M.J.' was would be like looking for a leaf in the forest—even going on the assumption that she was an immortal who was murdered. Whoever wrote this journal was careful not to reveal too much detail."

I stared at him in surprise. "Murdered?"

"Skip to the last entry," he instructed quietly.

I skimmed the notebook until I reached the void of blank pages, and then slowly turned back to the place where the author had touched pen to paper for the last time. Whereas before the handwriting had been flowing, here it became a dark, desperate scrawl. The page was rent in several places with the force she had used to scratch the words onto it.

He came to me today. I have been using a spell to strengthen my resolve against him. When he tried to come to my bed, I denied him. He only laughed. When I struggled, he struck me and threw me to the ground. He bound me with rope and beat me as he raped me. I thought he would kill me. M.J. tried to stop him, but he struck her down with magic—a spell that I had given him. When he finally left me, I crawled over to help her, but her wounds were mortal.

There was nothing I could do. She faded into nothingness before my eyes.

Oh, my sweet M.J., what have I done?

I will kill him for this. I vow it. I will bide my time, embracing this blackness and hatred until my revenge is complete. He will curse the day he took my soul before I end his pathetic life—he and all of his evil kindred.

I shivered in horror as the words faded to silence on the page. They continued to spin through my shocked mind long after I finished reading them. When I swallowed, I tasted sour bile in my throat. I looked up at Sparrow, silhouetted against the growing darkness as he stood looking out onto the crashing waves.

"Sparrow," I whispered hoarsely. "That was one of the most disturbing things I've ever read. Surely someone could trace the emotion in that, no matter how old it is."

"'Tis a terrible tale," he agreed, his voice soft and remote. "Perhaps we could consult another empath."

The breeze picked up outside, ruffling his dark hair through the open door. A faint rustling sounded behind me and I looked over my shoulder to find the wadded slip of paper with the Hell Ride incantation lying discarded by the headboard. The torn fragments made a loose bundle that crinkled together as the air currents stirred it.

I scooted backward on the bed to grab it, listlessly making my way over to toss it in the trash near the vanity. We *had* to find out who had written that journal, and what the poor woman had to do with the goblin and the unaligned souls. The paper unraveled as it hit the bottom of the wastebasket and I smiled grimly as my eye caught the last two words of the crumpled incantation—*evil's afoot.*

I turned away, and then froze before slowly turning back to retrieve the wrinkled fragments.

A terrible idea had just occurred to me.

I held my breath and dashed back to the bed.

<u>Chapter 6—The Third Wish</u>

My amateur career in forgery began when I was in high-school, copying my mom's signature for the odd sick note or permission slip. Cindy had me forge hers and Leslie's all the time simply as a convenience. Sometimes vendors forgot to write their company names on invoices and I had to compare handwriting to figure out who was charging us for what.

The point was—I'd become pretty good at identifying people's handwriting. I smoothed the torn pieces of the Hell Ride incantation to lie flat against one of the pages of the journal, staring at them as dawning horror prickled across my nerve endings.

That was why the journal had seemed so familiar.

"Oh my Goddess. It's Lauringer," I croaked past my tightening throat.

I leapt up with the proof clutched in my shaking hand to show Sparrow. A stunned slackness crept over his face.

"Sparrow, I stood at Lauringer's kitchen table and watched her write that incantation myself!" My head spun with disbelief. I sat down hard on the edge of the bed and began pulling on my discarded shorts.

"What does this mean?" I asked faintly as I pushed my head through the neck of my t-shirt.

"It means that the most powerful mage alive belongs to the death djinns," he answered in a bleak voice. "And it explains why our mages haven't been able to trace the magic on the unaligned souls. Lauringer has always been in a league by herself when it comes to spell craft."

I stared at him. "But you read that journal—she hates them! There's no way she's helping them take hundreds of unaligned souls," I denied.

Sparrow crossed the room and began donning his own clothing. "If they hold her soul, they can force her to do whatever they want, Sydney."

"Just wait a minute and think this out with me, *please*." Frustration was evident in my tone, and Sparrow paused in his harried search for his shoes to glance at me. Whatever he saw made him straighten and join me on the bed.

But the softness was gone from his face. It was replaced by the professional intensity that had made him the best detective on the Seelie Police Force. I could almost see the wheels of his brain turning behind his eyes.

"Something's not right here," I insisted.

"There's a lot that's not right here," Sparrow agreed.

I grunted in response to the veiled sarcasm. "If Lauringer were stealing souls for the death djinns, I doubt they would keep getting caught at it. She's too good. And they're not that stupid. And why would Balthus tell us anything that could possibly lead us to her?"

Sparrow's eyes bored into mine. "Then what are you suggesting?"

I puffed out a thoughtful breath. "Well, I'm obviously no expert on this kind of stuff. But put yourself in her place."

I found it all too easy to do that.

"You sign your soul over to a death djinn, thinking you're going to get your heart's desire, plus immortality in the bargain. By the time you realize you've made a huge mistake; it's too late. The bastard ends up raping you and killing your best friend. You vow revenge on him and his entire race. And you have pretty much unlimited magic at your disposal with which to get it.

"What would you do?"

"I'd kill the bastard," Sparrow stated, his tone level and hard.

"How do you kill a death djinn?" I asked, knowing I was getting off track, but unable to help my curiosity.

"Not easily. But there are ways."

I waited, but Sparrow didn't seem willing to elaborate. I frowned. "Maybe that's why she's so secretive and she makes herself so difficult to find. Because she killed him and she's on the run from the rest of them."

A considering look crept into Sparrow's eyes. "King Moab would most likely sentence her to death for murdering one of his own. But even if he spared her, he would certainly take a powerful soul such as hers for himself. And if Moab held her soul, no magic in the realm would be strong enough to hide her from him.

"So that leaves two options. Either she works for them; or she found a way to kill the djinn that held her, and they had kept their secret so well that none of the others knew her soul was claimable—which would mean she works for herself."

He exhaled as if he'd been punched in the stomach. "And she still wants revenge. She wants to discredit all of them and nullify their contract entirely. And she's framing them with stolen mortal souls to do it."

"No," I whispered. "I talked to Lauringer. She seemed to truly want to help me. She wouldn't rip the souls from hundreds of people, rendering them comatose and leaving them to die, just to satisfy her revenge. You still haven't found any of the people those souls belonged to. You don't know for sure that's what's happening."

"We found the woman Balthus' belonged to," Sparrow interjected.

"Alright, so you found *one*," I agreed impatiently. "But surely if Lauringer had taken all those souls, you would have been able to match some of the others up to missing or comatose people by now. There's something we're still not seeing."

"People disappear every day, Sydney, and no one cares enough to report them gone. We have no way of knowing what Lauringer is capable of, considering what she's been through. Why do you think Firzag ended up dead? Lauringer wouldn't have shown this journal to anyone. He must have taken it, and she found out and went after him."

My eyes widened. "I told her about him."

"It's not your fault, Sydney," Sparrow said, gentling his tone.

My brain spun. I didn't want to accept that Lauringer would end all of those lives so ruthlessly—especially after what had been done to her and M.J. But I supposed it was possible. "Maybe," I conceded with reluctance. "We'll need to apprehend her to find out for sure."

"Apprehend her?" The hint of a grin teased Sparrow's lips and I narrowed my eyes at him, feeling suspiciously like he was laughing at me.

"You know, you're actually pretty good at this detective stuff."

My ire was curbed by the sincerity of his words. "I've been working, and playing, with the best," I answered with a smile.

Humor and desire flared in Sparrow's gaze as he chuckled. "You're a silver tongued little witch," he said in a soft brogue. His grin faded. "You realize this means we won't be discrediting the death djinn contract after all."

The truth of his words dropped into my empty stomach like a lump of lead.

His fingers brushed away several strands of hair that had strayed onto my cheek, moving down to settle on my shoulder with a steadying squeeze. "And we're going to need help bringing in someone as powerful as Lauringer. I have an idea that could solve both of our problems, though, Sydney. It's dangerous, but I've not seen you balk at danger before. And your luck is the devil's own, so maybe—just maybe—it will work."

∞∞∞∞∞∞∞∞∞

"You want her to do WHAT?" Lorien shouted, startling Jasper from his nap and earning a look of feline disgust. He was already disgruntled because I had neglected to fill his food dish this morning. It wasn't completely empty, but he liked me to top it off about the same time each day—just to prove I cared.

Sparrow sighed around a mouthful of General Tso's chicken, looking beleaguered beneath the stares of my best friend and my faerie guardian. I sat back with what remained of my honey garlic chicken, secretly enjoying the interplay. I was on board with Sparrow's plan, but I was perfectly content allowing him to defend it to Sunny and Lorien.

He glanced at me with a half formed smirk to let me know how much he appreciated being thrown under the bus. "So this must be what the Inquisition was like," he muttered. He finished chewing and worked his face into a charming smile.

"Ladies, I fully understand your concern, and believe me—I share it. But in light of what we've discovered, I fear this is the best chance Sydney will have to nullify her contract. It's going to take a serious bit of blackmail to get her released, and this information is probably the most valuable bargaining chip we'll ever hold.

"Either way, I have no choice but to involve King Moab. He should be able to call Lauringer's soul, and that's our best bet at apprehending her. And if I'm right, she's the key to freeing his people. It's merely a matter of whether I present the information in an official capacity, or Sydney offers it up in return for the cancellation of her contract.

"An opportunity like this may never come again. So I believe we either go for it, or we pray she's able to live the rest of her life without ever uttering the word 'wish' again."

Sunny regarded him from narrowed eyes, arms crossed over her chest and shrimp lo mein forgotten as she considered his proposal. Lorien sputtered angrily as she paced a small span of air above the coffee table, shedding purple faerie dust into a partially-eaten container of wonton soup. In addition to her concern over Sparrow's plan, she seemed to be taking our accusations against Lauringer a trifle personally.

I finally took pity on Sparrow and spoke up. "Look—I know you guys are scared. Frankly, the idea of walking into the death djinn palace and trying to blackmail Old Moby into forcing Balthus to release me scares me to death. But I agree with Sparrow. It's either this, or accept the fact that I have to keep one eye over my shoulder for the rest of my life. And if I slip up," I snapped my fingers, "Poof! My soul is gone forever.

"Then all I have to look forward to is being a sex slave for the next couple hundred years. Not that I'd mind if it were with the right master." I gave Sparrow a suggestive look, and could have sworn he blushed. At the very least it wrenched a reluctant smile from Sunny.

"But I'd have to watch all my friends and family die," I added soberly. "And then comes the real kicker—do I use my little vial of immortality to fend off the insanity, or do I take a ride on the crazy train and hope it makes me incoherent enough to forget about the endless misery my life has become. Not to mention what it would do to Lorien."

"Loopy locomotive," she mumbled in favor of her preferred term. Then she sank to the edge of the table in a heap of wretchedness.

"Loopy locomotive," I agreed gently.

Sunny rolled her eyes and began picking at her lo mein again. "Well, you've obviously already decided what you're going to do, so we know there's no use trying to talk your stubborn ass out of it."

She transferred a clump of noodles to her mouth with the wooden chopsticks and chewed slowly, shifting her gaze to Sparrow as she swallowed.

"And you've certainly changed your tune. You didn't even want her to see Balthus before. Now you're suggesting she go into the middle of death djinn city, or wherever, and stand before the lot of them while she tries to blackmail their king."

Sparrow flinched at the accusation in her voice.

"Oddly enough, though, I think you're right," she added in a softer tone. "It's Syd's life and it's her chance to take. And I'd rather see you offer her the choice, than tell her how to make it."

Sparrow gave her a grateful look and she smirked. "But that doesn't mean I have to like it. I'm the one who's gonna be stuck here alone, frantic with worry, imagining worst case scenarios about my best friend's torture session with the death djinns."

I blanched at the word *torture* as I scooted over to hug her. "It'll be okay," I said, trying to reassure myself as much as her.

"I'll blink in to give you updates," Lorien grumbled in a resigned tone.

I kissed my finger and touched it to her small cheek in gratitude.

"So we're all agreed on our course of action, then?" Sparrow asked.

The question was greeted by three nods of acceptance, followed by Lorien's mumbled, "I still can't believe Lauringer is behind this."

Sparrow spared her a sympathetic glance before returning to the business at hand. "Then we should get going. Despite what you'll be telling King Moab, I can't, in good conscience, keep Lauringer's involvement from the department for long, Sydney."

Part of me wanted to demand that he do just that, but the other part of me knew he was right. And it was best to get started before my courage left me completely.

"I'm ready when you are," I told Lorien, with hardly a quaver in my voice at all.

"Just one more thing," Sparrow added. My spine stiffened in alarm at his serious tone. "And heed me well, Sydney, because what I'm about to say is very important, and I fear it may turn out to be your most difficult challenge in dealing with the king."

Nerves taut, I waited for his advice.

"Do not, under any circumstances, refer to King Moab as 'Old Moby'," he instructed sternly.

I blinked in confusion, and he cracked a small smile, looking pleased with himself. I threw a couch pillow at him.

∞∞∞∞∞∞∞∞∞∞

Lorien released the breath from her lungs in a nervous wheeze. "Thank Titania I got it right this time!"

"Good job, Lorien!" I encouraged, feeling a weight lift from my own chest.

"I've been practicing with Obie's pet frog, Buster," she admitted.

I grinned at the vision of tiny golden frogs falling from the sky.

Her goal had been to transport us to a point near King Moab's palace. We had both been tense, considering she wasn't all that familiar with the area, and in light of what had happened the last time she'd transported me to the faerie realm.

But true to her word, she had gotten it right. An imposing structure, which I could only assume was the palace, perched like a scowling sentinel several hundred yards away. It looked as if it had been hewn from a soot-blackened mountain born of rough, volcanic stone. Its high, sharp turrets stabbed at a rusty haze of smog, draped like a funeral pall across the darkening sky.

The land was parched and barren, sprawling out before us in an endless rocky plain that looked as if it had been scoured by fire. The air held a hot, acrid tang that seemed to suck all traces of moisture from whatever it touched. It made my throat burn and my eyes dry and scratchy.

I guessed the fire djinns weren't named solely for the emerald fire in their eyes. I found it difficult to picture Balthus in these surroundings, with his perfect clothes and refined manners.

Although I supposed if I looked deeper, I could make some comparisons to his blackened soul.

Sparrow was to blink in separately and unseen. He wanted to keep an eye on us, but didn't want to cast suspicion on the ruse that I was offering my information to the king instead of turning it over to the Seelie Police.

It was Lorien's job to keep me from accidentally making a wish, as well as to play delivery faerie for the journal in the event that Moab accepted my proposal. We had decided that it wouldn't be prudent to bring it with us.

I wasn't sure what Sparrow could do if things started to go south. I supposed he could intervene if the king started to use his mojo on me to coerce me into making a wish. Or maybe he could rescue me if Old Moby decided to torture me for what I knew instead of agreeing to set me free for it. I tried to push that thought out of my mind as I steeled myself to approach the old fiend's castle.

It was intimidating enough without indulging in visions of dungeons and dank cells stocked with implements of torture. There was that word again. *Thanks so much, Sunny, for planting that image in my head.*

We reached the castle's iron gates all too soon, despite the fact that I had to keep my pace to a crawl so I wouldn't twist my ankle on the loose rocks scattering the ground like a plague of stony locusts. Thank Goddess for sneakers. Although my feet were too warm inside them, it was better than bloody toes.

Lorien hovered above my right shoulder, a tiny beacon of light shining in the gloom. She broke our grim silence with a whispered, "Remember, Sydney—don't use the word 'wish' for any reason. Don't even think it."

I nodded my assent. And rather than being annoyed at her statement of the obvious, it shored me up with strength and comfort. A strange calm fell over me, giving me the courage to meet the glittering eyes of the two guards manning the palace gate. They each held a tall, iron pike that resembled the thick spikes from which the gate was constructed.

They had watched the progress of our approach without comment. Now one of them continued to stare at me in heavy silence, while the other's lips twisted in cruel amusement before he opened them to speak. "Be you here to choose your master, girl?" he asked with a raspy laugh.

His words were like shrapnel, harsh and gravelly, the syllables poking out in random places. His laughter was worse, prickling through my head like noisy stinging nettles.

"I am here to see King Moab," I stated, my voice surprisingly firm and even.

He laughed harder at that, and I had to restrain the urge to cover my ears against the sound. "You aim high, then," he growled. "But the king has so many pretties to play with. How about turnin' your head toward a lowly soldier? I can grant your third wish just as well as he, and I'll give you all the attention you deserve."

He leered at me, his gaze raking over my body. I felt as if a coating of filth was left in its wake. "I promise I'll never tire of paying attention to *you*," he ground out in a guttural slur, punctuating the words with an obscene flicker of his tongue.

Furious black dust sifted from Lorien's wings, their buzz of agitation a warning that she was about to let loose and fly at his ruddy, pock-marked face like a maddened hornet. I found my voice quickly.

"I have information that will exonerate the death djinns of all accusations regarding unaligned souls. I will present it only to your king."

The guard narrowed his eyes at me. He lacked all of Balthus' grace and charm. In fact, he was an entirely repellant creature. The only similarity was the emerald fire burning within the murky depths of his eyes. "What sort of information?" he demanded.

I remained silent, trying to pull off a look of bored contempt, though my heart beat so loudly I was sure both men could hear it. I turned my attention to the other guard, still watching mutely from several feet away. "I guarantee you that King Moab will be interested in hearing what I have to say. This information will assure the release of all those who have been wrongfully imprisoned for the possession of unaligned souls—including Prince Balthus."

Interest flickered across the unspeaking guard's face. But his crude companion seemed to have decided that I was a nuisance. Or maybe my dismissal of him had ticked him off. He reached for me with a grubby fist. I tried to step back, but his quick fingers grasped the neck of my shirt, yanking me forward.

Before I could react, the second guard swept his pike down hard on my assailant's wrist. It connected with a crack, and he let me go, howling as he cradled the injured appendage to his chest. I stumbled away, struggling to keep my feet, as Lorien darted angrily between us.

She hovered there with a mutinous expression, her tiny fists clenched and black dust pouring from her nearly invisible wings. I didn't know what she planned to do if he came at me again, but her protectiveness both warmed my heart and made me fear for her safety.

"Wha'd you hit me for?" the other guard demanded. "I was only out for a bit of sport. She's probably lying anyway." His muddy green eyes were sullen slits as he stared at my rescuer, but he made no move to retaliate.

The mute guard stared back at him. His skin was a deep shade of espresso that brightened the green of his eyes and made his teeth appear startlingly white. His dark face betrayed no emotion, but his eyes conveyed a singular disdain for his ill-mannered associate. When he finally spoke, his voice was smooth and melodic, his answer delivered in quiet, measured tones.

"In addition to our prince, my brother is among those being held on the charges about which this human speaks. She must be brought to our king unharmed so that he may ascertain the validity of her claim. It is neither your, nor my, place to determine her fate. If she lies, King Moab will see that she regrets her arrogance with a retribution that far outstrips any which you or I could deliver."

He gave me a severe look that cut through me like ice despite the acrid, heated air. "You walk willingly into the dragon's den, little human. Be warned."

Fabulous. What was I doing here again? I was *so* going to have my head examined if I made it out of this one alive and soul intact. On second thought, I probably shouldn't waste my money. I already had a pretty good idea what the diagnosis would be—especially if I started talking about faeries and death djinns and succubi and...well, scratch that idea.

I gave the nice guard a cheerful grin. "Lead on. I've always been fascinated by dragons."

Surprise flitted across his face. It faded into a slow, breathtaking smile that put a zing into my blood. The growing heat in his eyes held interest and something that could almost be identified as respect. "Follow me then, feisty one. I will arrange your audience with the king. And if you so choose, I would be honored to grant your third wish."

His voice was a throaty rumble that reached deep inside me and stroked my traitorous libido to life. And he was only a soldier. I had yet to get past the gate and pit my will against death djinn royalty. I was in so much trouble here.

Lorien turned and darted forward to hover in front of my face, flying backward as I fell in step behind the guard, her violet eyes knowing. She held my gaze for a moment in silent warning, and then returned to her place above my shoulder. I took a deep breath and attempted to calm the fire in my blood.

"Although I appreciate the offer, I don't plan on doing any wishing today," I said to his back.

Lorien jerked against my ear and let out an anxious little hum. I glanced at her and grimaced in apology. It was nearly impossible to tell someone you weren't going to do something without actually verbalizing what it was you weren't going to do—if you catch my drift.

The guard laughed, a warm echo that resounded through the wide tunnel, bouncing off the porous rock walls and buffeting my skin like a playful caress.

"How do you guys do that, anyway?" I asked, and then added, "Know I'm on my third, that is." I didn't want him to think I was asking how he managed to seduce me with the sound of his voice. I was pretty sure he knew what effect he had on me, but I wasn't about to acknowledge it.

He turned to flash me a heated grin over his shoulder. Subdued light spilled from the iron lamps lining the walls. It glistened against his pearly teeth and gave his complexion the sinful hue of dark chocolate. "Your uncompleted contract. It clings to your soul like a delicate film of silk kissing the body of a beautiful woman. It teases and beckons us to stake our claim and unwrap the prize within."

I shivered against the desire invoked by the poetic imagery of his words.

"That's a lovely turn of phrase," I commented, trying to sound unaffected.

"I judge that you are someone who appreciates a subtler form of speech than that thrust upon you by my uncouth colleague. Let me take this opportunity to apologize for his behavior. A woman of your allure deserves a delicacy of which he is incapable."

He was really laying it on thick. Only moments ago I had been a 'little human'—now suddenly I was a woman of allure. But his smoky voice still curled through me like a lover's touch. Damned death djinns.

Don't let him know how much he affects you. Don't let him know how much he affects you, I repeated to myself.

My internal mantra faded to silence as we exited the confines of the austere tunnel and stepped into a vast entry-hall that was its diametric opposite.

This was more the sort of place I expected Balthus to call home. A grand marble staircase, framed by gilded scrollwork banisters, swept up to a first floor balcony. The cathedral ceiling stretched even higher, rising to a dome above a second tiered balcony that overlooked the first.

The rug beneath my feet looked large enough to carpet my entire penthouse and was a rich study of color and intricate design. Dark wood paneled the walls, reaching up their towering heights to meet a carved moulding border that outlined the room.

A mosaic of tiny tiles sprawled across the whole of the ceiling. At first it appeared to be a random pattern of subdued colors, but as I focused, I realized the tiles depicted a massive work of art whose intricacy rivaled that of the Sistine Chapel. The similarity ended there, however. Lofty religious images had been the last thing on this artist's mind.

Men and women in various states of undress cavorted across its breadth, performing intimate acts upon themselves and each other, both with their own bodies and with various other apparatus—some of which, quite frankly, looked more painful than pleasurable. There were far more women than men, but it was obvious that the men were dominant, giving it the feel of a harem scene.

Upon closer inspection, I saw that the entire circumference of the moulding border was carved in the likenesses of female nudes. When I lowered my shocked gaze, I noticed that even the paintings on the walls and the room's bronze statuary, despite appearing to be museum quality antiques, were all explicitly sexual in theme.

The guard stopped to watch me take in the room. My eyes met his above a smile that blazed with blatant invitation, and my cheeks grew so hot I felt like there was steam rising from them. "Quite something, is it not?" he inquired.

I was still floundering for a reply when Lorien offered her own thoughts on the matter. "Death djinns," she muttered in disgust. "It's always sex, sex, sex with you guys. It's so crass. Just because you display it wherever you go doesn't mean you're better at it than everyone else."

A nervous titter escaped my lips. To my relief, the guard also chuckled. "Touché, little sister. It may seem ostentatious to you but, with a few exceptions, we are sensual creatures who are inspired by such visual stimulation. It is not meant to be a boastful statement of our prowess, yet rather an honest reflection of our desires and the heights of passion to which we aspire."

Lorien snorted. I knew I should feel the same, but his speech, combined with the erotic imagery, stirred my blood.

"Come. You can relax in the drawing room while I arrange your audience with King Moab."

Relax—yeah, right.

He turned and escorted us around the side of the colossal staircase. We passed a door on the right that led beneath it, then another sharply arched doorway to the left, and continued forward until we reached a third door that opened into the rear wall.

This room was smaller than, but just as opulent as, the entrance hall had been. Sparkling crystal chandeliers hung from the raised ceiling and more profane artwork decorated the space. Overstuffed couches and chairs, upholstered in rich velvet, were placed to provide optimal viewing of the pieces displayed.

A massive painting hung above the fireplace, serving as the focal point of the room. It depicted a woman gagged and bound by a complicated series of knots that left her suspended in midair with her hands and feet meeting at her back. There was an unlikely expression of unbridled ecstasy on her face.

A well endowed man with blazing emerald eyes, dark hair and a beard stood nearby with a long, multi-pronged whip. They were both nude.

As I looked at the man's features, and the three small golden hoops piercing his left ear, I realized he was a younger version of King Moab.

"It was commissioned by the king himself. Do you like it?" the guard asked.

I glanced at him, unsettled. "I find it disturbing." I didn't want to admit, even to myself, the disquieting idea that part of me found it arousing as well.

He merely smiled. "Please, have a seat." He indicated one of the couches. "And now I must apologize for my own boorish behavior, for I have neither introduced myself nor asked your names. I am Seraven."

"I'm Sydney and this is Lorien."

A frown marred his ebony forehead, as if he was trying to remember something, and then his eyes widened. "Am I to take it that you are the female our prince covets for his own?"

I should have said something earlier. It might have saved me some discomfort, I thought wryly.

"That would be me. And I happen to know he'll be pissed if anyone else lays a hand on me. So feel free to spread the word to your buddies."

"I would have known the moment I touched your soul," he murmured. "And as a faithful subject, I would be honor-bound to hand you over to him untouched. However, some would be neither so loyal nor so considerate. You must not rely on Prince Balthus' claim, Sydney."

He studied me with those burning green eyes a moment longer before turning for the door. "Wait here, please. It would not do to have you wondering the castle alone. Do you wish anything before I go?"

"NO!" Lorien and I exclaimed in unison.

He gave us a mocking grin and pulled the door shut behind him.

"Tricky bastard," Lorien grumbled.

I shrugged. "He seems a decent sort—for a death djinn."

Lorien's eyes rose to her hairline. "A stray hormonal surge has fried your brain, Sydney. Repeat after me: There are no decent death djinns!"

"Alright, alright," I submitted with a chuckle.

She looked unconvinced. "King Moab is going to be a hundred times worse than Seraven. If you can barely hold up against him, maybe we should just call this whole thing off. I can blink us home..."

I scowled at her. That line of thinking was too close to the one I had just been stubbornly trying to ignore. "I'm holding up fine." *Sort of.* "Anyway, we've had this discussion. I'm not missing out on what might be my only chance to get out of my contract. Now, will you please blink in and let Sunny know we're okay before Seraven comes back?"

She glared at me, but she must have realized that it would only waste time to argue, because she vanished without another word.

I sat on the couch and tried not to stare at Old Moby's self-congratulatory S&M portrait. There were plenty of other interesting things to look at. Take that reclining marble statue of a man and woman engaging in mutual oral gratification. Personally, I'd always found that particular position to be a bit distracting as far as both the giving and receiving of pleasure—but maybe it would be different if I tried it with Sparrow.

A shiver traveled through my already heated blood at the mere thought. I began to fantasize about it, and then I shook myself. What the hell was I doing? I needed to put my sex drive on ice for my meeting with Moab—not fire it up more!

I stiffened when I heard voices coming closer in the hallway outside. Shit, where was Lorien? I took a steadying breath and tried to shove down my panic as I listened. The voices echoed stridently in the cathedral ceilinged entry-hall. And they sounded angry.

One resolved into the gravelly tones of the guard who had grabbed me outside. "I don't care who you are. I caught you sneakin' around the palace like a rat sniffin' round an imp den."

"I am a Seelie police officer carrying out an official investigation. If you don't release me, I'll have you arrested and thrown in a jail cell for so long you'll wish you could die like a mortal." The voice was cold—and achingly familiar.

The guard ground out a vicious laugh. "Try again, *Officer*. We both know you have no leave to trespass here, no matter what you're investigating. I think it's you who'll be coolin' your miserable heels in our dungeon. Until the king decides what to do with you, that is. And Moab don't take kindly to spies."

He laughed again, the sound loud and grating, and just outside the door.

"Watch your step, Officer. Wouldn't want you to have any nasty accidents..."

I heard a pained grunt. The guard sniggered and the voices began to fade.

I jumped up, nearly tripping on the leg of the table that held the reclining marble statue, and sprinted across the carpet toward the door. My heart felt like it would beat out of my chest as I pulled it open a crack and looked into the hallway. I was just in time to see the arched doorway along the right wall ease closed with soundless finality.

"What are you looking at?"

I jumped and let out an undignified squeak. "Goddess, Lorien!" I breathed. "You scared me half to death!"

"Sorry."

When I glared over my shoulder at her, she didn't look sorry at all.

"They've got Sparrow!" I whispered impatiently. "That asshole guard is taking him to the dungeon! Can you look out for Seraven and warn me if he comes back? I need to follow them!"

I peered out into the empty hallway, then pulled the door open further and slipped through.

"Wait!" Lorien hissed in my ear, keeping pace with me as I tiptoed toward the arched doorway.

I made a face at the pile of faerie dust accumulating on my shoulder like sparkly red dandruff.

"Are you *insane*? You can't just go wandering off around the death djinn palace! If you get caught, you'll ruin everything—this was *not* part of the plan!"

"Shh!" I put my ear against the cool, grainy wood of the door. Silence greeted me. I turned the knob and held my breath as I pushed it open. It led onto a cramped flagstone staircase leading steeply downward. It was walled in by rough, grey blocks of stone and illuminated by the same iron lamps that lit the entrance tunnel.

I glanced at Lorien, my every sense alert with tension and sending out feelers for the approach of a death djinn. "Sparrow getting thrown in the dungeon wasn't part of the plan either," I whispered furiously. "I'm going to find him. You can come with me and keep telling me what a crappy idea it is—or you can keep lookout in the entrance hall and blink in to warn me when Seraven comes."

I started down the staircase, trying to keep my steps quick and silent.

"Please, Sydney," Lorien beseeched. "Sparrow's a big boy. He can take care of himself."

The desperation in her voice made me hesitate. Then I shot her a smile rife with understanding and determination. "I'm sorry, Lorien. It's my fault he's here, and I can't leave him. I'll be as careful as I can."

I continued downward toward the castle's lower level, my resolve overshadowing my fear. Lorien made a soft, disgruntled sound and then disappeared, leaving me to descend the passage alone. A chilly dampness bit through the air, accompanied by the odor of old mildew, as if I was entering a deep underground cavern.

When I reached the bottom, the staircase widened into a corridor that branched right or left before me. Indecision knotted my stomach as I listened for a sound to put me on the correct path. But there was nothing. I turned left on arbitrary instinct.

The passage was a series of turns, shadowy in the dim light. Unnerving silence and cold, damp air crept into my bones, gradually eating away at my courage and replacing it with a mounting panic. I crept along the rocky wall, its coarse texture snagging at my shirt and scraping my bare skin, peering around each corner with my heart straining upward as if it wanted to jump out of my throat.

Every wind of the passageway made me feel as if I was becoming lost within the castle's subterranean depths.

I finally came to a junction that continued forward, branched right or branched left. As I approached it, my eyes darted compulsively between the spaces that opened up to either side. All I saw was lonely, empty corridor. I rushed through the intersection, feeling vulnerable and exposed, and remained on the straight path.

My fear of becoming lost in the labyrinthine passages was too overwhelming for me to chance taking one of the turns.

Suddenly, a sound broke the silence. It was barely audible to my ears at first, but it grew into a horrible sort of croaking that echoed through the tunnels as it moved nearer. It was impossible to tell from which direction it approached, and I went stock-still, flattening myself against the uneven surface of the wall.

The sound grew closer and I stopped breathing, trying to make myself smaller, willing myself into invisibility. I realized it was singing—tone deaf and ear splitting, but singing nonetheless. As the voice became clearer, I was certain that it belonged to the obnoxious guard that had assaulted me at the gate.

I might have found some humor in his lack of singing prowess, but my terror at him catching me alone in the bowels of the death djinn palace killed all traces of mirth.

The confusing echo receded and his footsteps thumped against nearby flagstones to my left. My legs sprang to action before I knew my brain had formed the command. I fled deeper into the corridor, throwing myself around the next twist in the passage and struggling to tame my gasping breath.

My entire being was centered on the effort to listen and gauge his direction, and I waited with sick apprehension. Then, to my immense relief, the awful singing ebbed into an indistinguishable croak once more. When I risked a peek around the corner, I caught sight of the guard's back disappearing up the passage. My terror faded into a dull nausea and I pressed my shaking hands against my belly.

Lightheaded, I ventured back the way I had come and made a cautious left at the tunnels' intersection, hoping against hope that it would lead me to Sparrow. Not far ahead the stone wall was broken by a large wooden door with a small, iron-barred window. I approached it and placed my palms against the splintery timbers, then rose onto my toes to peer through the dusty grate.

On the other side of the door, a rickety old table and chair sat in the shadows of a spare entry chamber. Past that, a deserted hallway stretched out into indeterminate darkness. I could see iron bar facings on either side, as if for jail cells, but no one had bothered to light the wall-mounted lamps beyond the first few.

Oh, Goddess, please let me find him. Please let him be alright.

I grasped the thick iron handle and pulled. The door swung open on creaking hinges and I stepped into the dungeon. It was cold and damp here too, but the smell of mildew was overshadowed by something more rank and pungent. It drifted up from the unseen darkness that lay beyond the last iron lamp lighting the row of cells.

I heard a soft moan and hurried forward with fear and hope heavy in my heart. There, in one of the first metal-barred cells, sat Sparrow. His head hung forward onto his chest and his ankles were chained to the legs of a chair that was bolted into the filthy stone floor with fat, rusty screws. His shoulders strained backward, as if his hands were bound behind him.

"Sparrow," I whispered, my voice desperate.

His head jerked up and cobalt eyes met mine, hazy with pain in his bruised and bloodied face. "Sydney! What are you doing down here?" he demanded roughly.

"Getting you out!" I retorted, my fingers tightening around the cold iron bars. "How badly are you hurt?"

"I'll be fine." There was impatience in his tone, but his weak groan belied his words. "You need to go. You can't let them find you here."

"I'm not leaving you in a death djinn dungeon! Help me out here, Sparrow. Why can't you just blink away?"

Sparrow made an irritated sound. "Binding spell."

My eyes flew to the keyhole in the metal plate on the cell's door and then to the silver padlock on Sparrow's chains, incongruously shiny against the rusted metal of the chair. "There have to be keys," I muttered. "Do you know where the keys are?" I called behind me as I jogged toward the beat-up table and chair in the entryway. "Please don't let the guard have taken them," I added softly.

Stony silence was my reply.

The table had a single drawer built into its scratched edge. I pulled it open with a wordless prayer, the loose knob jiggling in my hand and its uneven legs rattling noisily against the stone floor. I exhaled in a whoosh. A large metal key-ring containing at least fifty keys lay there like a prize within.

I rushed back to Sparrow's cell and began trying keys. Some of them were obviously the wrong size and could be easily dismissed. Others fit into the keyhole, but refused to turn. I stubbornly kept trying, but my hands began to tremble so badly that I had trouble fitting the pronged tips into the small opening. Finally, after I'd gone about half-way through the key-ring, the lock clicked open.

I was at Sparrow's side in an instant. His head lolled on his chest and I was afraid he had lost consciousness. I knelt beside him and brushed my fingers gently through his dark hair, wincing as they came away sticky with blood from an ugly gash on his temple. He didn't respond.

"Sparrow, I'm going to get you out of here." My voice hitched with helpless tears as I shakily began trying keys on the padlock by his feet.

This keyhole was smaller than the one on the cell door, but I forced myself to methodically go through each key in clockwise order. I couldn't risk missing the right one.

I flipped through key after key, but none of them worked and I grew frantic. How much time had passed? Should I try to free his hands first in case I had to beat a hasty retreat and leave him to free his legs himself? And even if Lorien blinked in to warn me, would I be able to find my way back through the labyrinth of tunnels and up the stairs before Seraven discovered I was missing?

"*Stop it*," I ordered myself aloud, my voice hoarse and tight. I wasn't leaving him like this. And I wasn't going to give up and switch to his hands. I must have already gone through half the key ring again. If I moved now I'd have to start all over.

Goddess—the chains were so tight. His ankles and feet must be completely numb. I had to get them off! The key I was holding turned in the lock and the thick metal tine sprang free. I sobbed in gratitude and pulled it from the links, dropping it to the floor with a thunk. As I unwrapped the heavy chains, a shock of energy passed through my fingers. I prayed that it was the binding spell being broken.

Sparrow jolted awake with a grunt and stared down at me, wild-eyed, as if fresh from a nightmare. "Sydney," he muttered gruffly. "I told you—you have to go."

"I have the keys." I rubbed briskly at his ankles through his pant-legs, trying to help get the blood flowing again. "I'm going to free your hands now."

I maneuvered to the back of the chair and began working the final lock with the key-ring.

"The chains were spelled to drain my power," he said, sounding more alert. "I think I can free my hands. But you have to go—now," he insisted.

"Sparrow, I wish you would just shut up and let me rescue you," I said, the words coming out on an exhalation that was half laughter, half crying. "Ha!" I gasped in triumph as the lock sprang free. I quickly dropped it and unwound his hands, chafing gently at his bloodless, abraded wrists.

The intricate tattoo beneath his elbow was glowing a fierce yellow in its attempt to replenish his waning strength. I shuffled around to face him as he slowly pulled his arms forward, his shoulders cracking with the effort. My smile faded in concern as I looked up to find his jaw clenched and his blue eyes filled with unspeakable sorrow.

"What's wrong?" I asked worriedly.

"Personally, I would have wished for this one to keep his mouth shut for far longer—but your wish is my command," a horribly familiar voice grated behind me.

Dread overtook my body, leaving me feeling cold and sick as I crouched on the grimy stone floor of the cell. I couldn't move, couldn't turn to face that terrible voice, could only stare, stricken, into Sparrow's fathomless eyes. And the anger I found there was an awful thing. His tattoos began to thicken and swirl, blackness bleeding outward to overtake the surrounding skin.

"This is going to hurt you far worse than it hurts me," the voice behind me ground out with a guttural laugh. "And then we'll see what kind of fun we can have together, you and I."

An agonizing force slammed into my back and my face flew toward Sparrow's knees. He may have caught me, but the pain was so intense I couldn't tell. It felt as if I had been struck by a bolt of lightning. It seared across my nerve endings, burning like hellfire. It grew hotter and hotter until I was sure I would disintegrate.

The sensation pierced my chest, and it felt as if my heart was being ripped out. No. Not my heart—my soul. The sense of loss was so profound that, outside of the pain, my only thought was that I couldn't bear to continue living. The fire flared through me, white-hot and blinding, then abruptly faded to nothing. Black desolation overflowed a hollow well inside me, from which I knew I would never again be able to draw light and courage.

I sank to the dungeon floor and embraced unconsciousness.

Chapter 7—Trials

When I came to, I kept my eyes closed. I had no idea how long I'd been out, but I fervently wished I had stayed that way.

I guessed I didn't have to worry about the wishing thing anymore, although there was cold comfort in that. I should have killed myself like Sparrow's mom while I'd still had the chance. Now I was going to have to spend eternity as a death djinn slave.

At least I'd freed Sparrow. Was there any chance he'd gotten away? Maybe he could still use the journal to bargain for my soul the way I had been planning to do.

No. This asshole guard was probably going to make me tell him everything I knew as soon as he realized I was awake.

And he'd made it clear he had other plans for me as well. I shuddered and tried not to think about that. As much as I hated Balthus—given the choice between the two…

I made an effort to keep my breathing deep and even. I shifted minutely. The floor was gritty beneath me and the cold from the paving stones leeched through my clothing to steal the warmth from my skin. It smelled strongly of earth and mildew, tickling my nose with an unpleasant tang.

With a small burst of courage, I blinked my eyes open and cautiously gazed around. I lay alone on the floor of Sparrow's cell. The rusty underside of the metal chair was above me and the discarded silver chains were piled nearby. My eyes flew to the door and found it ajar.

My heart beat faster. Why was I in an unlocked cell? Should I even bother trying to escape? And where were Sparrow and Lorien?

I sat up slowly, taking stock of my condition. I was a little achy, but otherwise seemed physically okay. I searched myself for some evidence of being soulless, but couldn't feel much other than the numbness and fear. The distant clank of iron against iron echoed down the hallway, like a cell door being closed, and I froze. Footsteps approached, their pace rapid and purposeful. Cold sweat broke out over my body and the confining walls of the dungeon seemed to crowd tighter around me.

I stared with rapt horror through the bars and down the hallway where it disappeared into darkness. The outline of a figure moved forward through the gloom, tall and hulking, and I cowered back into the chair.

The figure resolved into Sparrow's form, and tears sprang into my eyes as I rose and stumbled toward him. In the doorway of the cell I threw my arms around his shoulders and squeezed like I never intended to let go.

When he flinched I loosened my grip and leaned back, but I couldn't bring myself to release him completely. He had ripped one of the sleeves off his shirt and used it to bind his lower arm. It looked as if the fabric had been singed.

"What happened to you?"

He glanced at the bandage. "Nothing. Sydney—you have to go, *now*, before Seraven comes back."

"How do you...? Do I still have my soul?" My voice tightened and cracked.

Sparrow ushered me forward. "Yes. And Lorien's still standing watch. You have to get back upstairs."

"What happened to the guard?"

"I killed him before he could claim you." Sparrow opened the heavy wooden door and pushed me into the hallway.

"How?" I asked faintly.

"Inwa."

"Inwa?" I repeated in confusion.

"I'll explain later. Go. Now." His eyes looked haunted and every muscle in his body was taut and rigid.

I stared at him for a split second and then rose up on my toes and pulled his grim lips down to mine. "Thank you, Sparrow," I whispered against his mouth.

At first he remained stiff and unyielding—then suddenly, as if emotion had broken through a dam of resolve, he took control of the kiss and returned it with a ferocity that stole my breath. His arms banded around me and he crushed me to him.

When he pulled away at last, he reached out to stroke my hair, his hands betraying a slight tremble. "For you, Sydney—any time. Now hurry!"

I smiled at him. "Be careful. I don't want to have to rescue you again."

His soft snort rang out behind me as I turned to jog back up the corridor. My mind whirled with unanswered questions, but first things first. I still had the chance to save my soul.

"*Left*," I whispered as I approached the intersection, sure I was going the right way but still nervous about losing myself beneath the castle. Who knew what other sorts of nastiness lurked down here. And it was a wonder that Seraven hadn't returned and found me missing yet. Even cats only had nine lives—I must be perilously close to using up all of mine.

I wound my way back through the twists and turns of shadowy passageway, sweating with effort and anxiety despite the chilled air. It seemed to be taking an interminably long time and I was beginning to wonder if I wasn't lost after all. Just as I realized I was turning the corner that led to the stone stairwell, my sigh of relief was interrupted by a frantic Lorien.

"Seraven's coming!" she squeaked.

I put on a burst of speed. Lorien kept pace at my shoulder, her wings sifting red dust as she chanted the word—*hurry*—over and over again in a mantra that ground against my skull. My legs pumped up and down on the stairs so fast that my calves felt as if they might shatter.

"I'm going as fast as I can," I forced out between teeth gritted.

She took the hint and shut up.

I leapt the last two steps and pulled the door open. Struggling to calm my labored breathing, I slipped into the hall and turned to sprint toward the drawing room.

"Sydney?" a deep voice called out behind me.

It echoed in my ears like an accusation and my heart stuttered to a stop. The stairwell door whisked shut behind me, and I knew I was caught.

Lorien spun in the air beside me and made an aggravated sound. "How could you leave her like that for so long without a bathroom? She was almost ready to use one of your vases! Not that anything she left inside it would have made it any more disgusting than what's already painted on the outside."

Thank Goddess Lorien's brain hadn't suddenly morphed into a piece of moldering cheese the way mine had. I turned to face Seraven with my best imitation of crossed legs and a desperate grin.

Full lips twitched in amusement beneath sparkling green eyes as he strode toward me. "Your pardon, Sydney. It's here." He indicated the door leading beneath the grand staircase.

"Thank you," I mumbled.

I shambled forward with a stiff-legged walk and Seraven moved to hold the door open for us. I gave him a chagrined smile, and Lorien gave another exaggerated huff of annoyance, as we made our escape into the sanctuary of a lush powder room. The door swung shut behind us and I sagged with relief.

Trees and flowering plants lined the walls, draping over the edges of hanging baskets and counters, giving the room the feel of a garden oasis. A fountain burbled in one corner, the water spilling down in a soft shower to spray a circle of stone figures carved to resemble muscular and fully erect men.

It was definitely the women's room.

I moved into the next area, which was tiled in gold-veined white marble from floor to ceiling, and provided a row of roomy private stalls. Discrete prints of male nudes were interspersed with more thriving foliage, and I decided the women had far better decorating taste than the men.

I really did need to pee, though, and I pushed my way through the first swinging door.

"Uh, I actually am going to use the bathroom," I warned Lorien.

She darted over to hover above the polished brass fixtures of the pedestal sink, but didn't leave the stall. I shrugged and unzipped my jeans.

"It's not too late to call this off, you know," she offered tonelessly. "I can blink us home in an instant."

I shook my head and sent her a crooked smile, not bothering to respond. "What's 'inwa'?" I asked instead.

She frowned and gave me a blank look.

"When I asked Sparrow how he killed the guard downstairs, he said 'inwa'."

Lorien raised one tiny brow. "Supposedly if you take the petrified pit of a certain type of fruit and cast it with enough magical force at a death djinn, it will kill him. There's not much else said to be capable of taking one out. And the blowback from killing with an inwa is supposed to be fierce."

I absorbed that in silence.

"You almost lost your soul down there, Sydney." Lorien pinned me with strangely emotionless violet eyes.

I met her unblinking gaze and returned it with a slow, serious nod. "It was a slip of the tongue when I thought Sparrow and I were alone."

A pained look crossed her small, pointed face. "I should have been there," she whispered.

I shook my head. "No. You were exactly where you were supposed to be—keeping watch for Seraven."

The corners of her lips drew down and I knew she was about to suggest I give up the plan again. I spoke to preempt those useless words.

"I felt my soul being ripped from my body." She flinched. "It was the most horrific thing I've ever experienced, including the Hell Ride. And all I could think was that I should have had the courage to kill myself before it happened, like Sparrow's mom did.

"I won't be making that mistake again."

Lorien's silvery glow paled and she sank to the edge of the sink.

"You know I'm right." The smile I gave her felt bitter on my lips. "But we're not going to let that happen, are we? We're going to keep to the plan and get this ridiculous contract cancelled. Because the alternative is unthinkable. Right, Lorien?"

She swallowed and made a visible effort to regain her composure. "Okay, Sydney," she agreed in a tight voice. "It's your call."

∞ ∞ ∞ ∞ ∞ ∞ ∞ ∞

As we ascended the grand staircase behind Seraven, I gazed up once more at the extensive mosaic that was set into the cathedral ceiling. It truly was an amazing work of art, despite its subject matter. We crossed the first tier balcony overlooking the entry-hall, our steps hushed against the muted colors of the finely woven carpeting, and entered a set of double doors that led onto a wide, warmly lit corridor.

Unseen rooms and more erotic art graced its walls. Each piece was displayed to advantage by soft lighting from tasteful brass wall sconces and chandeliers with brass chains. As we traversed the length of the hallway, the sound of classical music drifted toward my ears.

A second set of doors, punctuated by two burly guards, marked the end of the passageway. Their green eyes were watchful as we approached, assessing the situation, but betraying no expression. Both were magnificent specimens of masculinity, tall and muscular, with close-clipped goatees and small silver hoops piercing their left ears.

One resembled a younger version of King Moab, with the confident bearing of a man in charge and no sign of gray yet marring his coal black hair. The other was swarthy and dark, a heated intensity burning in his forest green gaze and a rugged sensuality to the full curve of his lips. I caught my breath as their attention narrowed in on me.

It was as if a wave of raw sexuality rolled into my body, moving over my nerve endings with relentless mastery, coaxing a response. They nodded at Seraven as they held the doors, neither speaking a word. But their lips curled upward in twin, knowing smiles and they pressed closer as I passed between them.

The word *wish* suddenly whispered through my brain. It trickled forward onto my tongue with an unexpected sweetness, like the promise of a first kiss, and the breathless anticipation of what would come after. Their shoulders brushed mine, enlivening my skin with a deluge of sensitivity, and I slowed, mired in a thick, honeyed swirl of desire.

These two liked to share. The knowledge sizzled in my blood as they cocooned me within their combined aura of eroticism. Images of the three of us, together, were painted with clear brush strokes in my mind, and I shuddered with an intense carnal need. Sounds fell from my lips, and it was only when I sneezed into a red warning cloud of faerie dust that I realized I had begun to voice a wish.

Lorien floated in front of my face, glaring. I blinked away the heavy fog of lust with difficulty, and found Seraven looking back at the two guards with an expression of disapproval. He reached for my hand to pull me forward into the dim alcove beyond the doorway. His warm palm slid against mine as his strong fingers wrapped around it, and a rush of liquid heat shot through my core.

I stumbled into him, my breasts pushing against the solid width of his chest and my entire body flooded with wanton craving. I flushed with the realization that I didn't care who satisfied it.

"This one is not for you," he stated quietly. His voice slipped through me, as smooth and tantalizing as melted chocolate.

The low vibration of laughter rumbled from both guards. "We were simply testing her resolve for the king," sounded one's resonant reply.

I didn't look to see which had spoken. *Testing my resolve.* I'd heard that before from both Balthus and Moab. Well, my resolve seemed to be pretty piss poor at the moment. I stepped back from Seraven and shook myself, my cheeks going up in flames at how easily I had been tempted to exchange my soul for a ménage a troi with two hunky death djinns.

"You would have enjoyed our games, little human." The accent was slurred, curling around the soft words in a way that made me shiver from head to toe. I imagined it coming from the darker of the two guards, but I stiffened my spine against the compulsion to look around. I was afraid that if I turned toward them again I would once more become ensnared in their spell.

Seraven's eyes bored into mine. When I looked down in mortification, his fingers gently urged my chin upward until I met his gaze. There was no seduction in his touch, but the comfort it offered was a lure of its own.

"You have nothing to be ashamed of, Sydney." His tone was so low I had to strain to hear him. "Theros and Besame are highly gifted masters of erotic enchantment. Alone, they are second only to the king and the prince. Together they are unrivaled. Few humans, if any, would be able to refuse them."

I mustered a smile and Seraven returned it, his bright green eyes crinkling at the corners. "Thanks for pulling me away," I murmured unsteadily.

"You're welcome, Sydney. I will do all I can to aid your resistance until you are able to rightfully complete your contract with Prince Balthus. Come. It is time for your audience with the king."

My smile faltered as I fell into step behind him. Lorien shot in front of me to give me a smug 'I told you so' look before resuming her place above my shoulder. Seraven's words were a blunt reminder of the fact that, no matter how helpful he seemed, he wasn't really on my side.

The alcove we'd been standing in opened onto a cavernous room that glowed with reddish light, making me feel as if I had stepped into the vast inner chamber of a dormant volcano. The rocky walls swept outward from the doorway to cage the enormous space within a vaguely circular shape. They were rough cut and glittered with embedded chunks of dark crystal that glinted deep claret in the fiery light. Stalactite formations of the crystal dripped from the rippled ceiling high above.

The effect was breathtaking; as was the realization that the room was crowded with death djinns. At least a hundred eyes were suddenly focused on me, gleaming eerily green in the ruby phosphorescence, peering out from both masculine and feminine faces of striking beauty. I inhaled a startled gasp and the tips of Lorien's wings brushed my cheek in a feather-light caress, reminding me that I wasn't alone.

I forced my feet to keep pace with Seraven's as he led us down a center walkway, hemmed in on either side by large half moon areas where the room's occupants were gathered. They lounged among intimate groupings of sofas and chairs, upholstered in dark earth tones. My gaze was glued to Seraven's back, but I could feel their scrutinizing eyes following my progress.

The glow grew brighter, taking on an orangey quality. The strip of floor beneath me turned opaque, becoming as translucent as glass within a few steps. I teetered on the dizzy edge looking down into an abyss, a ribbon of molten lava flowing in its depths far below. Seraven was already several strides ahead, walking out over what appeared to be empty space above a fall that would bring certain death.

"Keep moving!" Lorien hissed in my ear.

Whispers and laughter erupted around me. I took one ginger step into nothingness...and my foot came in contact with solid ground. To my great relief, my second and third steps met with the same. Still disconcerted, I wrested my eyes from the treacherous chasm beneath me and hurried forward to catch up with Seraven.

The invisible walkway ended at a raised dais of rock. At its center was an impressive throne carved entirely from a massive block of the same claret crystal that was strewn throughout the walls of the cavern. It looked as if it had grown straight up out of the floor, like a huge, oddly shaped stalagmite.

And there sat King Moab, on a thick burgundy cushion atop it.

Resplendent in a three piece suit of dark grey with a deep red shirt and matching pocket handkerchief, he was flanked by a pair of guards who stood at attention with their hands folded loosely in front of them. At his feet was an exceptionally beautiful, almost nude woman. She lay draped across a pile of pillows, her skin like cream-tinted mocha against the sheer white of her short, diaphanous robe. Her hair fell to her shoulders in waves of onyx silk.

A trio of female musicians were assembled in chairs to the right, their instruments the violin, flute and clarinet. All three were extraordinarily lovely, clad only in long, filmy robes. The color of each woman's robe was a fine complement to her complexion, and left little to the imagination as far as her form beneath.

Moab flicked an impeccably manicured finger in their direction, the gesture so rife with command that I nearly jumped to do his bidding. Annoyed, I held myself rigid as the lilting tones of a waltz whirled through the cavern. Moab's chiseled lips spread in a slow smile above his neatly trimmed salt and pepper goatee, his piercing green eyes catching the reaction I had attempted to hide.

"My lord," Seraven announced in a booming voice, "may I present the prince's chosen…"

"Sydney and I have met," the king interrupted dryly.

I wanted to bless Seraven for trying to remind everyone in the room of Balthus' claim on me, despite my determination to escape it. He looked as if he would say more, but Moab pinned him with an irritated gaze and he bowed low instead.

"Thank you, Seraven, that will be all."

It was an unmistakable dismissal. Seraven straightened to his full height and pulled a crisp salute. His eyes held mine for a brief moment, imparting both courage and caution, and then he faded into a vaporous outline and disappeared—along with whatever tenuous protection he had provided.

"Sydney, I can't tell you what a pleasure it is to see you again," Moab drawled, his tone turning rich and smoky as he devoted the full force of his attention to me. "And that you would travel so far to visit me in person truly warms my heart. May I offer you anything? A drink? Some more comfortable attire, perhaps? Surely one of our robes would be more relaxing than what you have on now."

His gaze roved my body with appreciation and flagrant hunger. It was a bold seduction, confident in its assurance that the path to ecstasy would be found in surrender. It made my blood quicken, and I hated him for it.

Moab smiled as if he knew exactly what I was thinking—and took immense pleasure in it. Long fingers moved up to stroke his goatee as he studied me with heated emerald eyes. "Red, I think, is your color, with your fair skin and passionate nature."

He snapped his fingers and one of the suit clad sentinels that flanked him disappeared. The guard returned in a flash to step forward and bow. A waterfall of deep red silk overflowed his massive forearms, as he offered me an elegant robe similar to the ones the musicians were wearing.

It was exquisite—a long, simply cut whisper of the finest fabric I'd ever seen. It drifted to the floor to gather in a soft pool between us. The shorter red silk negligee I'd worn with Sparrow last night might as well have been a burlap sack by comparison. It was truly beautiful. I started to reach for it and caught myself. *What the hell was I thinking?*

"I'm not here for a fashion show," I snapped, a bit more harshly than I intended.

Moab's eyes cooled to green chips of ice and Lorien's wings buzzed a warning in my ear. I was keenly aware of the dead silence pressing against my back from the group of onlookers, in jarring juxtaposition to the light, frolicsome melody now echoing throughout the chamber. I took a deep breath and forced a smile, reminding myself that I was trying to ingratiate myself with the bastard, not incur his wrath.

"Although I appreciate your hospitality, I'm quite comfortable as I am, thank you. I'd prefer to get down to business, if you don't mind. As I'm sure Seraven told you, I have some information that..."

"You mortals are always in such a hurry," he complained.

His voice was mocking, but I took comfort in the fact that his expression defrosted. He reached out to the woman reclining before him and idly stroked the graceful curve of her exposed neck. She arched toward his hand, practically purring in response, a mahogany flush creeping across her creamy skin.

"Immortality is a far more harmonious state. So many of your anxieties would simply disappear, if you would but surrender them and accept the gifts we offer. Isn't that so, my pet?" he murmured fondly, deft fingers gliding across the woman's collarbone to disappear beneath the low-cut neck of her sheer robe.

When his palm curved around her breast, she shuddered and a raw moan tore from her throat, a painful utterance of both agony and ecstasy. One delicate hand fluttered into restlessness, willow-thin fingers tipped with perfectly trimmed nails flickering over the slim cocoa expanse of her thigh and hovering to a stop near the silk-draped arc of her hip.

"An eternity to explore the pleasures of the flesh," Moab whispered, his voice a low, seductive rumble. "There is so much we could teach you, Sydney...so much freedom to be found in abandoning your inhibitions."

With a flick of his wrist, Moab parted the woman's robe. It fell open in a gossamer sigh, exposing small rounded breasts above a gently curved belly, and unveiling the intimacy of crisp dark hairs at the juncture of shapely legs. He took her trembling hand in his own and directed it to that vulnerable place, pressing her fingers against it in a teasing massage.

The woman's head dropped back and she whimpered, her hips lifting of their own volition. A hum of male appreciation rippled through the crowd behind me. As if in acknowledgment, Moab reached lower to spread the woman's knees wide, laying her secrets bare to their audience. A pent-up gasp rushed from her lips, and her free hand fluttered down to join the other as she began to pleasure herself.

Discomfort made me avert my eyes and I noted that Lorien had also turned away. She met my gaze, her expression stark with anger and pity. Behind us, the male death djinns were rapt with attention upon the fervid display. Some of the women watched as well, but I was surprised to discover that most sported expressions of long-suffering tolerance.

I wondered if it was simply because they weren't interested in the sexual exploits of other females, or if it could be that their disapproval went deeper.

The woman's breathing quickened into a desperate crescendo of sound as her climax overtook her, and then gradually softened back into inaudibility. I turned to find Moab stroking her raven hair as he looked down at her with an indulgent smile.

"Thank you, my dear. Your performance was rousing, as always."

He leaned back into his throne of blackened crystal, breaking their physical contact, and the woman's eyelids flickered open. She appeared dazed for a moment as she stared down at herself, and then her dark eyes cleared to reveal a hint of panic. But just as quickly, it was gone; to be replaced by a look of detached serenity as she pulled her robe closed and retied its pearly silken belt.

When scattered applause erupted behind me, her only visible reaction was a slight staining of the espresso and cream skin above her high cheekbones.

I wondered who she was, and what Moab had tricked her into accepting in exchange for her soul and the right to turn her into a one-woman-show for the pleasure of his court. I wasn't sure if he'd expected to titillate or embarrass me with the shocking act. Perhaps it merely amused him to flex his power in front of an audience.

Either way, I found myself having to pry my jaws apart to speak to the man again. I fixed him with a stony glare and somehow managed to pick up where I'd left off.

"King Moab, I have information regarding who is responsible for stealing the unaligned souls that so many of your people have been arrested for possessing."

His self-satisfied smirk faded and his gaze flicked over me thoughtfully. "Yes," he answered with a slow nod. "So Seraven has reported. And I appreciate you coming to me with this information. You have but to tell me what you know, and whatever you wish shall be yours."

It was my turn to smirk. "That's not quite what I had in mind."

He cocked a dark brow and his firm lips turned upward in an almost boyish grin. It took years off his face and transformed it into an eerie echo of Balthus'. "It *was* worth a try," he said with a chuckle.

"Very well, Sydney." He tipped his head to me charitably. "I shall grant you one free wish and leave your contract unclaimed. It would create an unpleasant political situation with my heir apparent if I took you for myself in any case."

Interesting to know that he cared, but still not where I wanted to be.

"You misunderstand me, King Moab," I replied quietly. "I want my contract cancelled altogether."

Moab stilled and all good humor fled his visage. "Impossible." The word dropped through the air, heavy as a stone.

Sparrow had warned me he wouldn't concede so easily.

"Not impossible," I contradicted, my tone soft but firm. "And I would think the freedom of your people would be more important to you than the collection of one human soul."

"You dare to blackmail me?" he demanded, his tanned face mottling with rage.

I forced myself to stare him down and hoped the inconvenient weakness that seemed to be developing in my knees wasn't too noticeable.

"Blackmail is such a nasty term," I answered with laudable calm. "I'd much rather refer to it as 'turnabout is fair play'. I never consciously wanted to die, and I certainly never wanted to give up my soul and become a plaything for a death djinn. I was tricked into my contract, King Moab, and I want it cancelled. In exchange, I'll give you the proof you need to free your people and clear your name."

Moab's form shimmered, and abruptly he was standing mere inches from me, glaring down from his height of over six feet. I flinched and Lorien cursed. I craned my neck to meet his eyes, my throat so tightly constricted it hurt. Although he hadn't touched me—yet—menace flowed off of him in waves.

"What makes you think I won't just *take* whatever proof you have, you little witch?" he snarled.

"Because..." My voice cracked and I forced a cough before trying again. "Because it's hidden, and only Lorien and I know about it." The words came out thin, but audible.

Moab's eyes narrowed and darted to my right. Before I could react, his hand flew toward my shoulder and his fist snapped shut next to my ear. I let out a strangled scream, staring in horror at his tightly closed fingers, hovering just where Lorien had been.

Frozen, my stomach clenched with nausea, I watched him relax his grip. His once handsome face contorted with fury as black dust began to sift down over us. We both looked up to find Lorien suspended in the air above, her wings whirring angrily, now well out of Moab's reach.

"That was a mistake, djinn," she hissed with shocking vehemence. Her violet eyes had darkened to jet and her usual silvery glow was streaked with obsidian. I'd never seen her so pissed—it was downright freaky.

"You have no claim over Sydney, and you will *never* have any claim over me," she ground out, enunciating each word with sibilant contempt. "You will release her from her contract, or I will destroy the only evidence you will ever find to clear your name and keep your miserable contract intact. Because you and I both know that's where this unaligned soul thing is headed if the Seelie Court finds you guilty. Make your decision. I'll be waiting for Sydney's call."

And with that, she was gone.

Something flickered in Moab's eyes as he lowered them back to mine. If I hadn't known better, I would have said it was fear. But before I could begin to process what had happened, a wave of heat passed through me, like a wall of pheromones soaking into my skin, sweeping away all rational thought. It felt so damned good that I nearly swayed into him.

The entire surface of my body felt tingly and alive, as if balanced on the edgy brink of release.

Moab brushed his hand down my arm, and what should have been a chaste caress inundated my senses with erotic awareness. He smiled as his warm palm gently engulfed mine. When his other hand came around to rest against the curve of my lower back, it was if a loose circuit had been completed, sending an almost unbearable sensual buzz flowing like quicksilver through my veins.

He whirled me into a dance, his movements smooth and sure. The music permeated the chamber with vitality and beauty, its vibrant swell carrying us along and making me feel as light as air. Moab gazed down at me with the tenderness of a lover, his eyes smoldering with deep sparks of emerald. His face was handsome and rugged beneath his goatee, its maturity hinting at an enticing blend of experience and finesse.

Some part of me knew that I was being enspelled, but the enchantment was impossible to resist. His stern lips softened with desire as he lowered his mouth to mine. I wanted his kiss like my body wanted its next breath of air, the need so primal I didn't know how to combat it. I closed my eyes and felt his whispered exhalation as he closed the distance between us, his touch the faintest brush of velvet.

With an effort so painful it brought tears to my eyes, I turned my face away.

"I'd rather die than belong to you."

He eased into stillness, the music still swirling dream-like around us. His hold on me neither tightened nor faltered. We stood like that for what seemed an eternity before I found the strength to look at him again. To my surprise, pain and uncertainty warred in his eyes as he gazed down at me, so raw it hurt to watch.

I forced my next words out with a gasp. "But you know all about that, don't you, King Moab? You've driven an innocent woman to her death before, at least once that I know of. I suppose I should be thankful that I don't have a young child to leave behind as an orphan."

He thrust me away as if touching me burned him. I stumbled to a halt, barely finding my feet. I fixed him with an emotionless stare, my insides churning with a queasy mixture of fear, anger and relief.

"I should have known. His stink is all over you. You're lovers."

I nearly choked. "That's none of your business."

Moab laughed then, the sound rife with bitter amusement. "What a double edged sword our Agent Sparrow has turned out to be. First my own chosen mate's affections for that sniveling half-breed brat steal her from me—and now, years later, the same half-breed has found his way into the affections of my heir's chosen mate."

I was livid with disbelief. "She was his *mother*. You stole her from him, not the other way around, you selfish bastard. And just so you know, where I come from, the word 'mate' implies a desire to be together from *both* parties."

A mask of anger descended upon his features. "Watch your tongue, you impertinent little witch. This is my court, and I've killed for lesser insults." His lips quirked up in a nasty grin. "And furthermore, dearest Sydney, you didn't seem to be lacking any desire for me a few moments ago."

Black hatred smothered me. I gritted my teeth and struggled to rein in my temper. The fact that he had just called me a 'little witch' for the second time wasn't helping. But starting a battle with him wasn't going to help my situation.

My face contorted into an expression of loathing. "All you need to know is that Lorien will destroy that evidence if you don't release me from my contract. And if you enspell me into completing it? It'll be up in flames before you even touch my soul," I bluffed.

Right then I was feeling what must have been only a fraction of Lauringer's all-consuming anger at what she had suffered. I realized that if it came down to it, destroying the evidence was exactly what I would want Lorien to do. I could easily watch King Moab and his djinns go down for Lauringer's crime—in a heartbeat and without the slightest remorse.

"What guarantee do I have that your so-called evidence will exonerate my people?" he demanded.

"We'll make a binding contract right now," I spat. "Upon receiving my evidence, you will release me from the contract for my soul. In the event that the evidence does not aid you in getting the unaligned soul charges against your people dropped, you can reinstate the contract for my soul *exactly* as it was. No harm, no foul."

Except for him. He was the foulest creature I'd ever met.

He considered my words with care, no doubt searching for hidden loopholes to betray me. I had done my best to leave him none. "Fine," he answered abruptly. "I accept your terms and agree to be bound by your contract as stated."

A gasp went up around the room from the audience I'd forgotten, and sweet relief coursed through me. Sparrow had told me that a formal statement like the one Moab had just given was as binding as me uttering a wish out loud in front of him.

"Lorien!" I called quickly, eager to be done with the death djinns once and for all.

She blinked into the air before me with a pop, and immediately sank downward with the weight of the aged green journal she held. I caught it in my hands and gave her a tremulous smile as she released it. She glowed silver once more and her eyes were luminous as she darted up to take her place above my right shoulder.

Wordless and stiff, I held the journal out for Moab. He reached for it with suspicion heavy on his face.

"What's this?" he asked as he began flipping through the thin, well-worn pages.

"If you read this journal, you'll see that it was written by someone who contracted their soul to one of your death djinns. Although it doesn't mention names, I happen to know that it belongs to Lauringer."

Moab paled and his eyes flew to mine. The staggering disbelief in his gaze released some of the tension from my body. I was pretty sure Sparrow and I had pieced the puzzle together correctly, but Moab's reaction only added to my certainty.

"Somehow, she managed to keep the whole thing a secret all these years."

"That's not possible," he whispered hoarsely.

"She's quite talented with magic—or so I hear." I raised one brow in thinly veiled sarcasm. "Apparently, she got pretty pissed when the djinn raped her and killed her best friend. Not that I blame her. If that's not enough to make a girl vow revenge, I don't know what is. Anyway, it's all there in the journal."

His eyes dropped back down to the notebook in horror. I doubted it had anything to do with sympathy for what had happened to Lauringer.

"I would hazard a guess that she figured out how to get rid of the bastard, and she's been itching to abolish your slimy soul contract ever since. Framing a large population of your people for the possession of unaligned souls is a pretty ingenious way to go about it, wouldn't you say? But you don't have to take my word for it. Why don't you see if you can claim her contract and ask her yourself?"

I cringed as I spoke the words. I hated that I was trading Lauringer's freedom for my own, but Sparrow was going to bring her in with or without me blackmailing the death djinns for my soul.

Moab's eyes were glazed with disbelief as he stared at me for a moment more before closing them. A remote look came over his face. Concentration tightened his jaw, and lines of strain appeared there, as if he was in the midst of an internal battle.

A fine sheen of sweat broke out across his forehead. "Lauringer Eloise Baumbirn," he bellowed, causing me to take a nervous step backward. "I call you forth by right of contract. Appear before me *now.*"

And suddenly, there she was—the famous Lauringer, the most powerful mage alive, wearing a comfortable-looking navy pajama set, her long blonde hair sleep-tousled. Her strange golden eyes were wild with confusion and fear as they darted between Moab and me. And an awful sense of guilt crawled through my chest.

Lorien's wings made a shrill peal near my ear as Lauringer collapsed to the ground, shaking her head and mewling in denial. The breathy, high-pitched murmurs from the watching djinns gained a desperate intensity. Moab, who had appeared almost as surprised as Lauringer, recovered himself quickly.

"What have you done, mage?" he snarled, yanking her up by the elbows to face him. "I see that Devlin of the Firestone clan laid claim to your soul over two hundred years ago! He was a tricky devil, keeping such a powerful asset a secret. Yet he disappeared nigh on a hundred years ago, and your contract was never passed on. How have you hidden yourself from us?"

He was shaking her so hard that her head whipped back and forth on her slim neck. Yet she remained limp in his grasp, her eyes blank, as if she had retreated into her mind. Lorien was making horrified little noises from her perch above my shoulder.

"Stop, please, you're hurting her!" I shouted, unable to stand watching it any longer.

I may as well have been a fly buzzing in his ear for all the effect I had.

"Are you responsible for planting unaligned souls in my people's containment safes?" he shrieked at Lauringer, continuing to ruthlessly manhandle her.

"That's enough." A woman rose from the crowd of djinns seated behind us and stepped forward, tall and slender, her face tranquil with quiet dignity. "Your anger is justified, Moab, but you are damaging the woman upon whose testimony our son's release depends. A less physical form of questioning will reveal quicker and more reliable results."

"I tire of you overstepping your bounds, Calypso," Moab snapped. He aimed a sneer at the female djinn but, although he didn't release her from his grip, he stopped jostling Lauringer about like a rag-doll.

The woman's unusual hazel eyes flashed with grudging satisfaction as she resumed her seat. I felt like I'd seen her before, but I was too distracted to figure out where.

Moab sighed in aggravation and made a visible effort to calm himself. He rearranged his hold on Lauringer so that his hands were gentle upon her shoulders, and with disturbing swiftness, a practiced cloak of charm fell across his handsome face. "Lauringer," he appealed in a cajoling tone, "I have called you here to answer some questions. You will answer them truthfully for me."

Lauringer blinked and looked up into Moab's guise of kindness with all the trust of a lost child. "I need my gold-dust," she murmured softly.

"Why would you need gold-dust, Lauringer?" Moab asked with amused indulgence.

"It helps me remember." Her earnest expression brightened into a sudden smile. "And it makes me pretty, see." She held out her arm for Moab's inspection, her loose sleeve falling back to reveal skin that glittered a fiery gold in the reddish light.

Comprehension dawned as I stared at her. She must have been fighting the insanity caused by the long separation from her soul with a spell—just like the one she'd given Emily for Ophelia. But she must have used so much of it for so long that her body had begun taking on its hue. And I saw something else as she twisted her arm around, gazing down with admiration at the effect of the room's ruby glow on the golden shimmer of her skin.

There was a tattoo of an infinity symbol inked into the middle of her now ungloved palm.

"I can help you remember," Moab urged. "Just look into my eyes."

Lauringer abandoned her fascination with her arm and obediently focused her attention on Moab. "Your eyes are such a pretty green," she said shyly. "They remind me of something...someone..." She frowned.

"Devlin," he prompted. "My eyes remind you of Devlin's. He granted you three wishes and took you into his service. But he disappeared. Tell me what happened to him, Lauringer."

"Devlin?" she repeated, her gaze narrowing inward. Her breath quickened and grew shallow. "He hurt me," she gasped. A storm-cloud of rage and horror descended upon her brow. "No! He killed M.J.!"

She struggled savagely to free herself from Moab's grasp, her golden eyes wide and unseeing. A frigid chill swept across the cavern and an eerie wind picked up, whistling mournfully through the peaks and valleys of the crystalline stalactites that littered the ceiling.

A fearful murmur went up amongst the seated djinns and the music came to an uneven halt as the whistle grew into a piercing whine. Plumes of frosty air rose with the gasping exhalations of the room's inhabitants, and I shivered as my own breath condensed into a visible puff before my eyes. Lorien crowded closer, a swirl of purple dust stirring around her as her agitated wings brushed the fine hairs on my neck.

"NO!" Moab roared. The word echoed around the chamber, resounding loudly, as if at battle with the shriek of the frozen wind. "*You will not use magic unless I command it!*"

The order didn't seem to have its desired effect, and surprise stained Moab's features. He focused with deepening intensity upon the viciously thrashing Lauringer. Strain lined his face as he fought for control, and slowly, she began to calm.

The deafening howl receded and the temperature abruptly returned to normal, as if the cold had been sucked from the air. Lauringer gentled to stillness, her golden eyes glittering up at Moab in the vacuum of silence that was left behind. He stared at her, awe-struck.

"So much raw power to be harnessed," he murmured. There was stark hunger in his voice, and it chilled me in a way that had nothing to do with the temperature to think of what he would do with Lauringer's considerable talents at his disposal.

Moab took a deep breath, as if to remind himself why he was there questioning the mage. "The unaligned souls—hundreds of them have appeared in my people's containment safes without their consent. What do you know of this, Lauringer?" he asked, wisely leaving the topic of Devlin alone.

"I put them there," she answered simply.

The death djinns sounded a collective exclamation, and even Moab appeared stunned, as if he hadn't believed it was true until he heard her say it. "How is that possible? How did you get them into our private safes without setting off our security?"

Lauringer smiled, appearing pleased with herself. "I have lots of really good spells." Her eyes twinkled and she leaned closer, whispering loudly to Moab. "But it wasn't getting into the safes that was the problem—that was the easy part. It took me forever to figure out how to mark myself with the ancient magi seal of eternity so I could manipulate the unborn souls."

"Unborn...souls," Moab repeated falteringly.

Lauringer beamed and shook her head in enthusiasm, her eyes taking on a fervent glow. "It was the perfect plan. There was no way to trace them because there were no bodies to trace them back to. I snapped them up as they were leaving the Sea of Souls to be born, and more just popped up to take their place."

Realization came crashing down as The Shepherd's words drifted back to me, '*Strange happenings here lately. More souls being reborn than usual.*' No wonder the Seelie Police hadn't been able to connect the unaligned souls with anyone. Lauringer had taken them before there had been anyone to connect them *to*.

It was an ingenious plan. And it seemed a victimless crime since the souls would be returned to the Sea when the police were finished with their investigation. Well, victimless except for the death djinns taking the fall, but oddly enough that little detail didn't trouble me much.

So why was it that the very thought of what she had done twisted my insides and made my skin crawl, as if my body felt a wrongness that my mind was unable to discern?

"Mad. Utterly mad," Lorien whimpered in my ear. "What she's done is an aberration." I tilted my head and looked at her askance. Her violet eyes were huge in her pale face.

I wanted to ask her why she was so upset, but another glaring inconsistency occurred to me. "Wait," my voice piped out against the uncomfortable hush. Now every death djinn eye was turned my way, and it seemed I had the floor whether I wanted it or not.

"Uh, what about the woman whose soul Balthus was arrested for having? The one he says he won from a goblin?"

Moab glanced from me back to the captive woman in his grasp. "Answer her," he commanded.

Distaste distorted Lauringer's shining features. "I never should have sought assistance from a goblin. They're sneaky, conniving creatures, and I should have known this one would be no different. But I needed someone to run errands and gather information for me, someone who wouldn't be noticed hanging around the gambling circuits frequented by the death djinns. Firzag seemed perfect."

She pouted. "I guess it wasn't surprising that he got greedy. He stole some of my books and journals and found out about the eternity mark. He cooked up his own scheme to take souls from promising humans and then turn a profit by selling them to the highest bidder.

"But he was unskilled in magic, and failed to realize that his methods would leave the soul unaligned. When he saw what happened with his first attempt, he panicked and slapped one of my temporary illusion spells on the soul to make it appear aligned. Then he pawned it off on the next death djinn he met. The little idiot almost ruined my entire plan—putting a traceable unaligned soul in the hands of the death djinn prince."

Lauringer grimaced. "I had to get rid of him. I had no choice."

So that was why Firzag had been so eager to give away the poor woman's soul. And Balthus had only ended up with it because he'd been in the wrong place at the wrong time. Lauringer must have magically concealed whatever she'd done to Firzag in order to cover her tracks.

I found I couldn't work up too much sorrow over the death of such a creature. Although I'd bet old Ezrega on the Hell Barge would give a pretty penny to know what had happened. Maybe she'd even be agreeable to exchanging the blood she'd taken for the information. But there was no freaking way I was going back into Lady Nightwing's domain.

My musings were interrupted by King Moab's astonished demand. "And you did all of this...why?"

Lauringer blinked as if the answer was obvious. "To incriminate the death djinns and push the Seelie Court into reexamining that horrible contract allowing you to enslave mortal souls."

Moab glared at her. "Our contract was deemed fair by the Seelie Court ages ago. We take mortals who are miserable and asking for their lives to end. We grant them their hearts' desires, renewing their will to live, and then bestow them with immortality. In return, they enter into our service."

"You take people as slaves," Lauringer railed, trying to jerk free of Moab's grasp. "*Nothing* you can offer is worth the price of freedom."

"Be still, woman!" he commanded forcefully.

She quieted in his arms and a blank, glassy look came into her eyes.

"She's right," I said softly. "You take people into your *service* for eternity, and they have no idea what they're getting themselves into."

Moab's gaze flew toward me, as if he'd forgotten I was there. "You," he scoffed. "No one asked your opinion, you blackmailing little witch. Although I suppose I should thank you in the end. After all—you did present me with the evidence needed to clear my people. And you returned a long lost soul to us in the process. What a boon to discover that the most powerful mage in the realm is ours to command.

"Her soul is worth a thousand of yours," he added nastily.

"Then you release me from my contract," I stated, hating the question that still wavered in my voice.

He huffed in irritation. "Yes, Sydney Corrigan, it is done. Though Balthus will not be best pleased by it, you are now free from us. My prince will just have to settle for gaining his own freedom. And in truth, I believe him better off without you."

Lorien whooped happily at my shoulder and I grinned as she threw her arms around the side of my neck, her wings stirring against my hair. But my happiness was somewhat dampened by Moab's next words.

"And now, Miss Lauringer," he said with relish, "we have long unfinished business to conclude."

He looked into Lauringer's eyes, his muscular form going rigid with taut control. "Lauringer Eloise Baumbirn, I rightfully claim your soul in repayment of your debt to Devlin of the Firestone clan."

I cringed as the blankness in her eyes was replaced by sheer panic.

Moab caught my reaction and grinned. "That's right," he drawled. "Lauringer, my dear, you can thank Sydney here for returning your soul to us." Though he was straining with exertion, it was obvious that the bastard was taking great pleasure in both her fear and my dismay.

Lauringer's eyes shot to me, her face a mask of pain that I forced myself not to look away from. "*I'm sorry*," I whispered. And I was. If I could have spared her this, I would have.

I held her stare, sick with misery, and watched as a sense of calm descended over her. For the first time since Moab had called her, she looked every inch the powerful, collected woman she had seemed when I'd met her—despite the pajamas. She smiled at me serenely, and then spoke in a voice that carried throughout the cavern.

"It's alright, Sydney. I have prepared for this eventuality, as well."

And then she vanished.

Moab jerked with surprise, blinking at the empty space before him. His eyes snapped shut and moved rapidly beneath his lids, his fists clenching and unclenching at his sides. Then he erupted in a howl of rage and his gaze settled over me. He advanced one menacing step and Lorien darted forward to hover between us.

"What is the meaning of this?" he screamed. "She is gone! Gone without a trace—as if she no longer walks this world!"

"I don't know!" I stammered, shaking my head back and forth.

"Treachery!" he cried. "You have reneged on our deal!"

"Don't even try it!" Lorien was abruptly in his face, shaking a tiny finger at his proud nose. "You have your evidence, as promised, not to mention a witnessed confession. That's more than enough to free your people and help protect your vile contract for a little while longer. It's not Sydney's fault that you can't hold onto one rogue soul."

Moab's mouth opened and closed soundlessly, his eyes flashing green fire. "OUT!" he bellowed, pointing to the chamber's entrance. He turned his back on me and whispered furiously to the guards by his throne.

I didn't have to be told twice. The voices of the death djinns escalated into a dull roar, and going by their glares in my direction, they were none too pleased with the turn of events either.

Lorien flitted to a quivering stop above my head and pulled her pouch from a fold in her color-shifting dress. Despite her bravado with the king, I could see the pouch trembling in her hand. And there was no mistaking the anxious purple hue of the faerie dust sifting down over me. "Are you ready to go home, Sydney?"

"More than you'll ever know," I answered emphatically.

She exhaled on a shaky grin. "Don't forget to close your eyes and lock your knees."

I was in the process of doing just that, when the sounds of a new commotion echoed through the cavern. I reopened one eye to find the entrance doors being thrown wide by a grim-looking Seraven. Thinking that couldn't bode well, I squeezed my eyelid shut and turned my face up to Lorien with a whispered, "Hurry!"

And then I heard a voice that sent prickles of dread spiking through my blood. My eyes shot open to find Lorien's transport dust floating down over my face in a silvery stream. I ducked frantically, dropping to the ground and scrambling away as it sprinkled harmlessly to the floor.

"For the love of the Seelie Court!" Lorien swore. "I don't have an endless supply of that stuff! What in the realm would possess you to..." she faltered into silence as she saw what I was staring at.

Seraven proceeded down the center aisle of the room, every eye riveted on him, through a silence so thick I could have choked on it. Behind the guard, with his legs shackled in bright silver chains, stumbled a groaning prisoner.

Sparrow hadn't escaped after all.

<u>Chapter 8—Tribulations</u>

"And what have you brought me this time, Seraven?" Moab asked. He appeared bitterly amused as he reseated himself on his dark crystal throne, one guard still flanking him and one having disappeared. At an impatient flick of his hand, the white-robed woman's head snapped up and the musicians began a solemn dirge.

All four women looked nervous, and I feared that the coming day was going to be particularly unpleasant for anyone whose soul belonged to King Moab.

Seraven crossed the invisible plot of floor above the lava flow far beneath, and halted before the king's dais. I recoiled at Sparrow's pained groan when the guard yanked him forward and forced him to his knees. His head hung low and I didn't think he was even aware that Lorien and I were there.

Seraven was sporting a split lip and the beginnings of a black eye, and I was guessing that Sparrow had put up a fight.

"My liege, this prisoner was discovered skulking about in the passages below the palace. Another guard and I subdued him and brought him to the dungeon. It was then that I discovered..."

"Lift his head so that I can see his face," Moab interrupted.

Seraven obliged by grasping a fistful of Sparrow's sweat-damp hair and cruelly snatching it upward. He looked far worse than he had when I'd left him earlier. The makeshift bandage he'd wrapped around his arm had slipped down to reveal a raw, blackened mass of flesh. It was concentrated on a large, vaguely circular patch of skin, and I realized that it was precisely where his healing tattoo should be.

His clothing was torn and soiled, and there were fresh bruises darkening his face beneath a crust of dirt and drying blood. But his eyes, as they lifted to meet King Moab's, threw sparks of fierce, rebellious blue.

Part of my paralyzing tension dissipated upon seeing that there was still some fight left in him.

Surprise flitted across Moab's features before it was quickly hidden behind a bland smile. "Agent Sparrow. If you wanted to come by, you should have called, son. You know that surprise visits to the palace are frowned upon. Security, and so forth."

He gave a vague wave of his hand.

"However—security or not—what, pray tell, were you doing *skulking* about my catacombs?"

Sparrow's jaw grew tighter with each word. I had a feeling that being called 'son' by Moab had nearly unhinged him. When he spoke, his voice was cold and rigid with control.

"Your people are under official Seelie investigation for the illegal possession of unaligned souls. You should well know that, as the detective in charge of this case, I have every right to pursue all reasonable leads."

Seraven made as if to interject, but an imperiously raised brow from Moab silenced him.

"And just what sort of *lead* might you have been pursuing in the passages beneath my palace?" Moab asked in a casual tone, as he shifted himself into a more comfortable position on the burgundy cushioned seat of his throne.

Sparrow's lips compressed into a thin line. "I'm afraid that's confidential."

Moab's eyes flashed and his expression hardened. "And *I'm* afraid that you're a bit behind the times, Agent Sparrow. Did no one within the Seelie police organization think to notify the detective in charge that his case has been solved?"

He clucked his tongue.

"How embarrassingly shoddy and disorganized that it falls upon me, as the falsely accused, to relay such information. My guard has informed me that my people have already been pardoned and are in the process of being released."

Sparrow stared at him as if weighing the information. "If that is so, then it must be an extremely recent development, and you have my apologies for wasting your time. I would appreciate it if you would release me so that I may return to my office for an update. I'm sure that I will be needed to help close out the case and process the release of your people."

The king snorted mockingly. "Just like that? You don't sound terribly surprised at this turn of events, Agent Sparrow. Could it be that you had some fore-knowledge of my people's innocence?"

His eyes narrowed on me before traveling back to consider Sparrow.

"And there is still the matter of your trespassing," he added with an unpleasant grin.

"As I said..." Agent Sparrow began, impatience coloring his voice.

"Sire," Seraven interrupted, "there is another urgent matter about which you should be aware. I discovered the remains of Zortho, a fellow guard, in one of the dungeon cells. I have determined that this man was responsible for his death. An inwa was used."

Chaos thundered throughout the chamber as its occupants reacted with shock and anger. I still wasn't clear on exactly what an inwa was, other than Lorien's hurried explanation about it being some sort of petrified fruit pit that could be thrown hard enough to kill a djinn. But apparently, the use of one was enough to cause quite a stir amongst the present company.

"SILENCE!" roared Moab. The noise died down to an incensed grumble. His incredulous gaze bored into Sparrow. "You snuck into my palace with an *inwa* in your possession? How did you even come by such a relic?"

Sparrow's reply was stony silence.

"Answer me!" Moab shouted. His eyes narrowed on Sparrow's chains and they flashed sharply silver in the crimson light.

Sparrow's entire body went stiff and he stifled a groan. When the silver flash faded, he looked as if he was struggling to remain upright. He glared hatred at King Moab.

"I came across it many years ago," he growled, "in a tin of useless trinkets at a human antique shop. The owner assumed it was junk and sold it to me for nothing. I kept it as a curiosity and brought it with me today, not intending to use it, but in case of an emergency—just such as the one I encountered.

"Your guard was unreasonably violent and would have killed me. I got to him first. It was self defense."

"My guards are trained to protect my person and my property. A trespasser would be considered a serious threat. You should have known that, Agent Sparrow. Have you anything more to offer in your defense?"

Sparrow remained silent, managing to look handsome and defiant even while beaten and kneeling in chains. Moab's smile stirred a sick feeling in my stomach.

"Very well. I fear I am forced to pass judgment for your crimes, then." Moab cleared his throat and intoned formally, "Agent Patrick Sparrow, for the offense of murder, executed on my property and against one of my people—who was at the time only in pursuit of carrying out his duties—I sentence you to death by fire."

"NO!" I shouted, the word tearing from my throat with the force of a bullet.

Sparrow cursed and swung his head around violently. Every other set of eyes in the room locked onto me as well, but I only saw Sparrow's. They echoed surprise and pain to find me there, and then anger, before they hardened into a frightening resolve.

"Lorien. Get her out of here. *Now.*" The words were harsh with command. He turned away without sparing me another glance, dismissing me as if I no longer existed.

Lorien flew forward a pace and looked from Sparrow back to me, her small face twisted by anxious indecision. I gave her a desperate warning shake of my head.

"Yes, Ms. Corrigan. Why *are* you still here?" Moab interjected drolly. "I distinctly remember suggesting that it was time for you to leave. Ohhh... that's right. You and Agent Sparrow have become lovers. How deliciously tragic."

"You can't kill him," I pleaded. My voice sounded high to my own ears and I couldn't seem to catch my breath. "He was just doing his job. And he says killing your guard was self defense."

Moab sighed as if bored. "These issues have already been addressed. And I do hate to repeat myself, Sydney."

My eyes filled with tears and I resisted the urge to blink them out. "But you didn't sentence Lauringer to death!" I exclaimed desperately. "And she killed one of your people without just cause!"

I didn't believe that was true. I believed with all my heart that Devlin had deserved to die, preferably after excessive torture. But I was frantic to defend Sparrow.

Moab leaned forward and captured me with his dangerously glittering gaze. "Lauringer, my sweet, would have paid dearly for her crimes. Have no doubt of that. She was, however, a mortal, and not necessarily subject to the same consequences as those who reside in this realm. Furthermore, she was far too valuable to lose."

He stared at me with such irate accusation that I shuffled backward a step before I caught myself. Then he smiled and leaned into his throne, his gaze turning thoughtful but never breaking with mine. Sparrow remained stiff and silent between us.

"I am not completely immune to such a poignant dilemma, however," he pronounced.

I stilled in suspicion.

"Perhaps Agent Sparrow's death could be averted. I might see my way to accepting his claim of self defense and lessening his sentence if I were offered the proper incentive."

Moab gave me an expectant grin.

"Such as?" I prompted hoarsely.

"Well, it's really quite simple, Sydney. Tit for tat. I will reduce Agent Sparrow's sentence to a hefty fine, and allow him to keep his life, in exchange for your soul."

"No, Sydney!" Sparrow yelled.

Seraven backhanded him and Sparrow spat blood. But he was no longer ignoring me. He snapped his head around to look at me and his expression held a stark plea.

"Don't do it, Sydney," Lorien whispered.

I stared numbly at King Moab. "That's pure blackmail."

He barked a short laugh. "And I prefer to call it negotiation, my dear. You aren't the only one capable of convenient definitions."

I closed my eyes and swallowed.

My soul for Sparrow's life. I hadn't been lying when I'd said I'd rather die than belong to Moab. And though no one but Angelica had actually voiced it, I was pretty sure that Lorien, Sunny and Sparrow agreed death was the better option as well.

But Sparrow wouldn't even be in this mess if it wasn't for me. He'd killed that guard to save my soul. So in a way, giving my soul in exchange for his life just returned things to the way they were before he'd committed the crime. Except I would belong to Moab instead of the horrible guard.

I felt nauseous and feverish.

"Tick tock, Sydney," Moab chirped. "Djinn law waits on no human."

I noticed that the temperature in the room had risen by several degrees, and opened my eyes to find that a visible band of heat shimmered in the air several yards away, behind where Seraven stood. Moab inclined his head at the guard, who proceeded to force Sparrow to his feet. Turning him so that he faced away from the king, Seraven pushed Sparrow forward toward the sweltering strip of air.

I realized with trepidation that it was rising from the aisle of invisible floor that looked down onto the river of lava. Oh, Goddess. Death by fire. They were going to push him in!

The tears that I had been holding back began to fall, drying instantly in the hot air as they rolled onto my cheeks. Sparrow was about to die and I was the only person who, with one miserable choice, could stop it. Seraven pushed him again, and he stumbled, as if teetering on the edge of an unseen abyss.

Moab raised a questioning brow at me.

My eyes found Sparrow's. His jaw was set with iron determination and resolve, and he shook his head at me in warning. He looked...resigned. As if he had already accepted his fate. And I wanted to scream with the tidal wave of rage and grief that swelled inside me.

But I still couldn't make myself do it. I couldn't give my soul to Moab. And I despised myself for it.

"No?" Moab inquired politely. I wanted to smash the look from his face. "Well, not to worry, Sydney. It's a quick death. He'll be ash before he ever hits the river below. And I completely understand your reluctance. I've always felt that self sacrifice is highly over-rated."

He nodded at Seraven, who grasped Sparrow by the shoulders, centering his weight in preparation to push. A funeral march swelled into the thickened air from the instrumental trio, somber and heart-rending, and agonizing despair tore through me.

"I wish I was dead!" I screamed suddenly. Lorien made a vexed sound, but didn't even bother with the warning dust.

"Sydney, no," Sparrow groaned, his blue eyes scorching mine as they echoed my torment.

Seraven froze and turned back to King Moab with an uncertain look. Watchful death djinn faces stared daggers at me from the crowd. But none of them spoke a word.

"I wish I was dead," I repeated breathlessly, looking out over the occupants of the room. "One of you—take my contract." My voice cracked on the plea. "I wish for Agent Sparrow to be absolved of all charges."

No one moved or uttered a sound. I slowly scanned the group, searching for a flicker of interest, a glimmer of greed—anything other than the cold silence of refusal. My gaze lingered on the graceful older woman, Calypso, who had referred to Balthus as her son, and I thought I saw a twinge of pity in her hazel eyes. It was then that I realized where I'd seen her before.

She was the woman I'd accidentally run into as I was going into Hannah's shop the other day.

Before I had a chance to process the thought, Moab broke into a chuckle behind me, the sound as grating to my ears as nails against a chalkboard. I turned to find his face alight with condescending amusement.

"Interesting move, Sydney, but I'm afraid you won't find anyone in this room willing to risk my wrath—at least not in such an open manner," he added with a sardonic twist of his lips.

"And, although I admit that I find your desperation quite...*arousing*," he said, his voice dropping into a husky purr, "I'm afraid that your counter-offer is not enough to satisfy me. However, my offer still stands if you would like to reconsider."

Bile rose in my throat as I looked back and forth between Moab's lecherous smile and Sparrow's beaten form. I squeezed my eyes shut, wondering if I'd ever be able to forgive myself for letting Sparrow die.

"Proceed, Seraven, and let us be done with this spectacle," Moab ordered grimly.

I held back a sob and squeezed my eyes shut tighter, unable to watch. A soft, tingling wetness brushed my neck, like drops of spring rain, and I realized Lorien was crying too.

"Please, I really do wish I was dead," I whispered brokenly.

There was a loud snap. I flinched as I pictured Sparrow toppling over the precipice, the thick silver chains around his ankles clipping the edge as he fell, a single horrible frame catching over and over on a movie reel in my mind.

"Seraven, stop." A familiar rich and cultured voice rang out in calm command. "I will take your contract, Sydney. What do you wish, my love?"

My eyes flew open and I nearly collapsed as my knees swayed beneath my weight.

"Balthus," Moab growled in warning, "What do you think you're doing?"

"I wish for Agent Sparrow to be absolved of all charges," I gasped quickly, before either of them could say another word. Despite my morbid imaginings, Sparrow still stood, drenched in sweat, on the verge of the abyss. But all it would take to change that was a single nudge from Seraven.

Balthus strode up the aisle between the seated members of Moab's court, a picture of relaxed power in his tailored slacks and black silk shirt, chestnut hair gleaming in the ruddy light. He fixed me with an intimate smile, filled with both the fiery heat of seduction and the easy warmth of reassurance.

Death djinn or not, I had never been so glad to see anyone in my life.

In the blink of an eye, the shimmering haze in the air disappeared and the room's temperature began to drop. Seraven still held Sparrow, but it looked as if he was supporting his weight rather than trying to restrain him. The silver shackles were gone.

The unbearable tension that had been building inside me left my body in a rush, turning my muscles to water and sending tears of relief streaming down my face.

"Forgive my late arrival, Father," Balthus said coolly. He detoured from the center path to give his mother a light kiss on the cheek. She hugged him tight, her delighted smile lingering as he left her and continued forward toward Moab.

"I'm afraid I was a bit delayed with the release paperwork. But you'll be pleased to know that everything is in order—the charges have been dropped and all of our people have been cleared to return home. I'm told we have Sydney's detective work to thank for that."

He winked at me over his shoulder and turned back to grin at his father.

"Clever, capable *and* beautiful—what more could I ask for in my chosen mate? By the way—I'd like to thank you all for respecting my claim to her." His voice rose to address the entire room, but there was a hard sparkle in his eyes as they remained fixed on Moab.

A low growl sounded from Sparrow's direction. He appeared to have found the strength to stand without Seraven's aid, and was glaring his hatred at both father and son. He held his control and his tongue with admirable restraint.

"Son," Moab said with a smile that didn't quite hide his irritation. "I'm sure we are all eager to celebrate the safe return of our prince and an end to the ridiculous charges that have imprisoned so many innocent djinns these past weeks—perhaps none so much as myself. However, you have interrupted the rightful pursuit of justice here. Agent Sparrow has committed a grave crime against us and he must be punished accordingly."

Balthus frowned. "I see. Of what crime have I absolved him?"

"He murdered one of our guards, the sentence for which, as you know, is death," Moab answered, his tone frigid.

"A serious offense indeed," Balthus agreed, his eyes never wavering from his father's. "Which guard was killed?"

"It does not matter which one it was," Moab snapped. "It matters only that the crime was committed."

Balthus raised a calm brow. "I was only thinking that perhaps reparations can be made to the guard's kin. I will personally see that they are taken care of, as it was my interference that robbed them of their justice. I'm sure they will understand that I am unable to renege on a contract with my chosen mate—especially seeing as our first contract was nullified without my consent," he added pointedly.

"Your *chosen mate*," Moab sneered, "was so eager to be rid of you that she blackmailed me and forced my hand into releasing her from your contract. If I had not done so, she would have destroyed the evidence that proved your innocence, leaving you rotting in a Seelie prison and possibly jeopardizing our entire way of life.

"Now, by granting her newest wish, you have not only set a murderer free—but you have given your so-called mate's lover back to her."

I cringed, fearing Balthus' reaction to his father's words—all of which were completely true and definitely aimed at pissing him off.

But he merely flashed me an indulgent smile. "She is a feisty one. She likes to play hard to get, my Sydney does. But I shall win her in the end."

Moab looked furious.

My father has no cause to keep either you or Agent Sparrow here any longer.

I started as the soft tendrils of Balthus' voice curled through my brain.

It would be wise for you to take your leave now, my love. Have a care, though—be polite, but do not show him any weakness.

I cleared my throat and bowed stiffly. "Uh, thank you again, King Moab, for granting me an audience. It's time for Agent Sparrow and me to be going, so we'll leave you to your reunion with the prince." I gave him a respectful nod and looked away from his irate glower as I forced my legs into forward motion toward Seraven and Sparrow.

Lorien darted in front of me, her violet eyes open wide, wordlessly begging to know if I had any inkling of what the hell I was doing. I tilted my head in an imperceptible nod at Balthus and she grimaced.

Seraven directed a questioning gaze toward the dais behind me, and must have received the permission he sought, because he stepped away from Sparrow.

Sparrow's eyes locked with mine, steely and unreadable.

"Can either of you blink us out of here?" I whispered.

"I don't have enough powder left for both of you," Lorien answered, wringing her small hands in worry as she hovered between us.

Sparrow's jaw tightened. "I won't be able to do any more magic until my powers have had a chance to recover." His voice was barely audible and laced with pain. "Lorien, you blink Sydney out. I'll manage on my own."

"Absolutely not," I hissed. "Can't you blink out and get some more powder?" I asked Lorien desperately.

She huffed her frustration. "It takes time and ingredients to make it, Sydney. And it loses potency quickly, so I can't just stockpile the stuff."

I exhaled a quiet curse. "Well, we're all walking—and flying," I added with a glance at Lorien, "out of here together, then. And don't bother arguing with me." I glared at Sparrow and grabbed his uninjured arm to pull him forward alongside me. "Let's go."

To my surprise and relief, he went without a fight. I realized why when I staggered beneath his weight as we began moving toward the doors. He was too weak to argue.

I shot Lorien a concerned look, struggling to hide from the death djinns the fact that I was half-carrying Sparrow out of there. They were silent and staring as we began the interminable walk up the aisle between them. I caught a glimpse of Calypso's face as we passed. She flashed me a small smile, her eyes gleaming with something akin to satisfaction and pride.

I'd ponder what the hell that was all about later, when I didn't have a two hundred and fifty pound half-sidhe using me for a crutch and the entire death djinn court watching my every move. I grunted as Sparrow shifted his weight and I nearly stumbled.

I'll be seeing you soon, love.

Balthus' seductive purr echoed through my head. I shivered, despite the fact that perspiration was making my hair stick to my neck in warm, uncomfortable clumps.

I was sweating buckets by the time we finally reached the double doors, still guarded by the hulking forms of Theros and Besame. I went rigid as we passed between them, and as if sensing my fear, Sparrow straightened for a moment to give them a formidable look.

I knew his show of strength was feigned as he sagged into my side in the hallway beyond, but it had worked—they had left us alone and we were through. Now all we had to do was get down the stairs and make our way out of the palace. I had no idea what we'd do then, but first things first—making it that far with Sparrow's heavy weight propped against me was daunting enough.

Lorien fluttered several paces in front of us and turned to take in our shaky progress. She shook her head in consternation, her small lips firming into a grim line. "We're going to need some help," she muttered. "I'll be back." And she blinked out.

"Where the hell is she going?" Sparrow grumbled.

"No idea." I reached forward with difficulty to push open one of the doors that led into the entry hall. "Do you think you can make it down these stairs?" I asked, gazing dubiously at the task before us.

"Better down than up," he grunted.

I snorted as I led him to the left so that he was sandwiched between me and the scrollwork banister. "Always look on the bright side of life," I sang, in what I thought was a passable English accent.

Sparrow groaned. I wasn't sure whether it was from the effort of descending the stairs, or if it was my paltry Monty Python reference. I chose not to ask, as I was feeling a bit strained myself.

It was dicey, but somehow we made it down without falling and breaking our necks.

We were inside the tunnel to the outer gate before Sparrow spoke again, his voice a thready, uncertain reverberation of sound in the enclosed space. "Sydney, I don't know if I can ever repay you for what you did in there. After everything you went through to get your contract cancelled—you know I never would have expected you to indebt yourself again in that way."

My throat tightened with emotion and made my response a husky rasp. "Sparrow, you put yourself on the line for me so many times—that first night with Balthus, letting me interfere repeatedly with your investigation... downstairs in the dungeon." I closed my eyes against the memory of feeling my soul being forcibly ripped from my body.

"You wouldn't have killed that guard if you hadn't been protecting me. And I'm ashamed that I almost allowed you to die for it by not taking Moab's offer," I admitted quietly.

Sparrow pulled me to a halt and leaned against the tunnel wall so he could face me. "I would *never* want you to do that, for any reason," he said fiercely. "It's bad enough that you did what you did. Promise me you won't give up your soul, no matter what happens. I would rather die."

"So would I," I whispered. "Ophelia, Lauringer, those women in Moab's hall—you didn't see what he made that one woman in the white robe do in front of everyone." I shuddered.

"I couldn't bring myself to become like that, even for you. And you saved me, Sparrow. Not just with Balthus and with that guard tonight—but last night too. I know you had to join your soul with mine to pull me from the Sea of Souls. And I know it created some sort of weird, unnatural connection between us."

"Sydney," Sparrow interrupted me with a pained look.

"No—let me finish," I insisted, the words beginning to pour out in a flood. "You called me your soul mate. It's a beautiful idea, Sparrow, but how can either of us know if it's true? There's been so much confusion, so much to cloud both our judgment.

"This whole mess started because my husband cheated on me. Do you know what my first wish was, after it happened? I wanted to be able to distract myself and forget about all my problems. It sounded good at the time, but it makes it kind of difficult to resolve things and move on when you keep pushing aside the stuff you're supposed to be dealing with.

"Then Angelica tells me that he was magically seduced by a succubus, and that it would have been damned near impossible for him to resist. So I can't really keep blaming him, can I? We're still married, and I have to stop ignoring him and deal with it.

"And you, Sparrow," I said, my gaze softening as I reached up to brush my fingers through the damp hair by his temple. "I think I may have fallen in love with you through all of this. But Lorien says we might need some time apart for the effects of the soul combining thing to wear off. And if that's what needs to happen, so that we can both be sure about what we want going forward, I'm okay with it.

"But also know that I will *never* regret what I did up there, because everything else aside, I would do just about anything, short of giving up my soul, for you." I faltered into spent silence.

Sparrow stared down at me, lamplight flickering in his inscrutable blue eyes.

"You shouldn't doubt yourself, Sydney," he said finally, his voice gruff and thick beneath his brogue. "You're one of the strongest people I know. And I promise you we'll find a way out of this again. You take care of what you need to take care of. I'll be waiting."

I nodded, my heart leaping at his words. I might have said more, but just then Lorien popped back into the air between us, hands resting on her hips and her expression tinged with exasperation.

"What is taking you two so long? Don't stop now—you're almost to the gate!"

I dragged my eyes from Sparrow's with a sigh of regret. "Just hold your horses," I grumbled, offering Sparrow my arm and tensing beneath his weight as we stumbled forward once more. "Sparrow and I didn't get to take the shortcut. You should be glad that we made it this far without falling and killing ourselves. I think a little rest stop was in order. And besides, where have *you* been?"

"You'll see." Lorien grinned as she flitted impatiently back and forth in front of us. *"Hold my horses, indeed,"* she repeated with a soft snort of laughter.

The tunnel grew gradually lighter, and as we crested a gentle slope and the spiked iron gate came into view ahead, I saw that a hazy dawn was brightening the sky outside. *Crap.* We'd spent the entire night inside the death djinn palace. And Cindy was sure to start calling the penthouse soon. I'd forgotten to tell her I needed another day off.

It seemed patently unfair that I still had to worry about such mundane nonsense after the night I'd just had.

A whickering sound caught my ears as Sparrow and I staggered through the gate, Lorien darting out ahead of us. I eyed the two new guards standing sentinel on either side, but to my relief, they made no move to hinder us. Balthus must have called ahead.

The air outside was dry and acrid, smoggy layers of clouds filtering the sun's light into a dull burning glow, while allowing its heat to gather into a smothering cauldron beneath. The first undiluted breath of it hit my lungs like a furnace blast and I gasped, wondering how much further I would be able to make it with Sparrow's increasingly heavy weight.

"Good morning, Miss Sydney," bellowed a welcome voice.

The tears in my stinging eyes were at least partially from gratitude as I turned toward the sound.

There stood Titus, a mass of powerful muscle beneath his glossy golden coat. His large, dark eyes assessed Sparrow as he trotted our way, his white tail swishing behind him as he ruffled the feathered tips of his immense wings.

"It looks like you could use some assistance there, Detective Sparrow," he rumbled.

Sparrow let out a pained chuckle. "Your assistance would be much appreciated, Master Titus. I'm sure Sydney is becoming rather tired of carrying me around."

"You know each other?" I asked.

"For many years. Detective Sparrow here is a good man to have on your side," Titus boomed with a horsey grin. "We met a while back when my brother, Argyle, was having a spot of trouble with some vandals getting into his fields."

Sparrow perked up at the memory. "We had some fun with that one, didn't we?" he laughed.

Titus tossed his head and snorted. "It was the darndest thing—we couldn't figure out how they were getting in without being seen. Argyle's fields are well-hidden within high mountains, protected by jagged cliffs and binding spells to keep anyone from blinking in. The only access is by air, hence his brew's name—Argyle's Aerie Ale."

My eyes lit in recognition. "I tried it—it's good stuff."

"Apparently a rival brewer had hired some imps to sabotage Argyle's crops," Sparrow explained with a smirk. "And I was more than happy to help. After all, I couldn't let anything happen to my favorite beer."

Titus shook his coarse white mane and whinnied in disgust. "Nasty little buggers, imps. Small enough to hide in plain sight and able to camouflage themselves into almost any surface—quite the climbers too, as it turns out. Wreaked a good bit of havoc before we caught on."

I grimaced in commiseration, recalling my own unpleasant experience with the Hell Barge's imps.

"Speaking of which, I could use an ice-cold Triple A or three right about now," Sparrow sighed wearily.

Titus whickered in consternation. "Forgive me for prattling on with you in such a state. I'd be more than happy to drop you somewhere. I'm sure Argyle would be pleased to see you, if you have a hankering to visit the brewery."

"As much as I'd love to take you up on that, I'm afraid I'll have to take a rain check. I need to get back to the office," Sparrow declined.

"You can barely stand!" I exclaimed. "Shouldn't you be going to a hospital, or at least home to rest?"

"Although I appreciate your concern, Sydney, a major case—which I was supposed to be heading up—just cracked without me. I'm going to have enough explaining to do as it is." When I started to argue, he added gently, "And there are healers on staff at Seelie headquarters. I couldn't get any better care if I did go to a hospital."

I made a noise of reluctant acceptance.

"Lorien will blink you home." Sparrow's eyes moved to encompass her and she nodded. "I'll check in on you later."

He tilted my face up to his with his free hand and smiled into my eyes. Then he leaned down and proceeded to kiss me with slow and thorough precision. Somehow I ended up resting against him, despite his weakened condition. I couldn't think beyond the sensation of his mouth on mine and the teasing temptation of his fingers grazing the sides of my breasts through my shirt.

When our lips finally parted, Lorien and Titus had both turned their backs. But a glance at the two guards found them staring at us with avid interest.

A blush rose into my cheeks.

"We're ready now," Sparrow called, his face stretched in an unrepentant grin. At least he seemed to be regaining some of his strength.

Lorien turned and rolled her eyes at me. Titus closed the distance between us and lowered himself to the ground so I could help Sparrow climb onto his back, politely ignoring the fact that we had just made out like teenagers in front of everyone present.

"Hold on tight, Detective," he rumbled as he rose to his feet. "We'll be traveling the skies—it's too far to run and the ride will be smoother for you this way."

"I thought you didn't do that," I stammered, afraid that with his injuries Sparrow would be more likely to fall.

"You've seen me break that rule when the situation calls for it, Miss Sydney, and I never hesitate to help a friend." He fixed me with a steady gaze of reassurance. "Not to worry—I'll get him there safe and sound."

I nodded slowly, somehow believing he would.

"Thank you so much for coming, Master Titus," Lorien piped up.

"Pleasure to serve, Mistress Lorien." He tipped his head and stamped his rear left foot. "That hoof's still right as rain, thanks to you. You ladies feel free to call on me anytime."

He took a few steps forward and was off the ground with a single swoop of his massive wings. Lorien and I watched for long silent moments, until he and Sparrow became a pale speck against the angrily blistered sky.

When they had disappeared completely from sight, she blinked us home.

<u>Chapter 9—Twisting Fate</u>

Lorien dropped me off, with impressive precision, smack dab in the middle of my living room. Sunny practically knocked me over as I was trying to find my feet. Apparently she'd been wearing a hole pacing the carpet in front of the coffee table for quite a while. An empty pot of said beverage rested next to her favorite oversized ceramic latte mug.

"Where have you been?" she exhaled, while at the same time squeezing all the breath out of me. "I've been worried sick! Last time Lorien blinked in, she was picking up Lauringer's journal for you to trade with Old Moby—but that was *hours* ago!"

She pushed me away so she could search my face, her hands tightening on my shoulders. "He did trade with you, right?" she asked worriedly. Her green eyes widened into glimmering pools. "You've still got your soul?" she whispered.

My laughter was tinged with hysteria. "Yeah—I've still got it. And yeah, we made the trade and he cancelled my contract."

"Oh, Syd!" she wailed, crushing my ribs again, "I'm so happy for you!"

"Thanks," I said, hugging her back. "But that was before they caught Sparrow and sentenced him to death for killing that guard down in the dungeons."

Sunny froze and drew back to stare at me with an expression of horror.

"It all turned out okay in the end," I assured her quickly. *"For the most part, anyway,"* I added on a mumble. "But can we sit down while I tell you about it?"

She ushered me over to the leather loveseat and I collapsed next to her with a grateful sigh as Lorien and I began recounting the night's events.

∞∞∞∞∞∞∞∞∞∞∞

"So Lauringer just disappeared?" Sunny echoed with disbelief.

I shrugged and glanced at Lorien, who sat with her feet dangling over the edge of the glass coffee table, lost in thought.

"She said she'd 'planned for that eventuality as well'—whatever that means," I answered.

"Huh," Sunny mused. "And she used unborn souls to frame the death djinns. So that's good, right? I mean—she didn't have to hurt anyone to get them, and the Seelie police will just release them back into the Sea of Souls now that they're no longer needed for evidence."

I nibbled the corner of my lip and snuck another peek at Lorien, remembering how appalled she'd been to learn what Lauringer had done. Her expression was solemn as she looked back at us, shaking her head in denial at Sunny's words.

"Her actions will have great repercussions for many years to come," she said sadly. "She's interrupted the destined timelines of countless souls—not only the ones she took, but possibly those who came forward to be born in their stead, as well as all of their counterpart souls with whom they may have played out karmic lessons during this lifetime."

Sunny and I stared at her blankly and she sighed.

"We touched on all this with Angelica, remember? Certain souls are fated to be together in specific relationships throughout their mortal lifetimes. The souls Lauringer meddled with will end up in those relationships eventually simply because it's meant to be—and some may still be born and meet in the current lifetime despite the disruption.

"But for others," Lorien winced, "the delays could take lifetimes to correct."

"Will there be any permanent damage?" Sunny questioned with a frown.

Lorien gave a resigned shrug. "The fabric of time won't be damaged, if that's what you mean—it just weaves the souls into their lifetimes as they come. But Lauringer altered the growth timelines of the souls she took, which in turn affects the growth timeline for every soul they would have come into contact with this lifetime. Take for example the souls of the parents they would have been born to. She said they were already in the process of being born when she took them—that means both parties had chosen to be in that relationship together this lifetime. It wasn't up to Lauringer to change it. And that's only one piece of the puzzle to consider."

"It really is like a giant tapestry on a loom," I murmured dazedly. "Thread one string into the wrong place, and the whole design can change."

Lorien dipped her head in a tired nod.

"I still can't believe you got your soul contract with Balthus cancelled, only to end up having to re-contract it to that arrogant bastard all over again," Sunny commented darkly. "That's one string I would happily snip myself. As a matter of fact, I wouldn't mind getting a little snip-happy with Balthus in general—starting with the source of all that over-inflated male libido."

I smiled at that. "On the other hand though, and in light of all this talk of destiny, maybe I've been looking at things all wrong. Maybe I'm *supposed* to have this connection with Balthus."

Sunny raised a disbelieving brow and Lorien sputtered, "When a death djinn takes a mortal soul as a slave, it unnaturally prolongs mortal life and interrupts the flow of karmic relationships. We've been over this—you've seen what a terrible thing it is!"

"I know, I know—take it easy." I chuckled and raised my hands in surrender. "I'm not saying I intend to hand over my soul. Believe me—I'll take the first opportunity I can find to get out of this new contract."

"Well I'm glad to hear that you haven't lost your mind completely," Lorien grumbled.

"*All I'm saying,*" I continued, "is that maybe everything does happen for a reason—even when it sucks as badly as getting yourself involved with a death djinn."

Lorien huffed and rolled her eyes.

Sunny grinned at me and shook her head. "I'm not sure whether you're incredibly enlightened, or tragically deluded."

I smirked. "Yeah—most days I wonder that myself."

The strident peal of the phone interrupted our shared humor. I glanced at the digital clock on the cable box and groaned. "Speaking of tragically deluded," I muttered as I got up to intercept Cindy's call.

"Salsa time!" Sunny announced cheerfully as she reached for the remote. She'd definitely had too much coffee.

The driving beat began to pound through the speakers just as I picked up with a tired, "Hello?"

"Oh—thank God you're there! I left you about fourteen messages on your cell phone. Why didn't you call me back? Things were crazy here yesterday and I really needed to talk to you. By the end of the day I *finally* ended up finding what I needed, but for a while there everything was falling apart."

Tell me about it, I thought dryly.

"So, what's cookin' this morning?" she asked.

The brightness of her voice made me wince. "My internet connection is down," I lied, "I'll have to call the bank to get the balances."

"Oh. Well call me back. Is, uh, your family emergency okay?"

"For the most part. I..."

"Good," she interrupted. "Gotta go—call me back as soon as you talk to the bank!"

I stared at the phone as the line went dead, my lips curving in a weary smile. At least some things never changed. I opened my laptop and pressed the start button, then headed to the kitchen to make myself a mega-cup of tea. That should get me through another conversation with Cindy and the shower I so desperately needed.

Then, hopefully, it would be one of those days when she left me alone. I needed sleep—a couple days' worth at least. *TGIF* was all I had to say.

Lorien followed me into the kitchen. "Listen, Sydney, if you're okay I should really be going. I think the Faerie Council is going to be interested in having a first-hand account of last night's events. And I need to track down Emily and have a talk with her first."

I blinked at her. "Faerie Council? And what's up with Emily?"

"The Faerie Council is the governing body of my people," she answered with only the faintest hint of irritation. "And I need to talk to Emily because I suspect she had a closer connection to Lauringer than she admitted. Considering how secretive Lauringer was, and how much she had to lose, I don't think she would have chanced supplying Emily with the memory spell she used unless she knew she could trust her."

"Oh." I frowned as I absorbed that logic. "Do you think Emily might know what happened to Lauringer?"

Lorien lifted her small hands and smirked. "That would be one of the reasons why I want to talk to her."

"Right," I replied in a distracted voice as I blinked at a funny noise my laptop was making. "Well, if you see her, would you ask her to pay me a visit? I need to talk to her too—about Ophelia."

Lorien gave me a crooked smile. "Sure thing."

"Thanks. I guess I'll see you later then?"

She nodded.

The disconcerting noise stopped and the normal screen popped up on my computer. I sighed with relief. I was too tired to deal with a broken laptop today.

"Lorien?" I looked up suddenly, pinning her with my gaze.

"Yeah?" she breathed on a small huff.

"I'm really glad you're my faerie guardian."

She beamed at me as she blinked out.

I stood there for a minute, staring into space with a small grin, before I shook myself back into action. Tea. Banking info. Call Cindy back. Shower...and call Jeremy.

I'd put it off for long enough.

<u>Chapter 10—Loose Ends</u>

"So how'd it go?" Sunny asked with a sympathetic wince.

I sighed and dropped my purse on the coffee table before slumping into the plush leather of the loveseat. It was Sunday, and I'd just returned from meeting with Jeremy. Sunny was stretched out on the couch with her laptop, which she closed in order to give me her full attention.

I dropped my head back onto the cushions and focused on a random speck dotting the ceiling. "I guess it wasn't as bad as I thought it would be."

"That's good," she prodded encouragingly.

"Yeah," I hedged with an uncertain breath. "And him dreaming about Angelica and then meeting her in person was probably actually a good thing. I don't think I would have been able to tell him the truth about everything that's happened otherwise."

She nodded and gave me the silence I needed to collect my thoughts.

"I told him the woman Edie, from his office, is really a succubus. And that he shouldn't feel too guilty for having an affair with her because she used her magic to seduce him."

"How'd he take that?" Sunny questioned, her eyes livid with curiosity.

"He was shocked, to say the least, but he took it pretty well. I mean, he still kept apologizing, but I think it was a big load off his mind that he wasn't entirely at fault. And he told me she quit."

"*Really?*"

"Mmhm. He said she came in late one morning with her hair messed up, no makeup on, and her clothes ripped. She said her house had been broken into." I smirked. "Then she got some phone call that scared the crap out of her, and after that, she just up and left. No one's seen her since."

Sunny chuckled. "What do you wanna bet our friend Angelica had something to do with her hasty departure?"

"I'm thinking imps," I replied with a mirthful snort.

We giggled over that for a moment before Sunny's face sobered and she asked, "So did he want to get back together?"

My smile turned bittersweet. "Well, I gave him the abbreviated version of the whole death djinn thing. I told him about Sparrow. And I said I didn't blame him for what happened anymore, and that a part of me would always love him—but that I couldn't go back to the way it was, and I wanted a divorce."

Sunny sucked in a breath of commiseration.

"Yeah," I said quietly. "We both cried a little, and he tried to talk me out of it, but I don't think he really meant it."

"Aw, Syd," Sunny consoled, her heart in her voice.

"Yeah." I sniffed, and she tossed me the box of tissues that rested on the end table nearby. Jasper wandered over and jumped into my lap, adding his furry support.

I dabbed at my eyes. "I told him that he shouldn't be afraid of Angelica—that she wasn't anything like Edie, and that I thought she really cared for him."

"That was good of you," Sunny commended.

"To be honest, I don't think either of us was truly happy before all this happened. I mean, we loved each other, but I'm not sure we were really *meant* for each other. You know?" I nibbled my lip and lifted my eyes to hers.

"I'm in love with Sparrow," I admitted. "I knew I was in love with him before the whole soul combining thing. And the sex, Sunny," I drew a shaky breath. "I know there's more to a good relationship than the physical part, but I never knew how unfulfilled I was in that department until I met Sparrow. And if I felt that way, I'm betting Jeremy felt it too. I think we're both going to be happier apart."

Sunny sighed. "So what are you going to do about this thing with Sparrow?"

I gave a teary laugh. "I honestly don't know. I'd love to dismiss the whole soul combining issue and just enjoy our connection for however long it lasts. But I'm done ignoring my problems. And I love him too much to take a chance that his feelings for me will eventually wear off with the effects of the soul combining. If we were together, and then he realized he'd never really loved me, I think it would kill me."

I tapered into silence as I stroked Jasper's silky back.

"Uh, excuse me." A small voice cleared its throat behind me.

I peered around to find Emily hovering uncertainly nearby. She was almost unrecognizable—her violet eyes were bright and her skin glowed with a silvery flush of health. Her wings were no longer tattered and her color-shifting dress was a study of rich earth-tones, as opposed to the dull, lifeless smear of brown and gray it had been the last time we'd met.

"Emily!" Sunny exclaimed with surprise. "You look great!"

She glanced down self-consciously. "Thanks, honey. Balthus is back—mostly thanks to Sydney, I hear—so Ophelia and I have been doing much better." She gave me a tentative smile. "Anyway, I hope I didn't interrupt anything, but I heard you wanted to talk to me."

"Right," I agreed, sitting up straighter. "So you spoke to Lorien, then?"

Emily colored. "Yes. She and I had a long talk."

"And was she right? Do you know what happened to Lauringer?" I probed with unconcealed curiosity.

"Oh, honey." Emily sagged. "What happened to Lauringer is a long and terrible story. You already know some of it from that journal you found. And maybe I should have come forward with what I knew before now, but

I didn't see what good it would have done anyone. I had no idea what she was planning."

"Why don't you sit down," Sunny offered, gesturing to the edge of the coffee table where Lorien always sat.

I made a hurried noise of agreement, appalled at my lack of manners.

Emily sighed and settled onto the glass. "I thought I was protecting her by not saying anything. I didn't want to see her soul passed off to another death djinn. That Devlin was a right bastard; he deserved exactly what he got," she said angrily.

"And she knew she'd end up claimed by King Moab if he ever found out—he would have stopped at nothing to claim her power for himself. We discussed her pleading her case to Balthus. He's nowhere near as horrible as his father, you know. But she was adamant about never belonging to one of them again."

Sunny and I nodded sympathetically.

"So she went into hiding, and became more and more isolated as the years went on." Emily gave us a guilty wince. "I knew she had to be suffering after being without her soul for so long, just as Ophelia was, but she had her memory spell. And she still answered my messages, although she became paranoid about meeting in person."

"Couldn't she reclaim her soul for herself using the infinity magi symbol?" I asked.

Emily's face hardened. "Honey, knowing her, she probably could have. But Devlin's last act before she killed him was to send it to the Sea of Souls. Most mortals would have passed on instantly, but not Lauringer. She had too much magic and too much will to live. I only wish it hadn't all been fueled by hatred and the need for revenge."

She sighed again. "She refused to join the Sea, instead choosing to remain in limbo, with the false immortality granted by her soul contract keeping her body alive. Maybe she hoped to reclaim her own soul somehow, when she hatched that plan to steal the unaligned souls as they were released to be born." Emily shook her head. "She must have been consumed by madness at that point. The Lauringer I knew would never have done such a thing."

I had a dream-like recollection of The Shepherd saying that only *one* other soul had ever refused to join the Sea as I had. And then a vague memory floated through my mind, of a dim, sad woman, with long blonde hair and an aura of gold, looking out at me from the shadows.

"She's finally at peace now," Emily said in a solemn tone.

"You mean she's dead?" Sunny whispered.

"She finally joined the Sea," I murmured, the revelation both wondrous and sad.

Emily gave a slow nod. "Her passing will be a great loss to the magical community. And to those who once counted her a friend. But I'm afraid she was lost long ago—starting when she gave up her soul, and ending when she lost M.J. Their bond was probably the only thing that could have saved Lauringer from the hatred that consumed her."

"Who *was* M.J.?" I asked.

Emily gave me a wobbly smile and a single crystalline tear made its way down her silvery cheek. "I once told you that I only knew of one faerie guardian who had passed on before her human charge. M.J. was Lauringer's faerie guardian...and my sister. I think that's another reason why Lauringer stopped meeting with me in person—I reminded her too much of my sister."

"I'm so sorry, Emily," I offered quietly.

Sunny reached over for the dwindling box of tissues and tore off a corner. She offered it to Emily on the tip of her forefinger.

"Thank you, honey," Emily sniffed, taking the wispy fragment.

"So, Ophelia's doing better now?" I asked after a moment.

"Back to her old self," she answered with a crooked grin. Her expression clouded as she added, "Balthus apologized to both of us. He swears he'd never have allowed us to get into such a state if he'd been able to help it."

"About that—I have something for you, hang on a sec..."

I jumped up, earning a peevish look from my lap-bound cat, and ran to my bedroom. I returned to set the small, green crystal vial next to Emily on the coffee table. Its gold stopper came even with the top of her head as she sat, the light inside still glowing like a faint star when I caught it with the corner of my eye. Emily's tiny jaw went slack as she stared at it.

"Do you know what this is, Sydney?" she breathed in awe.

I grinned. "It's a vial of immortality. I know she'll still be physically tied to Balthus, but didn't you say that if you give this to Ophelia, you'll never have to worry about her going mad from the loss of her soul again?"

Emily gaped at me. "Do you know how much this is worth, and how difficult it is to come by?" She looked as if she was afraid to believe I was really offering her such a thing.

I nodded. Both Lauringer and Sparrow had told me how valuable it was. I almost wondered why Lauringer hadn't taken it for herself. But maybe she really had been ready to let go and join the Sea of Souls.

"Please take it Emily. It's my way of repaying you for all the help you've given me."

She put her hand to her mouth and gave me a conflicted look. Then her eyes hardened with pained resolve as she spoke. "Sydney, Lorien told me what happened at the death djinn palace. I know you re-contracted your soul to Balthus to save Agent Sparrow. Maybe you should hold onto this for yourself. You may find you need it some day."

I swallowed and gave her a small smile. "I'm afraid I've come to the same conclusion that Lauringer did in the end. I won't be completing my contract, if it comes to that. Besides," I added with forced levity, "I know who this came from, and I'd rather not feel connected to him for eternity."

Emily searched my face. "You're sure?" she asked in a tight voice.

"It's yours," I said firmly. "Go ahead and take it to Ophelia."

She exhaled in a whoosh. "Thank you so much, honey. You have no idea what this means to us."

I nodded, and she smiled hugely at both me and Sunny before wrapping her arms around the vial and blinking out.

"Nice!" Sunny exclaimed. "Now maybe the next time we pay Ophelia a visit, I won't have to pretend to drink that tepid dishwater you guys insist on substituting for coffee. Girlfriend was a little scary with the whole mad tea party thing."

I sputtered in laughter.

"Well done, Syd," she said with a soft grin.

∞ ∞ ∞ ∞ ∞ ∞ ∞ ∞ ∞

"Have you seen my green flip-flops?" Sunny's muffled voice called from her bedroom.

I made a final keystroke and flipped shut the folder with the meager sales figures Hannah had given me. "I've hidden them. It's all part of my diabolical plan to keep you here," I retorted.

Sunny tromped out into the hallway with a baleful glare, her black bikini top in one hand and a single strappy black sandal in the other. "Is that why I can only find half my clothes? I only brought two pieces of luggage. And I've spent the entire time in one room. How could I have possibly lost so much stuff? Ugh. You know I hate packing. What time is it anyway?"

I chuckled. "It's almost three. We don't have to leave for another couple of hours. Check the laundry room. I dumped some of your stuff into the blue basket last time I used the dryer. And I thought I saw Jasper batting at something green beneath the couch. Maybe your flip-flops and your other black sandal are taking a page out of your book and having a ménage a trois under there."

Sunny sucked at her bottom lip and her eyes took on a mischievous twinkle. "The twins *have* promised to keep visiting me in Boston. Apparently when incubi track someone through their dreams, physical distance has no bearing on finding them."

"Damn, I was planning on using them for leverage to get you back."

"You *are* diabolical," Sunny gasped in horror. "Seriously though, I'll look into whether any positions in my field are opening up at the local colleges—before you retaliate with something even worse than trying to rob me of my nightly pleasures."

"*Nightly* now, is it?" I asked in a scandalized tone.

"Pretty much," she sighed in contentment. "Still want me to move in? Are you sure you want such disgraceful behavior going on beneath your roof on a permanent basis?"

"Are you kidding me?" I muttered. "Somebody's gotta do it. Otherwise, it might get downright boring around here."

"Somehow I doubt that." Sunny laughed.

"Besides, think of all the money you'll be able to save with no rent," I dangled enticingly.

"Alright—I'll check into it! But right now I'd better finish packing, or I'll miss my flight."

"Foiled again," I sniggered as she passed me on her way to the laundry room.

There was a knock at the door and I got up to let Angelica in for her Monday afternoon cleaning.

"Hey, Angelica. How are you?" I kept my voice light and friendly, hoping there'd be no lingering discomfort between us over the Jeremy thing.

"I am fine, and you Sydney?" she replied with an uncertain smile.

"Good, good. You probably won't have much to worry about today. I have to take Sunny to the airport in a little while and she's still packing up her room and bathroom."

Her face fell. "Sunny is leaving?"

"Yeah," I sighed. "I feel the same way. I've been trying to talk her into moving here, but she keeps going on about her apartment and her job. Personally, I think she's just sick of me," I whispered loudly.

Sunny shot me a dirty look on her way to the couch to look for her shoes. "Hi Angelica!" she called brightly.

"Hello, Sunny. I will be sorry to see you go," Angelica replied sincerely, her gaze uncomfortable as it took in our glowers at each other.

"Don't worry," I assured, "I'm just teasing her."

"Oh," she said, her eyes rounding in relief. "I am glad. And I will be quick, then." She backtracked out the door to grab some supplies from her cart.

"You're always quick," I called, returning to my office at the dining room table. "We're convinced you use your magic to help you along when no one's looking."

Angelica grinned at me as she set about dusting the living room. "I'll never tell."

We worked in companionable silence as Sunny rustled around finishing up her packing. More than once, I almost opened my mouth to bring up the subject of Jeremy, but I kept stalling.

Finally I decided I was being ridiculous and mustered up my courage. "I spoke with Jeremy yesterday," I told her in a casual tone.

She paused in swiping some glass cleaner from the sliding glass door, and then continued without looking around. "That is good, Sydney. I am glad to hear it—for both of you."

"I told him about Edie. I think it set his mind at ease to know that what happened wasn't all his fault."

"Good," she said again softly, her back still toward me.

"I also told him we couldn't be together anymore. And we agreed we'd look into getting a divorce."

"I'm sorry, Sydney." She stopped swiping at the door and her head drooped a little.

"And I told him that you were nothing like Edie, and that I thought it would be a mistake for him to shut you out of his life because of what happened with her."

She turned to face me, her blue eyes liquid and tremulous. "Thank you," she whispered.

"You're welcome," I replied, my mouth quirked in a gentle smile.

She took a breath and nodded at me. We locked gazes in silent understanding, and then resumed our work.

As she passed me on her way to my bedroom I looked up thoughtfully. "Just one more thing."

She sent me a questioning gaze.

"Edie quit her job at Jeremy's office."

"Oh?" she inquired.

I bit back a helpless smirk. "Mmhm. Apparently there was some sort of trouble at her house—a break-in or something. Jeremy said it shook her up pretty badly. The final straw must have been some nasty phone call she got, because he said after that, she just picked up and left without another word."

Angelica blinked at me, telltale points of pink flushing her cheeks.

"From the way he described it, it sounds to me like it could have been an imp infestation." I chewed my lip with the effort of hiding my smile.

"They are vile little creatures," she murmured in a choked voice.

"Oh well. Just wanted to let you know that's probably the last we'll be seeing of her. Karma can be a bitch—or so I hear."

Angelica nodded and turned away, her prim tone drifting back to me through the kitchen, "So can I."

A sharp bark of laughter escaped my throat.

∞∞∞∞∞∞∞∞∞∞

Sunny managed to find all of her belongings and we left in time to stop by D.J.D. and Haute Hannah's on the way to the airport. Cindy fluttered out the door to hand me a bag of bills and invoices, and I made it back into the car with no sign of Mr. H.

I wondered if an occasion would ever present itself for me to tell the miserable jerk I knew he was really a goblin, and that I'd held his lost immortality in my hands. I decided, for now, I was just happy not to have to see him.

Luck was still with me as I found a parking space close to Hannah's shop.

"Tell Hannah 'Au Revoir'!" Sunny called out the window as I left her in the car to go grab my paperwork for the week.

My pace was brisk as I walked up the sun-baked sidewalk toward Hannah's storefront. We still had plenty of time to get to the airport, but you never knew what kind of traffic you'd run into around 5:00 in South Florida.

The glass door was pristine as always. I pushed it open and was greeted by the shimmering tinkle of the bell, the sultry tones of French jazz...and a chorus of deep feminine laughter.

I paused as the cool air conditioning swept over me, staring around the myriad sparkling displays in confusion. Hannah's voice rose above the laughter and I moved toward it, although I couldn't see where it was coming from.

"*Merci beaucoup*, ladies! You are more than welcome any time. I will be making a buying trip to Paris very soon, and I promise that the next time you come, I shall have many more exquisite, hand-crafted pieces you will love! *Oui?*"

"Thank *you*, Hannah. We'll certainly be back," assured a warm, whiskey-dark voice.

I rounded one of the display cases just as Hannah straightened from crouching beside five exceedingly short women—one of whom was Galena, sans her high-heeled shoes. Each woman carried a sky-blue Haute Hannah's bag decorated with stylized puffs of white clouds to match the walls of her shop. Hannah held an impressive stack of cash, and from where I was standing, it looked like all large bills.

"Sydney!" Hannah exclaimed, her face going from ecstatic to flustered in a heartbeat.

"Hi Hannah!" I greeted with a cheery smile. "Hey, Galena—I knew you'd love Hannah's shop!"

"Sydney—good to see you," Galena boomed. "These are my friends, Thora, Salena, Dora and Nora."

She indicated the four female dwarves who accompanied her, all of whom appeared to favor glittery, ostentatious jewelry as much as she did. We nodded at each other as Galena added, "This is Sydney, that friend of Patrick Sparrow's I was telling you about."

Four sets of dark brown eyes widened, and then the women dipped their heads at me again, deeper this time.

"You did a noble thing for our Detective Sparrow," Thora commented in a gravelly tone.

"Uh, thank you." I flushed with discomfort, hoping Hannah wouldn't ask what we were talking about.

"Well, we should be going," Galena interjected, nudging Thora's arm and shooting a meaningful glance up at my boss. "Perhaps we'll get the chance to chat another time."

"Yeah, another time," I agreed. "I'm actually in a hurry now because I'm on my way to drop a friend off at the airport."

Galena winked at me.

"Thanks again, Hannah. Your store is magnificent!" she rumbled as she ushered her friends to the door.

"*Merci beaucoup!* I hope to see you again soon!" Hannah called, a nervous quiver marring the confidence of her voice.

As the door drifted shut behind them, I turned to her and smiled. "Looks like you've found some good customers there."

"*Oui*, Sydney…about that."

Hannah clutched the money tighter in her hand and I gave her a quizzical look.

"I would have preferred for you not to see…*Zut!*…This is difficult."

I blinked at her in confusion. "What do you mean?"

"Well, you must understand, Sydney—I have certain customers, like those women, who will pay me all in cash," she stammered, growing visibly more uncomfortable by the second. "And because I make so little during the summer, sometimes they will not appear on your reports that go to the government…" she faltered into awkward silence.

"Ohhhh," I breathed in comprehension. "Like that tall woman I thought I recognized in here last week?" I asked, suddenly giddy with relief.

She gave an abashed tip of her head. "That one is quite fond of my crystal perfume bottles."

I was betting Calypso didn't use them for perfume, but I still couldn't help my grin. Hannah hadn't betrayed me to the death djinns—Balthus' mom had been doing nothing more sinister than shopping! And of course people from the faerie realm would pay in cash.

"Hannah, please—don't worry about it for another minute. How you report your sales is your business." I reached out to pat her shoulder. "Do you think D.J.D. doesn't do the same thing? Along with probably every other store around here, for that matter?"

She gave me a tentative smile. "Really, Sydney? And you are not disappointed by this?"

"I honestly couldn't care less." Considering what I'd been afraid she was keeping from me, the thought was laughable.

"Are you sure? Because I could not bear for you to think of me as some kind of criminal!"

She fanned her face dramatically with the cash. When she realized what she was doing, a blush stained her pale cheeks and she quickly tucked the money away behind the counter.

"I could never have such a low opinion of you, Hannah. After all—you are my favorite employer," I teased warmly.

"To hear you say so is a great weight from my shoulders, Sydney," Hannah gushed as she handed me my stack of paperwork.

"Glad to hear it. Uh, I really do have to get my friend Sunny to the airport, though. See you next Monday?"

"I will look forward to it, *Cherie*!"

She was all smiles once more as she sashayed me to the door, bright gold and glittering gems winking at her wrists and throat, her perfume a persistent tickle against my plugged nose.

I said goodbye, grateful to have that mystery solved.

∞∞∞∞∞∞∞∞∞

Feeling a little melancholy as I unlocked the door to my empty penthouse, I trudged forward to collapse alone on my couch. I sat in silence and stared out the sliding glass door. The sun was down and the lights of early evening spilled out over the buff-colored sand of the hotel's private beach, reaching just far enough to illuminate the softly foaming waves as they rolled in to meet the shore.

I thought about calling Lorien, but it wasn't an emergency. And I couldn't think of anyone else I wanted to be with right now. Except Sparrow. But I had resolved to allow us some time apart to let the effects of the soul combining thing wear off.

At least I still had Jasper to curl up with, although he was currently nowhere in sight.

I decided a little champagne would lift my spirits and pulled myself back to my feet to plod over to the bar. When I checked the mini-fridge, I realized Sunny and I had polished off the last bottle from there. I grabbed a Waterford and headed into the kitchen for one of the backups.

A clattering sound from the direction of my bedroom nearly made me drop the bottle as I was about to pop the cork. I looked up, startled, to find Jasper tearing down the hallway toward me. He streaked past my jean-clad legs and disappeared into the living room.

I set the bottle safely back on the counter and frowned after him. "Great, Jasper, what have you been into now?" I muttered as I padded toward my bedroom.

I stopped dead in the doorway with a petrified hitch of breath. Balthus' tall frame lay stretched atop the thick cream comforter on my freshly made bed. He looked devilishly handsome with his long-sleeved silk shirt pulling across his chest, lending definition to his lean muscular form.

Crisp black slacks draped the lengths of his legs above expensive Italian loafers.

He was propped on one elbow, smiling up at me from beneath smoldering green eyes, fingertips gently mussing his chestnut hair where his head rested against them.

I blinked at him, my heart racing. "What are you doing here?" I blurted, wishing my voice had come out more indignant and less squeaky. Whoops. Better not even *think* that word around him.

"Sydney," he drawled in a throaty tone, "I thought I'd pay you a visit to see how you're doing after your adventure at my father's palace. Not to mention that I never properly thanked you for discovering the evidence that resulted in my release."

"You can't just come here uninvited," I stammered, my annoyance overshadowing my fear. "Would you get off my bed?"

"Your pardon, love." He moved with the slow grace of a panther, swinging his long legs to floor and rising to stalk toward me, making me regret my request.

I put my palms out to keep some distance between us as he halted to tower above me. "That's far enough," I grumbled.

He grasped my hands in his, his warm palms engulfing mine as he took a step closer. "Do I make you nervous, Sydney?" His low voice vibrated through me, a hint of cinnamon and mint drifting across my senses as his breath caressed my face.

"Stop it, Balthus," I demanded, breaking away with difficulty to move across the plush expanse of carpet beside the bed. My choices of destination were limited, so I continued toward the balcony to open the door. I stood for a moment, breathing in the humid night air and hating the fact that I was fleeing from him on my own turf.

"Why are you really here?" I crossed my arms over my chest and turned to face him again, relieved to discover that he remained several feet away.

He tilted his head, his gaze intent as he studied me. "I won't harm you, Sydney," he said quietly.

I shook my head and gave a humorless little laugh. "Physical harm isn't the only kind you can inflict, Balthus. You want me to grant you absolute power over me. No matter how you intend to wield it, I would still be losing my free will, and in a lot of ways that's worse than anything else you could do to me."

"I want you for my mate," he countered. "I would treat you as my equal, make you immortal, you would stand beside me as my queen when the time comes for me to rule my people."

"No, Balthus. You would *own* me. There can be no equality there."

He glided into motion and was before me in three long, fluid strides. His hands were gentle as they cupped my shoulders, his eyes scorching my face with the heat of their persuasion. "You're wrong," he said with certainty. "Just because I *can* exercise my power over you, doesn't mean I will."

Raw hunger flared in his expression. "I want you, Sydney." His voice was like roughened silk, his words a delicate torment to my weakening will.

Goddess help me—I wanted him too.

"I can *feel* your desire for me," he groaned, his head descending toward mine.

My breathing turned shallow and my lips parted.

Then I ground my teeth together and turned my face away so that his mouth grazed my cheek. "Damn it, Balthus! You're doing it right now!" I choked out angrily.

"And you are denying your desire," he whispered by my ear, the soft puff of air making me shiver.

"As is my right," I grated, trying to extricate myself from his grasp. His hands tightened briefly on my arms, and then he released me.

I turned my back on him, but there was nowhere left to run. I wrapped my arms protectively around my midsection and stared blindly out toward the ocean, speaking into the growing darkness.

"You may be able to make me want you, but I will never trust you. You claim you want me for your mate, but you don't even care that I don't want the same thing. If you care about me at all, you should know that I will end my life before you force me to hand over my soul."

His hand skimmed my hair, a feather-light caress down the length of my back. "It pains me to hear you say that."

"Does it pain you enough to release me from my contract?" I asked bitterly, venturing a glance at his face.

His lips quirked in a regretful half smile. "No, Sydney. I'm afraid not."

I sighed. I hadn't really expected any other response.

Suddenly my lips stretched in an acid grin as a new thought occurred to me. "How about we make an exchange for Princess Amalia then?"

He stared at me, his expression as close to shock as I'd ever seen it. "What do you mean?"

My grin widened. "It seems your sister was trying to claim my contract for herself, and decided it would be a good idea to possess my boss' son in order to get closer to me. I caught her at it and trapped her."

"Remarkable," Balthus breathed. "I wondered what she was up to. Father said he hadn't seen her skulking about lately. Oh, that's priceless." He threw his head back and laughed.

I lifted my eyebrows, nonplussed by his reaction. "Surely you want her released?"

His green eyes twinkled with amusement. "I regret to disappoint you again, love, but my sister and I are not on the best of terms. You may do with her what you wish. Truthfully, I shall rather enjoy having her out of my hair for a while."

I glared at him in disgust and turned away. That had been my last bargaining chip.

My gaze wandered to the ceiling and I frowned, noticing that the silver plate covering the air conditioning vent was askew. One of the screws hung loose from its mooring.

My eyes flicked to Balthus and I traced my teeth with my tongue, my mind racing with suspicion. "Why are you really here?" I crossed my arms. "I don't think you came to see me tonight at all."

He straightened. "No?" he queried, his expression carefully blank.

"No," I replied with a knowing smirk. "I think you were looking for something," I inclined my chin toward the vent, "something small and valuable, that you hid here."

He gave a slow, appreciative chuckle. "Apparently I didn't hide it well enough. That's a costly little token which I've held onto for some time, with a history that you may find interesting. Would you like to hear about it?"

"Mmm," I murmured derisively. "If it involves how it belonged to a certain goblin, who was cursed into an equally unpleasant human form, I'm afraid someone else has spoiled the surprise."

He arched one dark brow. "You never fail to amaze me, Sydney. I don't suppose you'd be inclined to return the object to me?"

I blew out my cheeks in feigned contrition. "Sorry, Balthus. I'm afraid it's already been put to a better use. My downstairs neighbor was having some problems recently, and I found myself quite sympathetic to her plight. I gave it to her."

He stared at me for a moment, and then his emerald eyes went wide with comprehension. "You didn't."

My expression turned smug.

"You realize I had intended that for you," he stated quietly.

A small jolt of surprise traveled across my nerve endings, rendering me speechless for a second. I took a deep breath and managed a rueful smile. "Although I sort of appreciate the thought—as I've already said, I won't be needing it."

Balthus shook his head in amusement. "You aren't at all what I thought you would be, Sydney."

"People seldom are. If you cared enough to try to get to know them before ripping out their souls, you'd realize that. And thanks for the visit," I added, "but I'd appreciate it if you called before you came over next time."

I hoped he'd take that the way it was meant and get out.

He took my hand in his and gently brushed his lips across the backs of my knuckles, his eyes drawing me into their fiery depths. "As you wish, Sydney," he whispered.

"Don't even try it," I said dryly.

He gave me an intimate grin as his voice sighed seductively through my head, S*ee you around, love.*

Then he took a step back and his form turned hazy and disappeared.

I stood unmoving for several minutes, collecting my frazzled nerves. Then I headed back to the kitchen for the bottle of champagne. I needed it after that little episode.

And I did have reason to celebrate, after all. I'd just had my first encounter with Balthus' renewed efforts at seduction, and I'd come away no closer to losing my soul. And although contract-free would be best, I was still better off than I had been. At least I had the buffer of two wishes between us, instead of only one.

I turned down the lights and settled back into the couch with a sigh, champagne glass in hand. After a few minutes I leaned toward the bottle for a top-off, and found Lorien sitting beside it, her feet swinging over the edge of the coffee table.

She had a mischievous air about her.

"What are you grinning about?" I demanded on a laugh.

"You really held your own with Balthus just now," she said, her smile widening.

"Spying on us, were you?" I smirked.

"Yep," she answered, unabashed.

She produced her tiny earthenware mug from the folds of her dress and helped herself to a dip of champagne. Jasper peeked around the side of the couch, and then strolled toward us, his green gaze fixed on Lorien's fluttering wings. I almost expected Sunny to pop out of her bedroom and grab a glass.

I sighed, feeling her absence all the more.

"I'm surprised you didn't intervene," I told Lorien.

She shrugged. "I would have if you'd needed it. But I've been thinking about what you said before. Maybe there *is* a reason for your connection to Balthus. Maybe you're giving him something to think about, helping to change his perspective a bit before he takes the throne from Dear Old Dad."

"One can only hope," I muttered over the rim of my glass.

"Couldn't let you drink your champagne alone, though," she added as she downed her jug and darted forward for a refill.

"Thanks for that," I said, torn between gratitude and amusement.

She hummed happily into her jug as I flipped on the classical station and we settled back to sip our bubbly in companionable silence. After a while she leaned forward to sprinkle green faerie dust over Jasper's upturned face. He dropped to the carpet and began rolling playfully on his back, joining us in our revelry.

"Think we'll ever get to relax completely, without you having to worry about saving me from the dire clutches of fate...and my own mouth?" I mused with a tipsy grin.

She lowered her hand from covering a small stream of hiccup-bubbles, and sent me a giddy smile.

"I did pick a rather troublesome human charge, didn't I? After all, the worst thing most faerie guardians ever have to deal with is nudging their humans away from a car accident or a mugger. But not mine, nooo, that's far too easy—mine has to make friends with succubi and make wishes in front of death djinns and..."

The rest of her complaint was muffled by the Kleenex I dropped over her head. Her small hands found the edges and she pulled it around her like a blanket, openly laughing at me.

"You asked," she chortled merrily, hiccupping again and producing more bubbles that floated down toward Jasper. "But by Titania's wand—I wouldn't have it any other way."

I smiled at her. "Me neither.

<u>Chapter 11—There And Back Again</u>

I'd made it through a whole work week without Sunny, Sparrow, or Balthus and any of his death djinn nonsense. I'd seen Angelica when she came to clean, and Lorien had dropped by a couple of times to check in, but other than that it had been pretty boring.

You'd think I'd appreciate the reprieve from near death experiences, but the truth was that it left me feeling empty. Or maybe it was how much I missed Sparrow that made me feel that way. It had only been a week, and I was trying not to whine to Lorien about it since she seemed busy attending Faerie Realm meetings and being a witness to the Lauringer debacle. But the effort to stay away from him was like a physical ache in my chest.

I sighed as I popped the last of the penthouse's stash of bubbly, ruminating over the fact that I was going to have to replace it with something much less expensive. There was a knock on the door and I started. I wasn't used to unexpected visitors knocking—they usually just appeared out of thin air.

I padded to the door and warily put my eye up to the peephole. A tall, thin woman stood in the outer foyer, dressed to the nines in an emerald green skirt suit with sparkling crystal buttons. The color picked up the embers in her hazel eyes, and I stopped breathing when I recognized her.

It was Balthus' mother, Calypso.

I was trying to decide what to do when she said, "I know you are there, Miss Corrigan. I can feel your uncompleted soul contract calling to me."

I swallowed a surge of panic. "How can I help you?" I asked, wincing at the squeak in my voice.

"I would like to speak with you. I have an offer that I think you will be interested in hearing."

She stared at the door as she spoke, as if she could see through the back of the peephole and into my eyes. It made me tense and uncomfortable, and afraid to look away. I cleared my throat. "What sort of offer?" At least my voice had lost its mousey cadence.

One delicate brow arched and her glossy lips twitched with a small smile. "You are stalling, Miss Corrigan. You do realize that if I wanted to come inside, your door would not hinder me. I am merely being polite."

The truth of her statement demolished my illusion of safety. I was cornered with the choice of fight or flight again, and I stiffened my spine as I chose the former. This was my home, damn it, and I wasn't going to cower like a frightened rabbit. I took a deep breath and opened the door, praying I'd be able to keep my wits sharp and watch my tongue.

"What sort of offer?" I repeated brusquely to her face.

Calypso tilted her head and regarded me with an enigmatic expression.

"I suppose you are wise to be guarded. After all, treachery is in my blood."

I snorted softly and she chuckled. "May I come in, Miss Corrigan, or do you intend for us to parley on your doorstep?"

I had been seduced, bullied, coerced and tricked by death djinns trying to gain possession of my soul. 'Mom guilt' over my manners was a new one. I shook my head and motioned for her to come inside. Like she said, she could come in anyway, so what did it hurt to be polite?

"I was just pouring a glass of champagne. Would you like one?" I offered.

"That sounds lovely."

I grabbed the bottle and two glasses and led the way to the living room. She lowered herself onto the loveseat, crossing her legs demurely, and I folded my jean-clad legs beneath me on the couch.

"This is a very nice penthouse," she commented.

"Courtesy of your son," I replied with a self deprecating smirk.

She smiled, her gaze thoughtful as it travelled over me. "Yes, Balthus is quite taken with you. I believe he is fascinated by your refusal to bend to his will."

I scoffed. "I can't be the only woman who's ever objected to him trying to rip her soul from her body."

She gave a surprised laugh. "You are refreshingly irreverent, Sydney. May I call you Sydney?"

I shrugged. "Why not."

She nodded. "You may call me Calypso. And though it may surprise you, Balthus has not had much experience with female rejection. He is, after all, the prince of his people. Not to mention, he's quite gifted at the art of seduction—or so I hear."

"I'll drink to that," I muttered.

She tipped her glass toward me and we both sipped our drinks. I barely wet my tongue, not wanting the alcohol to dull my senses. I hoped she would get to the point soon.

"It's not good for a boy to get everything he wants too easily. It makes him callous and spoiled. I have tried to be a tempering influence in Balthus' life, but his father..." she shook her head and sighed. "Well, spoiled or not, I am confident that he will make a better ruler than his father when his time comes to claim the throne."

She studied me over the rim of her champagne flute. "I feel that you have been a positive influence on my son."

It was my turn to laugh in surprise.

Calypso smiled at me. "Does that shock you? It shouldn't. You are a strong woman, Sydney. You have forced Balthus to acknowledge your differences of opinion. And whether he respects those differences or not, he will not soon forget the passion with which you defend them. It is always good for a prince to be reminded that his desires are not the only ones which need to be considered."

She chuckled. "The same goes for a king. I must tell you—I was very impressed with the way you handled yourself at my husband's court. Not many humans would have had the courage to do what you did. I would be proud to call you my daughter-in-law."

I choked on my champagne. "Uh, listen, Calypso," I sputtered, "I appreciate the thought, and I know Balthus has some crazy idea about me being his mate, but I really have no intention of becoming part of the family. I'm in love with someone else, and I never..."

Calypso held up her hand to silence me. "I'm not here to force you to accept me as your future mother-in-law. I merely wanted you to know that if my son insists on pursuing you, I am not opposed to the match. I *am* here, however, as a mother." She gave me a meaningful look. "I believe you are in possession of something, or someone, that I would dearly love to have returned to me. And I feel confident that what I have to offer in exchange will be of equal value to you."

My eyes widened in comprehension. I assumed she was talking about Princess Amalia. And though Balthus might not have been so eager to have his sister returned, apparently Calypso didn't feel the same way about her daughter. I moistened my suddenly dry lips, hopeful and afraid in equal measures.

"I gave Balthus my offer and he refused," I said, careful not to reveal too much.

Calypso's eyes grew stormy. "He and I had words over that. He was foolish to think that I wouldn't find out about his decision to leave his own sister moldering in a prison just so he could continue pining over an uncompleted soul contract."

I was relieved to hear her say it, but I knew I couldn't relax just yet. "I won't let her go for anything other than the cancellation of my contract."

She raised an eyebrow. "And despite the fact that you have already been granted a number of wishes by my people, I have no intention of arguing the point. I simply want my daughter returned to me safely." She held out one manicured hand and a piece of parchment appeared floating above her palm. "I believe you will find this to be a straightforward exchange agreement. We could have done it verbally, but I thought you might be more comfortable to receive it in writing."

"Lorien!" I called, excitement warring with nervousness as I took the yellowed paper from her hand and skimmed over it. The terms looked clear-cut: Amalia's release for the cancellation of my contract. There was a space for Calypso to initial when I turned over Amalia, and her official signature appeared at the bottom in a neat, loopy scrawl with a wax seal pressed into the space beneath it.

"LORIEN!" I called again with more urgency.

She blinked in with a cloud of sparkling dust. "What? I was in the middle of..." she stopped dead and gaped at Calypso. Her eyes darted warily from me to the death djinn queen.

"Is this for real?" I breathed, lifting the parchment for her to read.

It took a minute for her to go over it, while simultaneously trying to keep one eye on Calypso. Then all of a sudden a smile lit her face and her wings flashed iridescent silver as they sped up. "It's real!"

"Should I go get Amalia?" I asked, my heart pounding.

Lorien narrowed her eyes at Calypso, as if searching for signs of betrayal. "Hang on one minute. I'll be right back."

She popped out of the room and I gave Calypso a tense smile.

"The agreement is perfectly legitimate. I assure you," she said drily.

I forced an anxious laugh. "I'm sure Lorien is just being thorough—treachery being such a common death djinn trait, and all."

She lifted her lips in a well-bred smirk.

I took another baby sip of champagne, praying Lorien would hurry. My nerves were wound tight enough to snap. I reached over to top off Calypso's glass, needing something to do since I was all out of things to say.

It felt like an eternity before Lorien reappeared, and then my breath caught as Sparrow blinked in behind her.

"Agent Sparrow, how nice to see you again," Calypso greeted smoothly.

"Your majesty," he acknowledged, his eyes capturing mine. The sleeves of his crisp white shirt were rolled up to his elbows and his dark hair was tousled, as if he'd been running his fingers through it. I wanted to touch him so badly it made my hands shake.

"I thought it might be good to have another witness," Lorien piped up with a self satisfied grin.

"And you thought, *who better than a Seelie Police agent*?" Calypso drawled.

"Let me see this agreement, Sydney," Sparrow said as he strode forward to take the parchment from me. His fingers brushed over mine, gently squeezing as he slid the paper from my hand. His presence alone made me feel like everything was going to be alright.

"This agreement is legal and binding," he confirmed after a moment. "Did Nugratz's son, Mickey, want to press charges for Princess Amalia's illegal possession of him?"

I blinked at Sparrow's deadpan expression. The thought hadn't even occurred to me. I glanced at Calypso, who appeared to be grinding her teeth in annoyance, and realized that the thought had definitely occurred to her. In fact, it was almost certainly the reason why she was making things so easy for me.

I gave her a wan smile. "The last I talked to him, he seemed willing to forget about the whole episode. And as long as I can put my death djinn troubles behind me, I don't see any reason to stir up the pot."

"I'm glad to hear it," she said, visibly relaxing.

"Well, I'll go get Amalia then." I stood up and padded to my bedroom to get Hannah's horrible brooch from the back of the drawer where I'd stuffed it. As I returned to the living room I felt dazed. After everything that had happened, I couldn't believe it was really almost over.

"Initial here." Sparrow pushed the agreement between me and Calypso when I tried to hand her the chunk of crystal.

She looked as if she wanted to roll her eyes at him, but was too dignified. "Half a moment, please." She reached out and cupped one elegant hand around the gold-trimmed rock. She appeared to be listening to something none of us could hear, and then her lips quavered in a smile.

"My daughter seems to have quite a lot to say. I believe I will wait until we arrive home to release her, and save you the hearing of it."

"Thank you," Lorien and I chorused, having both had enough of angry death djinns for one lifetime.

"One more thing," I said hesitantly, as Calypso initialed the parchment and took the brooch, "Hannah from Haute Hannah's gave me that as a gift. I know you shop there and I'd appreciate it if you wouldn't wear it in front of her. I'm sure she'd recognize it—it's pretty hard to miss."

She sniffed as if at an offensive odor. "You needn't worry. This piece isn't exactly my style."

"Mine either," I muttered under my breath as she faded into smoke and disappeared.

"We did it!" Lorien whooped, darting over to kiss me on one cheek, and then the other. "You're finally free of the death djinns!"

I giggled as her wings tickled my ear and blew wisps of hair into my eyes. "I know. I can't believe it. It doesn't seem real." I grinned at her in bemusement.

"This calls for a celebration!" she exclaimed.

My gaze landed on the coffee table. "Well, I've got champagne." I gestured to the half full bottle with a flourish of my hand. "It's the last one in the case. It seems fitting somehow."

Lorien gave me an inscrutable smile. "I just remembered, though—I have somewhere to be. Why don't you two celebrate?" And then she was gone.

∞∞∞∞∞∞∞∞∞

I looked at Sparrow. "Um, champagne?" I asked, feeling suddenly nervous.

He breathed a soft laugh. "I'd love to celebrate with you, Sydney."

Unbidden, heated images filled my head and I shook them off. "Right.

Let me just get you a fresh glass."

When I came back from the kitchen, Sparrow was sitting on the side of the love seat furthest from the couch. I thought about keeping that physical distance between us, but it seemed weird, so I lowered myself onto the cushion next to him and poured our drinks.

"Congratulations," he said, clinking his glass softly against mine.

"Thanks," I replied, tipping the bubbles past my lips with a giddy smile.

"So, do you have any other last minute surprises you'd like to spring on me?" he asked conversationally. "Perhaps a leprechaun you're holding prisoner in your spare room, or a distant cousin who's a werewolf?"

I looked at him askance.

"You realize that today was the first I'd heard of you capturing the princess of the death djinns? Imagine my astonishment when Lorien popped into my office unannounced and babbling incoherently about you and exorcisms and Queen Calypso."

My eyes widened in horror. Oh Goddess. This was almost as bad as forgetting to tell him about Jeremy. Well okay, not nearly as bad as that, but still pretty thoughtless. "I'm so sorry, Sparrow! I didn't mean to keep it from you. It's just that everything was happening so fast, and you weren't speaking to me, and then I called the Hell Ride...and I honestly forgot."

His eyes twinkled with humor. "I'm only teasing you."

"Oh," I said, chagrinned. I collapsed back into the cushions and sipped my champagne. My eyelids drifted shut as I breathed in his woodsy scent. The heat from his body seeped into mine, relaxing my muscles and casting a spell over my senses. I straightened and shook myself, realizing I wasn't doing a very good job of maintaining a healthy distance between us.

He frowned. "That reminds me. I have something for you." He slid two fingers into the chest pocket of his shirt and pulled out an envelope twice the size of the space he'd pulled it from.

I shook my head as he handed it to me. "That magic pocket thing gets me every time."

Sparrow grinned. "This was hand delivered to me by a rather strange half-breed goblin yesterday. I would have brought it to you sooner, but I've barely had a moment to breathe. The station is still buzzing with inquiries over the death djinn releases and Lauringer's involvement with the unaligned souls and her subsequent disappearance."

The envelope had my name inked on the front in careful script. A thin gold seal held the flap closed, and when I broke it I felt a tiny surge of power at my fingertips.

"It was magically sealed so that only you could open it," Sparrow said with a bemused expression.

I unfolded it into a single piece of heavy cream stock paper and laughed out loud as I read it.

Dear Sydney,

I fear that I will never be able to adequately repay you for your kindness in using your boon from Lady Nightwing to request my release. I wanted to let you know that I purchased the two vials of blood that you gave to the old goblin witch, Ezrega, and I have destroyed both to prevent them from being used in dark magic against you. It is but a small token of my appreciation. If there is ever anything more I can do to offer you aid, it would be my pleasure.

Yours Truly,
Barnaby

I handed the letter to Sparrow and he chuckled. "You really do have the devil's own luck, Sydney. You've survived the Hell Ride, two death djinn contracts and an audience with their king, and come out relatively unscathed."

I put the letter on the coffee table and glanced at him uncertainly. "Speaking of unscathed, how are you after last weekend? You were feeling pretty rough the last time I saw you."

He shrugged. "Nothing a few healing spells and a little rest couldn't fix."

I studied his face. "Lorien said you caught some hefty blowback from using that inwa to kill the guard."

He rubbed his forearm and gave me a crooked grin. "My *leigheas* tattoo damn near burned a hole through my arm trying to keep me alive, but no lasting damage done."

I winced. "You told King Moab you found that thing in a junk bin at an antique shop. Was that true?"

Sparrow sighed and nodded. "It's true. An inwa is not an easy thing to come by and I found that one by accident many years ago. I held onto it with the intention of some day using it for revenge. It occurred to me that the occasion might have finally arrived when we were making our plans for you to meet with the king."

My eyes widened in comprehension. "You wanted to use it on *him*."

Sparrow gave a mirthless chuckle. "I would have preferred a less public venue. Killing the king of the death djinns in front of his entire court wouldn't have ended pleasantly. Even if I'd survived, my career in law enforcement most certainly would not have."

"I'm sorry," I whispered. He had sacrificed more than I'd known when he saved me.

His expression softened and he reached out to run the backs of his fingers over my cheek. It was a chaste caress, but desire bloomed in the pit of my stomach. "I was young and reckless when I forged that plan. And in any case, I'm sure my mother would have agreed that your life is far more important than my revenge."

I thought he was going to kiss me then, and my breath quickened. But he reclaimed his hand and took a swallow of his drink instead.

He cleared his throat. "And you Sydney—how have you fared over the last week? Are you fully recovered from your adventures?"

I thought about that. He was right—I was incredibly fortunate to have survived everything I had and come out with no permanent scars. Except for one very large hole in my heart. "I guess I should count my lucky stars. I had almost forgotten about those vials of blood, but it's nice to know that they won't be coming back to bite me in the ass."

"Charming," he intoned in a dry brogue.

I shot him a snide look and his lips twitched with humor.

"I've been missing Sunny, but I can afford to visit her in Boston more often now that I don't have a mortgage payment. And I'm working on talking her into moving down here," I said with a grin.

"So you've decided to stay here at the penthouse, then?" Sparrow asked.

I glanced at him and found his expression guarded. "Yes. I talked things out with Jeremy and we've decided to get a divorce."

He leaned back into the cushions and turned to face me more fully. "I was under the impression that his infidelity was not entirely his fault."

My pulse sped up. He and I had never really discussed what happened with Jeremy. I knew we needed to, but I was nervous. I still felt guilty for not telling him up front that I was married. And his forgiving me for it so easily was still at the crux of my fear that his feelings for me were clouded by our souls combining.

"It wasn't entirely his fault," I replied. "But I think if he had really been happy in our marriage, he would have been able to resist being unfaithful, despite the fact that she was a succubus."

He nodded, something like disappointment flashing in his eyes.

"And I've come to realize that I wasn't happy either," I added softly. "I'm not in love with him anymore."

His eyes held mine for a long moment. "I meant what I said before, Sydney. You *are* my soul mate, and I will always wait for you."

I wanted nothing more than to fall into his arms then, and the unfairness of holding back made tears prickle beneath my lashes. "I know it *feels* like we're soul mates, Sparrow. But Lorien told me that an unnatural connection was created between us when you combined your soul with mine to bring me back from the Sea of Souls. Think about it. You went from hating me for not telling you I was married, to thinking we were soul mates the next night."

I sniffed and wiped away a quick tear. "I feel the same deep connection to you, but I don't think I can survive the heartache if your feelings for me wear off in another month, or however long it takes for the effects of our souls combining to fade."

Sparrow gazed at me in disbelief. He opened his mouth as if to speak, and then seemed to change his mind. He leaned forward and placed one hand behind my head to pull my mouth to his instead. He kissed me hot and slow, his tongue pressing against mine in languid, shallow thrusts that sent tendrils of need curling through my veins. I wrapped my arms around his neck, pulling my body into his, unable to resist any longer.

I groaned in protest when he broke off the kiss, but he pulled me closer into the warmth of his chest and just held me there as he stroked my hair and murmured words in Gaelic.

"First of all," he began, "I was *upset* that you hadn't told me you were married. I never hated you." His voice was a comfortable rumble vibrating through me. I settled against him, giving into how good it felt to be there.

"And second of all, I knew you were my soul mate long before I brought you back from the Sea of Souls."

I leaned back to look up into his eyes. "You did?"

He smiled down at me and traced the curve of my ear with a fingertip, making my skin come alive with a shiver. "I did."

"How?" I asked, wanting badly to believe it.

He disentangled himself from my embrace and began unbuttoning his shirt.

"Um, not that I'm complaining, but how is undressing going to solve this?"

He chuckled. "Hush, little witch, and you'll see." He pulled the sleeve of his shirt down over his shoulder and biceps to reveal his striking Aegishjalmur tattoo. He pulled my fingers toward it and it began to glow red, throwing off sparks of energy as my bare skin brushed against his.

"That day in the hospital, when you asked about this tattoo, I told you it was designed to give me protection and irresistibility in battle. But it has one other important significance." He shut his eyes and pressed my palm into the design.

I gasped as a jolt of power shot through me. Heat and sensitivity trembled across every nerve ending, stealing my breath. It was as if some invisible cord connected me to Sparrow, heightening my awareness of him and allowing me to feel him with more than just the five senses I was used to.

Sparrow shuddered in response. "Yours is the only touch that can awaken its power in this way. It's why we feel each other's pleasure when we make love. And it's how I know, beyond a shadow of a doubt, that you are my soul mate."

Tears fell unchecked down my cheeks. "That's good to know, Sparrow. Because I am so far gone in love with you that I don't think I can even try to deny it any longer."

Emotions chased across his face as he reached to brush my tears away with his thumbs. "Sydney, I love you more than life itself. You will own my heart for all of my days." And then he was pushing me back into the armrest, his body pressing into me as he rained kisses over my damp cheeks. His lips found mine and my tears were salty on his tongue as I tasted him.

"I want to be inside you." He breathed the words into my mouth and they spread like oxygen throughout my starving body, awakening life and need and passion. I wept for him between my thighs, a fierce aching emptiness rising up there.

I struggled to undo my jeans, finally pushing him up off of me so I could remove them. He pulled me forward to kiss me again as I fumbled with his pants. I gasped as he stroked a finger through my wetness, pushing his fingertip into me and then rolling it over my clit. The ache was like a fire in my blood as I drew away to finish undressing him.

Sparrow tried to push me back down onto the cushions beneath him, but I shook my head and forced him to sit up as I rose to straddle him. "Stubborn little witch," he whispered, eyes blazing deep cobalt as he allowed me to take charge.

"I have it on good authority that this couch has the ideal angle and depth for seated positions," I panted.

His brows drew together in comic dismay.

"Angelica said so," I clarified quickly. I settled my knees outside his thighs and his expression cleared as I lowered myself onto him. He slid up inside me with one perfect thrust of heat and friction that made stars dance behind my eyes. He gave a hoarse shout of pleasure as his head fell back onto the cushions.

I lifted my body up his length and felt him swelling inside me as he brushed against my G spot. My legs turned to jelly and he grasped my hips with a soft curse, pulling me back down hard until he was seated fully inside me again. It only took twice more before we both exploded in climax and I collapsed against him, breathing hard.

Sparrow's fingers swirled in lazy caresses over my back as my pulse slowed, and I sighed in contentment. My mind drifted in a sea of warmth, and a singular realization came over me: My life was now officially perfect. My soul was out of danger and Sparrow truly was my soul mate. I'd literally had to go through hell to get here, but the end result was better than I could have ever imagined.

I hugged Sparrow tighter to me and he brushed his lips over my temple.

"Angelica was right about this couch," he murmured in a drowsy voice.

I smiled and kissed his shoulder. "Even *I* know you should never ignore sexual advice from a succubus."

The End

Dear Readers,

If you enjoy my books, I'd truly appreciate it if you would take a quick moment to add positive reviews on-line at Amazon.com, B&N.com, and/or your Goodreads.com shelf. Your recommendation is the best advertising!

An excerpt follows from *Passionate Magic*, which features Sparrow's best friend, Doyle. It is more of a traditional romance than *The Third Wish* Duology, but still has plenty of fantasy. I hope you enjoy it!

- Dawn Addonizio

Passion...

When Violet Hendrickson takes a tour in The Florida Keys and meets sexy boat captain, Doyle Thresher, the attraction is instantaneous. The warm summer sun, the mystique of the ocean, and the charming, chiseled Irish-man are more than she can resist.

Magic...

But something evil is lurking beneath the waves, lying in wait for Violet. And when she nearly drowns on Doyle's boat tour, he knows it's no ordinary accident. In order to keep her safe, he will be forced to reveal his most deeply held secret.

Will Violet be able to accept the magical truth of his identity? And will he be able to convince her of the existence of the evil that hunts her...before it's too late?

Chapter One of *PASSIONATE MAGIC*

The summer sun blazed down onto Violet's upturned face, soaking into her body to melt away the tension that had been building since she'd arrived in Key Largo two days ago. Dazzling points of sunlight glinted across countless rippling waves as the boat sped toward a nearby coral reef, the rush of wind softening the heat and sending her long, dark hair fluttering out behind her. The sweet scent of orange and coconut tanning oil teased her senses.

She was on summer vacation from her job teaching fourth grade, although it didn't feel like much of a vacation. She'd been putting off this trip, but with the end of the school year she'd run out of excuses. She couldn't believe it had already been two whole months since the day she'd stood beside the ugly upturned earth that marked her parents' graves.

Vicki and George Hendrickson had always loved the ocean, reveled in its mystery and magic, and they had instilled that love in their only daughter. Even now, being on the ocean soothed and calmed Violet—despite the fact that, in the end, it had been this very expanse of water that had stolen her parents' lives.

Violet sighed. She'd thought she was almost at peace with the unfair way in which they'd been taken from her. But two days spent alone in their cozy garden villa, going through closets scattered with Hawaiian shirts that carried traces of her dad's aftershave, and her mom's eclectic collection of hats, had stirred her grief back up to the surface.

She needed a break, intending to go for a walk down by the docks and maybe a swim on the beach. But she'd happened past this snorkeling tour just as it was leaving and joined it on a whim.

Maybe it was the boat's name that called to her—*Ocean Magic*—painted in bright, glowing blue against the vessel's crisp, white-washed stern. Or perhaps she was drawn by the challenge of embracing the ocean again after what had happened; proving that she held neither fear nor blame for it.

Violet couldn't help a small smirk as she admitted to herself that it also might have had something to do with the sexy boat captain rounding up customers from the dock as she passed. The husky timbre of his voice had lured her over, Irish if she wasn't mistaken. She was a sucker for that particular accent. Of course, it didn't hurt that he was built like a Celtic god.

She stole a peek at him through the dark lenses of her sunglasses. He stood at the polished mahogany captain's wheel, the wind ruffling his short honey-brown hair, all easy self-assurance as he chatted with a pair of women who sat nearby.

Just her luck, they both looked like supermodels. She inhaled the brisk salt-air and turned away to stare out at the fathomless aquamarine water, determined to enjoy her adventure with or without the attention of the handsome boat captain.

As the boat coasted to a halt, she peeled off her shorts and top, bending to retrieve her fluorescent orange snorkel vest and mask. She sucked in a breath as she rose in time to see the mouth-watering captain casually pull off his shirt, revealing a wide, well-defined chest and abs with just a hint of a six-pack. The pair of women beside him appeared to appreciate the view as well.

Violet refused to join them in their ogling, doubting he needed his ego inflated further. When he began instructing them on water safety, however, he drew her attention once more. He had the loveliest voice, with that rich Irish brogue of his, and his sea-green eyes sparkled with warmth when he smiled.

He caught her gaze for a moment, holding it as he finished his speech, almost as if he was speaking to her alone. He seemed to start toward her, and heat rose to her already flushed cheeks. Flustered, she looked away and hurried to the back of the line to await her turn to descend the ladder into the water.

∞∞∞∞∞∞∞∞∞

Doyle forced a smile at the scantily clad young woman sitting in front of him. She was tracing a manicured fingertip over her glossed pink lips in what was obviously meant to be an enticing manner. She and her giggling, gum chewing friend had rushed to sit by him as soon as they'd boarded the boat.

"Brittany and I were giving each other belly button shots at the bar last night. It was a blast." She gave him a coy look from beneath lashes thick with mascara. "You should come hang out with us tonight. If you buy the shots, we'll feed them to you."

Brittany giggled and Doyle laughed politely. "That's quite an offer, ladies."

They were certainly pretty enough, but he met the same type of girl day in and day out. He'd enjoyed his share of them, taking advantage of what they were only too willing to give, but he wasn't in the mood for another meaningless romp with a tourist.

It was his last snorkel trip of the day and he was eager to be done with it. He loved his business, but he was wiped out from the brutal heat and his four earlier groups. It wasn't so bad when he had a turn in the water and his partner, Manny, stayed on the boat to supervise the scene from above. But it was Manny's turn to swim.

He'd never thought anything could make him miss Ireland's wet, aching cold until he experienced mid-summer in the subtropics.

The flirtier of the two girls leaned into him. "That's not all I have to offer, handsome," she whispered on a drawn out breath. The cloying aroma of smoke and cloves nearly made him choke. "Come swimming with me and I'll show you."

Doyle gave a noncommittal chuckle and hid a grimace. Maybe sweating on the boat was the better alternative after all. He reminded himself that he couldn't complain. He'd said he wanted sun and sand, and he had it in spades here in the Florida Keys.

He'd never regretted his decision to leave Ireland. Although he wasn't sure his poor parents would ever get over the shock of it. That he'd chosen to venture so far from home was only a part of their dismay; it was more that he'd bucked convention and decided to live in the *human world*. Because, despite appearances, Doyle wasn't human.

I wonder if knowing that would be enough to make these two leave me alone, he thought dryly. But he would never reveal his secret, the satisfaction of chasing away overbearing tourists notwithstanding. He hadn't even told Manny, and they'd been friends and business partners for ten years.

Doyle steered the boat alongside the reef, giving his first-mate a nod to indicate they were stopping. Manny winked in salute as he dropped anchor, the wiry muscles of his arms and bare chest shifting beneath summer-darkened skin that had started out a deep, Costa Rican brown. Doyle stripped off his t-shirt with the *Ocean Magic*'s logo, ignoring the increased giggling from the college girls, and began to give his rote safety spiel before he sent the group into the water.

He almost stumbled over his words as his eyes fell upon the beautiful young woman watching him solemnly from the aft railing. He'd been busy piloting the boat and fending off advances from the 'girls gone wild', but he couldn't believe he hadn't noticed *her*.

She had a solitary air, standing apart from the couples who were helping each other with their lifevests, and not joining in the laughter of the other clustered groups of passengers. But she didn't look like she minded being alone. Her posture was selfpossessed and confident, though a veiled sorrow seemed to linger beneath the tranquility of her expression.

She was several inches shorter than he, with a firm but curvaceous body. Her breasts and hips were full and ripe, her pale golden skin clear and sunblushed. Her long, dark hair fell in waves to frame a soft face with extraordinarily blue, almost purple, eyes. She locked gazes with him as he finished speaking, and he began to move toward her, as if in a dream. But at the last moment she turned away and joined the queue to get in the water.

Disappointed, he faltered to a stop, oblivious to the giggling blonde who threaded her arm through his and asked if he would be her snorkel partner. He mumbled something about having to stay on the boat as he disentangled himself, earning a pretty pout.

Absorbed with thoughts of the mysterious brunette, and determined to introduce himself on the return ride, he picked up the clipboard with the passenger roster and tried to guess her name. As he scanned the page, he smiled in triumph. Hendrickson, Violet. The name reflected the color of her eyes. And she was the only passenger traveling alone.

∞∞∞∞∞∞∞∞∞

Violet admonished herself for being foolish as she waited, her mask looped around her wrist and fins dangling from her fingers. The captain was far too good-looking for his own, or her, good. Out of the corner of her eye she saw one of the blondes hanging on his arm, and she turned away, shoving him resolutely from her mind. What had she been thinking? There was no way he'd been about pass up that free lunch to come talk to *her*.

She reached the ladder and was soon lowering herself into the warm, soothing water; all other thoughts forgotten as the buoyant swells welcomed her into their embrace. She had forgotten how good it felt to be out here in the middle of the ocean. It was far different from swimming near the shore with the rolling whitecaps crashing onto the beach. Here it was like another world, with only an unbroken expanse of blue-green serenity as far as the eye could see.

She quickly donned her snorkel mask and fins, and worked her way out over the jumble of pitted and maze-like corals that made up the reef. Lacy sea fans waved lazily in the currents and multitudes of colorful fish flitted every which way. She lost herself in exploring the teeming marine life, following a couple of parrot fish that were chasing each other for a while, and then stopping to admire a large anemone with purple-pink tentacles.

She floated past a school of butterfly fish, flashing silver and yellow in the water-muted sunlight, and held her breath to dive down for a closer look at a huge grouper that she'd nearly missed. Its mouth gaped open and its fins barely moved as it hovered in a dark crevice, waiting for prey. Trigger fish darted by as she returned to the surface to clear out her breathing tube.

Violet's gasp of delight sounded hollow inside her snorkel as she caught sight of a sea turtle in the distance. She hurried toward it, trying to minimize her movements so as not to startle the creature. A large shadow moved past, and she blinked, jerking her face around to see what it was.

Something smacked hard against the side of her head and her vision went grey. She was stunned for a moment, and then pain crashed over her. She realized suddenly that she could no longer breathe. Her mask was filling with water, blinding her, and something was dragging her down, down, away from the air and the light. She panicked, struggling and flailing against its merciless pull.

Her lungs burned and tightened until they felt as if they would implode. No longer able to stop herself, Violet inhaled seawater.

∞∞∞∞∞∞∞∞∞

Excerpt from *Passionate Magic* by Dawn Addonizio

Doyle paced from stern to bow in frustration. The group had dispersed out over the reef, and from this distance he couldn't tell who was who. They were just a collection of bright orange blobs. They would be floating around out there for another half hour before he would get the chance to talk to the lovely Violet Hendrickson.

Who was she? And why would someone like her be vacationing alone? With his luck, she had a fiancée waiting for her back at her hotel room.

He continued his pacing, staring moodily out over the water, and then he went stock still. *That was odd.* He could have sworn he'd just seen a merrow's tail break the surface out beyond the reef, its large, silvery green scales sparkling in the sunlight.

The merrow were mer-folk, and notorious for keeping to themselves. There had been tales of sailors spotting them throughout history, but he'd never seen a hint of their existence in all his years in the Keys. It was strange that one would be anywhere near a place that was so populated by humans. His eyes scanned the water, searching for another glimpse.

Instead, he saw something that made his blood run cold despite the blazing afternoon heat. There was a single orange jersey floating about a hundred yards off the starboard bow, like so much abandoned flotsam.

Without a second thought he dove over the side of the boat and began a furious swim toward the empty snorkeling vest. He realized too late that he should have donned a mask, as he squinted through blurry, salt-stung eyes to gauge his surroundings. As soon as he reached the solitary jersey, he plunged deeper.

This was where the reef started to become the territory of divers. The seafloor dropped and the coral became a rocky landscape of peaks and valleys, jutting out to create hundreds of miniature caves. Many were large enough to conceal a human body. Had some fool decided to go exploring on their own and gotten stuck? Inadvisable though it was, he began feeling around inside the dark dens with his ungloved hands.

A perturbed moray eel shot out at him, its jagged teeth nearly clamping onto his fingers. He jerked his hand back and moved onto the next opening, growing frantic. The human brain could only go without oxygen for about five minutes. It must have been at least two since he'd jumped in the water. And though Doyle wasn't human, whoever had been wearing that orange snorkeling vest was. And they were running out of time.

A large, sleek shape rushed past him, creating its own wake beneath the surface. Doyle squinted at it, thinking it was a shark. But then he glimpsed something that seemed out of place on the seafloor below and he dismissed the creature as he lunged toward it.

A clump of dark wisps floated at the edge of a recess of rock, disappearing into a hidden cavity beneath. His fingers tangled in the mass, identifying the clinging strands as human hair. He reached deeper, past the curve of an unmoving head, to grasp a lifeless body beneath the shoulders. He tugged, and found himself holding an unconscious Violet in his arms.

He felt as if he was looking at her in slow motion. Her beautiful face was pale and eerily still, her long hair hovering in a weightless raven cloud. Then time caught up with him and he pushed off the rock, his leg muscles stroking for the surface.

"There they are!" someone shouted.

Doyle barely registered the sound as he rolled onto his back, pulling Violet's limp form with him, desperate to get her to the boat where he could perform CPR. His arms tightened beneath her ribcage as he struggled to position her, and suddenly she was choking and sputtering as she coughed up water and gasped for breath.

Doyle didn't think he'd ever felt such stark relief in his almost two hundred years of existence.

His first mate reached his side and began trying to pull Violet from him. Doyle's grip on her tightened reflexively, some primal instinct roaring to life, unwilling to relinquish her to another.

"Easy now," Manny soothed.

Doyle wasn't sure whether the calming words were meant for him or for Violet, but he relaxed his hold and allowed Manny to slide her down so that she was supported between them.

"We'll have you out of the water soon," Doyle assured her gently as they began working their way back to the boat. She murmured a sound of gratitude between coughing sputters.

The rest of the group bobbed in loose knots around them, treading water and staring. Doyle knew they were only concerned, but it was all he could do not to shout at them to get out of the way. He heard a faint, agitated buzz and looked up to find a distraught faerie hovering overhead, her wings sifting sparkling purple dust that scattered behind her on the wind.

She was a sprite, approximately three inches tall with dark shining hair that fell past her knees. Her skin glowed with silvery light and her pastel dress shimmered in shades of pink, blue and yellow. From the anxious stare she was directing at Violet, Doyle guessed that she must be the young woman's faerie guardian.

Faerie guardians bonded with certain mortals at birth, following them throughout their lives to bring them aid and protection. Most mortals had no idea of the existence of the faerie realm or any of its denizens. If they had a faerie guardian helping them they simply attributed it to luck, when they noticed it at all.

Doyle had a bone to pick with this particular faerie. Where the hell had she been when her charge was drowning, and why hadn't she steered Violet away from the danger?

"How the devil could you let this happen, little sister?" he muttered up at her, his jaw set in a grim line.

Her tilted eyes widened a fraction. "You're sidhe," she gasped in surprise.

He was just about to let loose a scathing reply, when he realized that Violet was trying to speak, her voice coming out stilted and hoarse from a throat raw with saltwater.

"Excuse me?" she managed finally. "I didn't *let* anything happen," she croaked. "Something knocked into me and dragged me under!"

She sent him a *how-dare-you* scowl and looked to the other group members for support.

"Of course it's not your fault, sweetie," a plump, motherly woman cooed. Her flowered rubber bathing cap was askew, leaving her kindly expression lopsided, but Violet smiled back at her in gratitude.

Some of the others nodded their agreement, staunchly remaining nearby, but several people were rapidly working their way back toward the boat. No doubt it had something to do with Violet's announcement that something had tried to drag her beneath the waves.

"I didn't mean you," Doyle assured her quickly. He directed an aggravated glance at the faerie as he realized his mistake. Of course Violet had assumed he was talking to her.

Violet shot him a disbelieving look. "Who did you mean, then?" she demanded, her voice still husky. "I'm fairly sure you weren't calling your friend here 'little sister'. He looks manly enough to me."

Doyle was forced to tamp down an unreasonable surge of jealousy toward Manny. "I didn't...I'm sorry, okay? Let's just get you back on board," he said with an irritable sigh.

"Captain Doyle's just a little hot with me for no keeping a closer eye on things," Manny said in a smooth tone. "He only wants to keep you safe, *lindita*." He gave Violet a reassuring smile, but a question flickered in his dark eyes as they traveled to Doyle's.

Doyle shook his head in silent apology and concentrated on guiding Violet to the ladder. He ignored the faerie now flitting back and forth in front of them. Apparently she found the situation humorous, her attempts to stifle her laughter with her small hands failing miserably. The dust from her wings changed from purple to green, and it drifted into his face as the wind changed direction, tickling his nose.

He sent her an irate glare. Most types of faerie dust made humans sneeze, and right on cue, Violet and Manny erupted in unison.

"Bless you," Doyle said, unable to keep the sourness from his tone.

The faerie shot upward with a muffled chortle.

"Just a little salt water in the nose, eh, *lindita*?" Manny chuckled.

Violet tilted a smile in Manny's direction and Doyle fumed.

They reached the ladder and Manny managed to ascend it first, helping

Violet up and leading her to a bench. Doyle scrambled after them and hurried to Violet's other side.

"Thank you, Manny. Can you get everyone back aboard while I tend to Miss Hendrickson?"

Manny gave him another questioning look, but rose and did as he asked.

Doyle placed a hand on Violet's shoulder. Though he felt her stiffen, he couldn't seem to make himself stop touching her. Her skin was warm and satiny beneath his palm. His gaze dropped to the rounded tops of her breasts where they peeked from the scooped neckline of her bathing suit. They rose and fell gently with her breath, the sight making his throat go dry.

He jerked his eyes back to her face and found her studying him with a puzzled frown. He swallowed. "I'm sorry." His voice sounded rough and he swallowed again. "I was just checking to make sure you had no visible signs of injury."

One delicate sable brow lifted. "Whatever it was hit me in the head." Violet reached up to gingerly explore her scalp.

"Of course." Doyle nodded quickly, his fingers brushing hers as he began his own examination.

Violet winced and sucked in a breath as he found a tender spot.

"Sorry," he said again, lightening his touch. "The skin doesn't seem to be broken, but you do have quite a bump. Does it hurt anywhere else?"

He gave the faerie, still hovering above them, a meaningful glance. She pulled a small cloth pouch from inside her dress and darted down to sprinkle silvery healing dust over the area he was probing with his fingers.

Violet shook her head. "No. I think I'm alright. It's already starting to feel better."

Doyle smiled and Violet's rosy lips quivered upward in response. She smelled of the ocean and sun-ripened fruit. Her hair was drying into shining ripples of silk beneath his hand, and he longed to run his fingers through its length. She was so close, her eyes like wide pools of liquid amethyst. A man could lose himself in their crystalline depths. If he just leaned in a few inches, he would be able to taste her...

An annoying chorus of giggles broke the spell. Doyle shook his head to clear it and reluctantly pulled his hand back from Violet.

∞∞∞∞∞∞∞∞∞∞

Violet wasn't quite sure what had just happened. First the handsome captain had blamed her for almost drowning. Then he'd insisted on taking care of her himself and sent the other, friendlier man away. She could have sworn she'd caught him ogling her cleavage, but he'd insisted he was only looking for injuries. Her head *had* been throbbing. But when he'd touched her, his fingers had literally soothed away the pain, as if by magic.

Excerpt from *Passionate Magic* by Dawn Addonizio

To make things even more confusing, just now there had been a moment when she was sure he was about to kiss her. A shiver went through her, her lips still tingling at the enticing thought. His sea-green eyes had held such heat as they stared into hers. But he'd pulled away when his two girlfriends showed up.

"Are you okay?" gasped the woman in the red bikini. Her voice dripped with concern, but her eyes roamed the captain's muscular chest as she spoke. It was the clingy blonde he'd had on his arm earlier.

"What happened?" her friend asked in an anxious tone, steadily grinding a piece of chewing gum between her teeth.

Captain Doyle straightened and crossed his arms over the width of his chest, as if to distance himself from Violet. She felt a bright flash of annoyance at him, mingled with a touch of disgust for herself. She reached down to pull a towel from her backpack, using it as an excuse to scoot away from the fickle captain.

"Something big knocked into me from behind. It was probably a shark," she replied briskly, enjoying the discomfort that flitted across both women's faces as their eyes traveled from her to the water in which they'd just been swimming. "I felt it dragging me down before I passed out."

"Did it bite you?" asked the one with the gum, grinding it harder as she stared at Violet in horrified fascination.

"I..." Violet looked down to make sure she wasn't bleeding. It suddenly occurred to her that the only way a shark could have pulled her down was with its teeth. But all she found were a few light abrasions where her skin had rubbed against rock. Although relieved not to find any more serious injury, she discovered, with a surge of disappointment, that her favorite silver anklet had fallen off.

She looked up to find the woman still looking at her expectantly. "No, I wasn't bitten," she said, feeling foolish. She must have imagined being dragged down.

"Thank Gawd!" the woman exclaimed, appearing not to spot the inconsistency in Violet's shark story.

Violet glanced at Captain Doyle, sure he'd catch it right away. But he was staring off into space, not even listening to her. Apparently she no longer merited his attention. Miffed and a little hurt, she stood up and wrapped her towel tighter around her midsection. "Excuse me. I need to use the restroom."

∞∞∞∞∞∞∞∞∞∞

"It wasn't a shark," the faerie piped up as soon as the word left Violet's mouth. "It was a merrow. That's why I wasn't able to warn her away in time. Sometimes my signals get crossed when other magical beings are involved."

Excerpt from *Passionate Magic* by Dawn Addonizio

Doyle stared at her, frustrated with his inability to reply.

"I don't think this was an isolated incident. A couple of months ago...oh, Titania's wand!" she cursed.

"I have to go. My son found his way out of his playpen. Little tyke's getting much too clever. I'll find you later, when you can talk." She gave him an apologetic grimace and was gone.

Doyle blinked and realized that Violet was no longer at his side. He rose, skirting around the college girls, and began walking toward the bow in search of her. He thought he'd seen a merrow. But why would one of the mer-folk want to harm Violet?

Violet exited the head, pointedly avoiding his gaze as she returned to her seat, and Doyle sighed. Apparently he'd upset her again. He'd have to figure out how to make it up to her later. Right now, he needed to get his passengers back to shore.

"Ready to pull anchor, *amigo*?" Manny clapped him on the shoulder.

"Let's take her in," he grumbled.

PASSIONATE MAGIC is available now in print and for e-readers!

Dear Readers,

My novel *Grey's Magic* features Doyle's sister Scarlett, and has lots of cameo appearances by Sydney and Sparrow. It contains and exciting blend of fantasy and romance, though it is a bit darker than *Passionate Magic*. I hope you enjoy it!

- Dawn Addonizio

Scarlett Thresher doesn't like humans. She's an immortal warrior. She's lethal with a sword. And she can hold her whiskey better than most men. But visiting the human realm gives her panic attacks.

Too bad her baby brother is getting married there and skipping the wedding isn't an option.

But when Scarlett stumbles across FBI Agent Greyson Derrington at a murder scene, she realizes that his killer is quite literally inhuman. And he's going to need cooperation from the faerie realm to have any hope of stopping the monster.

As they close in on an insidious evil that's stalking human women through their dreams, Grey begins to awaken parts of Scarlett that she long believed were shattered beyond repair.

Can he help her to release her fear and let go of the past, before time runs out for the next victim?

<u>About the Author</u>

Dawn Addonizio lives in South Florida with her wonderful husband, who is a science teacher, and their beloved menagerie of pets.

When she's not working her day job, or staring into space, she spends her time writing fantasy and making jewelry, wine accessories, and all manner of other sparkly things.

You can visit her store at DawnsBoutique.Net, "like" her on Facebook/D.Addonizio, and read some of her musings at DAddonizio.blogspot.com. You can also follow her on Twitter @DawnAddonizio